Also by Ciara Smyth:
The Falling in Love Montage

Shortlisted for the An Post Irish Book Awards

'An outrageously comic, moving debut'
Guardian

'It's so special, so arrestingly heartfelt, and so
painfully, gorgeously real'
Becky Albertalli

'Funny, sexy and smart, *The Falling in Love Montage* is the
romcom to beat all romcoms'
Cat Clarke

'An emotionally stirring queer romance with witty,
playful dialogue'
***Publishers Weekly*, starred review**

'Audaciously fills a gap in queer romance.
Smyth paints each character as a complex,
messy, lifelike individual'
Kirkus

'[A] beautifully written rom-com about two girls'
Big Issue

'Smyth's love-flecked debut is a meet-cute drawn out in
the style of Jenny Han's *To All the Boys I Loved Before*,
and the moments are just as sweet and cinematic as
YA rom-com fans will expect'
Booklist

'Written with a light touch, lots of humour and

Not MY PROBLEM

CIARA SMYTH

ANDERSEN PRESS

First published in 2021 by
Andersen Press Limited
20 Vauxhall Bridge Road
London SW1V 2SA
www.andersenpress.co.uk

2 4 6 8 10 9 7 5 3 1

British Library Cataloguing in Publication Data available.

ISBN 978 1 83913 085 4

Printed and bound in Great Britain
by Clays Ltd, Elcograf S.p.A.

To Darren, for everything.
Maybe you'll read this one.

1

It started with Meabh Kowalska having a temper tantrum in the girls' changing room. You know a Meabh Kowalska. Trust me. The intense overachiever type, with no hobbies other than winning. The girl who will either run the world or become a supervillain dedicated to destroying it.

Or maybe they're the same thing.

She was weeping. No. Not weeping. She was wailing and writhing on the floor. Her pale skin had turned blotchy, and she was banging her fists. It was a full-on tantrum. She clearly thought she was alone.

No, I'm getting ahead of myself. It started in the PE hall about an hour earlier. Our form tutor, also our English teacher and the head of PE (that was her true love, much more than Emily Dickinson and Shakespeare), always took morning registration in the gym instead of a classroom, and we had to balance on those huge inflatable balls instead of chairs. I can't imagine what they're actually supposed to be for. Giant dodgeball?

"—so Mrs McKeever's class will be in room one-oh-three instead of two-oh-seven. If you want to audition for next term's musical, there's a sign-up sheet. It's somewhere.

You know what, just ask Mr Smith, he's usually involved with that—"

I rolled the ball under my bum from side to side, bumping into Holly each time I leaned left. I wasn't really paying attention. I was thinking about how Mam seemed off this morning and whether I should text her and make sure everything was OK.

"I'm going to ask Jill to read my article and give me notes," Holly said. "If she can tear herself away from that slimy knuckle dragger she calls a boyfriend."

We both glanced over at Jill and Ronan, who was about two seconds away from sticking his tongue in her ear. They'd been going out three weeks and I had no idea what she saw in him. Neither did Holly, though I didn't mind that Jill had less time to spend with the only person who actively liked me. Jill could hang out with anyone. I only had Holly.

I bounced up and down on my ball until Ms Devlin gave me one of her fed-up-with-your-antics glares and I stopped and pressed really hard into the rubber instead, watching the tips of my fingers turn white.

I wondered if I could text inside my bag. I slipped my hand in through the open zip and rummaged around.

"Finally, as you all know—Aideen? Do you need something in your bag that you cannot find?"

Ms Devlin was a sarky bastard.

"I was looking for my phone, but I think it'd be inappropriate to take it out now."

I heard Holly snort beside me.

"It would, Aideen. I think it can wait another minute. As can foreplay, Ronan." She shook her head, disgusted, and he rolled a few inches from Jill and shoved his hands into his pockets with a huff. "As I was saying, the student council elections will be held in three weeks, which is an opportunity for you all to exercise your democratic responsibility. Women died for your right to vote, girls; the least you can do is use it. Boys, you've had a head start – if you want to sit this one out, be my guest."

A few of the boys exchanged miffed expressions.

"Miss! You can't say stuff like that!" Ronan said.

Ms Devlin looked at him, waiting for him to explain why she couldn't say stuff like that.

"It's . . . it's not fair."

Ms Devlin looked extremely unmoved by his reasoning.

"I hope that any applicants to the student council will have more impressive debate skills. Just a thought."

I watched Ronan choke back a retort, his face contorting in frustration. It was like he'd never met Ms Devlin before.

"Anyway, as I was saying. The elections will be held at the end of the month and the president chosen this year will be your class president for the remainder of your senior cycle, so choose wisely, for God's sake. I don't want to be sitting in a consultation meeting with some eejit demanding no school on Fridays, all right? Just because someone tells you they can do something you like the sound of, doesn't mean it's remotely possible, and if they can't actually achieve it, then they're worse than useless to you."

Meabh Kowalska's hand shot up into the air.

Holly leaned over and whispered to me, "You know, I really don't think anyone died so the students at St Louise's could vote for Meabh Kowalska to kiss teachers' arses for two years."

I snickered. She had a point. The whole election was a formality anyway. For one thing, she was the principal's daughter, and for another, I couldn't tell you the name of anyone who'd been council president since I'd started at this school. No one cared. Usually only one person volunteered for it. It was extra work with no reward except maybe missing a few classes – and there was no point in that if you were missing them so you could sit and talk to teachers anyway.

"Yes, Meabh?" Ms Devlin pointed at her. She didn't have the weary expression many of the teachers had when they called on her.

Meabh stood up.

"She's going to make a speech," Holly said. I could hear the eye roll without having to see it.

"I'd just like to say a few words."

Groans.

"Shut your mouths, every last one of you," Ms Devlin barked. "Or you're doing suicide sprints before your first class. That's right, you can sit next to your adorable crush smelling like unwashed armpits."

4

The class collectively remembered we were terrified of Ms Devlin's wrath and we fell silent like she'd pressed the mute button on us. She was one of those teachers where you could have the craic with her, but when she reached her limit . . . well, no one tested what happened when she reached her limit, but the threats often involved an inhumane amount of exercise.

Meabh faltered slightly but drew herself up.

"I will be running for class president this year and I would like to ask for your support and give you some information about the initiatives I will be hoping to implement. Firstly, I have a green initiative, which includes reducing the shocking amount of unnecessary waste produced by this school. I will also be campaigning to have a Polish language class for the Leaving Certificate – as you all know, my family is Polish-Irish and there is a significant Polish community in this town as well as making up two-point-seven per cent of the national population. Thirdly, I will be seeking to address the issues in the school's application procedures that have created a worryingly homogenous student body. I hope that you will consider voting for me. I want to address the problems in this school that students really care about and my door is always open. I will take any questions you may have now."

She looked around the room expectantly, with the impatient air of a mother waiting for a toddler to tie their own shoes. Ms Devlin had commanded silence, but she couldn't make people listen. I followed Meabh's gaze as she took in people biting their nails and playing with their hair. Her brow furrowed. She had tried very hard to sound calm and collected. It was almost impressive, when I knew for a fact that she would rather beat us all into submission if that had only been an option.

"Very admirable and ambitious but not fucking absurd ideas, Meabh. Thank you." Ms Devlin's swearing brought the class back to attention with a few giggles. Meabh plopped back on her ball chair, her jaw visibly grinding. She took out a notebook and began scribbling furiously as Ms Devlin dismissed us.

"See you all second period. Helmets and shin guards. No excuses."

She looked at me when she said the last bit, and I pointed to myself and looked around, pretending there could be someone else that she meant. Ms Devlin rolled her eyes.

I grabbed Holly by the elbow and guided her out the door into the cold.

"Did you hear Queen Meabh?" she said as we crossed over the pitch to get to the main building. Then she mimicked her in a high-pitched voice: *I'm going to address the problems the students really care about.* I mean, if she wanted to address the problems students really have, she'd be printing fake IDs or getting us all tickets for Electric Picnic."

"There's an idea," I agreed. "Instead of flyers and badges, she could hand out test paper answers and bags of weed."

I checked my phone to see if Mam had texted. She hadn't. I pressed my fingertips into the sides of my jaw, where all the tension was, and found a painful knot. Who even knew you could get face knots?

Holly took my hand and squeezed. She looked down at me with her big blue eyes sparkling.

"Save me a seat for Geography?" she said. "I see Jill's escaped Ronan's clutches."

"Last time I saved you a seat, you ended up sitting with Jennifer Murphy and I was on my own."

We were in a lot more classes together this year because we weren't streamed by ability for transition year, but so far we hadn't spent much more time together than when we were separated for nearly everything.

"She's not in our Geography class," she pouted.

That was not the point. But it didn't matter either way. I didn't have to save her a seat next to me. No one would take it anyway.

"Thank you, thank you, thank you," she said, kissing my hands. I felt a flutter for a second and then a dull, familiar drop as I watched her run off, with her perfect wavy red hair bouncing in its ponytail.

I took out my phone and texted Mam.

Aideen
U ok?

Of course Holly was only just in time for Geography; she and Jill were still nattering about her article when they walked in and took two seats at the front. She texted me under her desk that she hadn't wanted to make a fuss and it would have been rude to abandon Jill. That was understandable.

I didn't get any response from Mam.

We were supposed to read a passage about plate tectonics and answer questions. It made my head swim. I tried to think about all the things Mam could be doing, and how that list was so much longer than the list of things I hoped she wasn't doing. Which meant statistically it was more likely that she was doing one of the OK things. She'd message me back on her coffee break.

Even with your limited knowledge of statistics, you know that's not how it works.

I ignored that voice. The mean one. I kept my phone tucked into the waist of my school skirt all through the class so I'd feel it vibrate when she replied.

Mam didn't reply.

I got all the answers wrong.

2

An hour later I was in front of Ms Devlin again. This time I had a slip of paper and she had a huge wooden stick. OK, the technical term was a camán and it was used to play camogie. For those of you who, like me, think all sports are just sticks and/or balls, this is another stick-and-ball game. For Ms Devlin and the girls on her team, it was life and death.

"I'm not reading that," Ms Devlin said. She was short, white, and sturdy, and she had a no-nonsense energy that I ignored.

"OK." I shrugged and put the note in my pocket.

"You're playing today," she said. Her voice had a very "this is an order, not a request" feel about it.

"No, I have a note," I said brightly, and produced the note again, smoothing it out.

She closed her eyes and breathed really hard. With her free hand she snatched the note from me.

"Please excuse Aideen Cleary from PE today. She has bubonic plague."

I coughed.

"You do not have bubonic plague."

"I do though."

"I could phone your mother."

"You could."

She'd threatened this a dozen times since September. But she hadn't done it yet. I had a suspicion my last form tutor had warned her there was no point, that my mam didn't care. Mam would absolutely eat the face off me if she knew I was skipping PE, but I had long since solved that problem. Unfortunately, I had a bad feeling about Ms Devlin. Like sooner or later she wouldn't be able to help herself from getting involved.

The rest of the class had changed into shorts and T-shirts and were messing around on the pitch even though it was the bloody dead of winter. Out of the corner of my eye I saw Holly stretching, the hem of her jersey riding up and revealing a few inches of bare skin. Holly was one of those girls who took camogie very seriously.

Ms Devlin narrowed her eyes at me, then threw her hands up.

"Whatever. Just do something productive. You haven't done your last two English assignments and you have one due Friday. I told you next time it's detention."

"Wow, gossiping about me with the English teacher. I would have thought you were above that kind of thing."

Ms Devlin turned red, ready to explode. "I *am* your English teacher, you ninny."

"Oh right, I thought you looked familiar."

She sighed and rubbed her temples for a second.

"Is everything OK at home, Aideen? Is there a reason your work isn't being done?"

A prickling sensation crept over my skin.

"Everything is fine."

"I don't know if there's anything I can do to help unless you talk to me. I'm not trying to give you a hard time. I want to see you get stuck into something. Anything. So you have some support."

"You're trying to make me play camogie to solve an imaginary problem. There's nothing wrong. Except for my bubons."

"Your what?"

"My bubons. I have bubonic plague. My body is covered in bubons. Under my clothes, though, obviously."

"You could at least read a bit more about these illnesses, you know, instead of simply choosing one off a list."

"Sounds like homework."

Ms Devlin shook her head at my back as I escaped towards the sports centre. I couldn't see it but I knew she was doing it. I could feel the head shake of resignation.

I made a beeline for my usual spot. There was a sort of balcony that overlooked the main hall; it had great reception, and last year I managed to talk a substitute teacher into giving me her log-in details to the teachers' Wi-Fi network when she couldn't work out the system. During PE I liked to sit up in the balcony and get all Netflix and cosy.

I tried ringing Mam before I settled in, but she didn't answer. She was supposed to be at work. She worked in a hairdresser's and they opened around ten. So it was fine. Her phone was on silent, that was all. Just as I found the show I wanted to watch I realised I needed to pee and sighed, thinking of how I had to walk all the way downstairs again. I left most of my stuff behind me because I didn't have anything worth stealing, but I put my phone in my pocket. Not that it was worth stealing either, but I'd still be annoyed to lose it if some waste of space nabbed it.

As I approached the changing room, where the toilets were, my ears picked up on some kind of unholy wailing. It echoed and bounced off the walls and the closer I got to the changing room, the louder it became. I blessed myself. This was it. There was some kind of ghost or demon in there. The school was an old convent and although the sports hall was a renovated building, it was definitely built on ancient ground. Although wasn't all ground ancient technically? The most likely scenario here was the disturbed spirit of some girl who had died while undergoing an aggressive exorcism. Probably because she had unnatural feelings (a gay) or disturbing thoughts (an opinion) or had been possessed by Satan (was horny?).

I was almost disappointed for a second that it turned out to be a regular, real-life teenage girl having a shit fit.

OK, that's potentially misleading on account of how it's a toilet, but I mean like a tantrum. All the crying and wailing was less interesting before I realised who it was. Meabh Kowalska. I watched for a moment, curious like I was getting to see rare footage of a creature undisturbed in its natural habitat.

Here we see the Perfectionist maximus *engaged in the ritual dance of her species. See how she flails her limbs? Soon she will progress to pulling chunks of hair from the head.*

She must have noticed me mid-thrashing, because she suddenly froze and then slowly turned her head and looked me dead in the eyes. Her blue eyes were red rimmed and puffy. I thought about how I must look to her now, in her moment of weakness, and I was very generous, picturing my out-of-control brown curls as lustrous waves and my blue eyes as sparkling and amused.

She let out a strangled groan. "You."

"Yep." I grinned broadly, and rocked back and forth on my heels. This was the best day of my life.

I have these two daydreams. One is catching my enemies in a moment when I have the upper hand and they're embarrassed and I get to act cool and aloof. The other is doing something amazing with my life and coming back to a school reunion and rubbing it in everyone's faces. I'd invent an app that everyone uses and I'd rock up to the reunion and people would be using it and they'd be like, *Oh, Aideen, nice to see you after ten years. Are you on Flubberygiblets?* and I'd shrug like I didn't even care. *I invented Flubberygiblets*, I'd say. Everyone would think I was class and then I'd be like,

13

Have you met my wife, Kristen Stewart? We're flying on a private jet to Maui tonight to have lots of sex and lip biting. Fuckity bye, arseholes.

This was obviously the first scenario, and for a second I worried that I'd peaked. Maybe it would all be downhill from here unless I could figure out what Flubberygiblets did and learn how to code. That wasn't likely seeing as I was pretty stumped by the time we had to create budgets in Excel for Business Studies and my figures wouldn't add the numbers together. I just kept getting this symbol a lot: Σ.

Calling Meabh Kowalska my enemy was kind of harsh really. Saying that I have enemies sounds like I have had epic showdowns with people and we're involved in elaborate plots to take each other down, when really it's a lot more basic than that. We've been in the same class our whole lives and "didn't play well together" in teacher speak. This is definitely a nice way of saying it. The same way those "Good Effort" elephant stickers on my homework was the nice way of saying I was stupid when everyone else got "Excellent" eagles or "Very Good" gorillas. After a few years it doesn't really matter why you don't like each other, you just don't. It's not like I remember every detail of how she made me feel smaller than all those inept elephant stickers combined or anything.

But it was 9th November 2013 at 11:00 a.m. and it was raining, not pissing rain, just spitting down, you know? We had this school project that was a shoebox model of a scene from a book and I had actually read the book and all. I really liked it and so for a change I was kind of into the homework. We split up the tasks. Meabh was going to construct the chairs for the auditorium scene and all the little people, and I had to make the background look like a stage. Well, I went round her house on Sunday night with my shoebox. I'd done my best trying to paint a stage and I'd cut a picture of a pair of red curtains out of a home furnishings catalogue and stuck them to the sides. I thought this was really clever. Well, sure didn't she take one glance at my creation and get a face on her like a smacked arse.

"What. Is. This?" she screeched, and picked up my box, holding it out from her body with her fingertips like she might be infected by my mediocrity.

I wish I'd told her to cop on to herself because it was only a school project, but I was shy and got embarrassed real easy so I looked at my shoes and swallowed hard.

"Do you think these" – she indicated a hundred tiny, perfectly constructed wooden chairs with real red velvet seats – "go with this?" She looked half possessed when she said it and waved my box desperately in my face. "These are one-twenty-fourth scale Victorian replicas and this has a picture of a pair of curtains taped on it. You didn't even use glue."

We didn't have glue. I'd had to search the junk drawers for the end of a roll of tape and had been so relieved when I found it because I knew there was no way Mam was going to go out and get a new roll just for this.

I've thought about that moment a lot over the years. It's the kind of thing that pops into my head when I'm trying to fall asleep, and even though I know that Meabh was the one being the dick, I always feel the shame all over again. It's like a dormant creature living in my stomach and every now and then it wakes up and crawls up my throat to choke me.

In the changing room, looking at Meabh's red eyes and blotchy cheeks, after all these years, I remembered something else about that day back in primary school: the way Meabh pressed all ten fingertips into her skull so hard it looked like the bones of her knuckles would break through the skin. I remember how her dad came into the room and Meabh winced when he took the box out of her hand.

"We don't scream, Meabh," her dad said, and she apologised. Mr Kowalski told me to ring my mam to pick me up because Meabh had homework to do. He wasn't the type to be cross or shout, but that made him scarier to me then. I didn't know how to handle his quiet disappointment. I didn't want to say I didn't have a phone. Or that we didn't have a car and that Mam had told me to get the bus. I didn't want to say that Mam hadn't given me enough money for the bus either, so I just walked home. Mam wasn't there and I didn't have a key for the flat so I sat on the stairs in the hall until she got home and hugged me with limp arms and kissed me sloppily on the forehead, her breath making my eyes water.

When we went back to school on Monday, Meabh had completely redone the shoebox. It had real tiny curtains and a cord you could pull to draw them open. The teacher went loolally over it, obviously, and Meabh never said that I didn't do any of it, but the teacher knew. We both got an A and I finally got a stupid eagle sticker. I peeled it off the page and stuck it to the inside of my pencil case. I didn't want to look at it, but I didn't want to throw it away either.

But I don't hold a grudge. Meabh is what she is. A hectic pain in the hole. I didn't like her, with her speeches and her being a relentless know-it-all, but Holly *hated* her. They were always in competition. When they were six, Meabh tripped her before their gymnastics yoke and Holly twisted her ankle. Holly was convinced it was some Tonya Harding shit. I don't know about that because I thought Meabh wouldn't want to beat her by default. She'd want to beat her by being better than her. And then she'd want to rub it in her face that she tried her absolute hardest and still lost. Last year Meabh had a party after the exams and her dad made her invite everyone in the class even though she wasn't really friends with anyone; I think the party was his idea really. So Holly invited a bunch of girls out the same night to the underage disco up at the hotel and her mam paid for us all to get in. It didn't help that Meabh had made camogie captain over Holly three years running.

"This must be pretty embarrassing for you," I said now.

"I thought you stopped having these tantrums years ago but obviously you just stopped having them in public."

"This is a school changing room. Technically that is a public place," she said, heaving herself into a cross-legged position on the floor.

"I love how you'd rather correct me on a technicality than deny you still have massive hissy fits at sixteen."

"I can hardly deny that now."

"True. But you're taking the fun out of this for me. I want to bask in your humiliation."

Instead of sniping back, she just sat there as a tear snuck out of her eye and rolled down her face. I couldn't help but feel kind of sorry for her. I was watching her sad little tear make its way down her face when—

"Did you . . . ?" I pointed, aghast.

"What?" She looked confused.

"You . . . you licked your own tear. It reached your mouth and your tongue popped out and licked it."

She shrugged. "It's salty."

I shook my head. "Uh, that doesn't make the kind of sense you think it does. *It's salty* does not explain ingesting liquid that came out your eyeballs. There's loads of things that are salty but you don't go round licking them all."

"Like what?"

I scrambled to think of something.

"Um . . . ROAD SALT," I finally said triumphantly. "Sand."

"A sweaty armpit," she said.

"A dick."

"Oh my God, Aideen. Gross." She groaned and wrinkled her nose. She was laughing though, and I forgot that I was supposed to be revelling in her pain.

That brings me to one of the other reasons Meabh annoyed me. Even if it wasn't technically her fault. In first year at secondary school everyone called me a lesbian because I was always hanging around Holly, and while she had lots of other friends from all her clubs and societies, I didn't. I was never really comfortable with her other friends either. There was stuff about my life only Holly knew and that was how I wanted it to stay. But it did mean that it was really hard to ever feel connected to anyone else. I always felt like I was lying. Anyway, I told another girl who I *thought* was my friend at the time that maybe I *was* a lesbian, and she told everyone, and for ages there were a few people who gave me a really hard time about it.

Until at some point a couple of years later everyone turned super woke and a few other girls said they were bi and Meabh said she was a lesbian too and the same people who made jokes about me acted like none of that had ever happened. Even though Meabh wasn't exactly Miss Popularity, no one was going to make fun of her for that now because being homophobic was no longer acceptable. Which is great, *obviously*. It just wasn't great in time for me. It didn't seem fair that it was easy for Meabh and Orla and Katia; I got all the hassle and they got to be brave and everyone else got to act like our school had always been this rainbow utopia.

"Are you going to tell me what you're yapping about anyway? Did you get a B in something?" I joked.

Meabh pursed her lips. "I'm going to lose."

"What, the election thing? You were junior president. You're a shoo-in. Besides, no one else is actually running."

"*Yet.* Some arsehole is definitely going to. And I have so much to do. I have so many policies to write and I said I'd do all this stuff and I don't even know where to start and I can't do anything."

Tears were streaming down her face. She was a hopeless case.

"It's a stupid election. You don't need any policies or initiatives. No one cares. Like genuinely nobody cares. And so what if you lose? You already have a lot going on, do you really need this too?" Aside from being camogie captain, Meabh always had her hand in something. She was for ever fundraising or making a petition or entering some kind of competition. Not a week went by without her lobbying the teachers for some kind of change. Last week she harangued the old caretaker until he agreed to only order energy-saving bulbs in future.

"You don't understand," she said. Not in a mean way, like I wouldn't understand because I'm a dope, although that's true, but in a way like she really wished that I could.

20

"I don't understand most things," I said, "but sure, why don't you tell me what it's like to be a smarty-pants anyway?"

Meabh must have been disorientated by her tantrum because she actually started telling me. Me. The girl who cut curtains out of a catalogue instead of sewing them from scratch. How the mighty had fallen.

"I already said I'd do all these things and I can't fail. I can't." She looked genuinely distressed, and I *didn't* understand. I dug deep into my empathy store and found a dried-up old raisin. Meabh had literally everything. She was a brainiac and her family's house had two sitting rooms, for fuck's sake. Still, I tried my best.

"Look," I said matter-of-factly. "I fail at things all the time. I promise you nothing actually happens. It won't kill you."

"That's what I'm worried about."

"You're worried it *won't* kill you?" There was no pleasing this girl. "Tell you what, if you do lose, I'll finish you off myself. How about that?"

She stood up, a scarily serious look on her face. The kind I assumed serial killers got right before they chopped your head off and wore it as a hat. I took another few steps back, but she stalked towards me. This is what you get for being a Good Samaritan. You die in a girls' changing room at the hands of a deranged overachiever.

"Do you know what will happen if I fail? What I'll learn from that?"

She kept walking towards me until I'd backed into the wall, which was damp with condensation from the showers. Her menacing expression was enhanced by the mascara dripping down her face. I would have laughed, but I was pretty sure if I did she'd unhinge her jaw and I'd be swallowed into the dark chasm of her stomach.

"I'll learn that failure is not the end of the world."

I opened my mouth to squeak out that this might not be a terrible lesson for her to learn sooner or later. It might cut down on the meltdowns. But she put her hand across my mouth.

"Then maybe I'll start to relax. I won't be so intense about my homework. I'll think, *Meabh, you can chill out. Wind your tits down to medium.*"

I laughed into her hand, thinking that her tits were indeed currently wound up to high and I enjoyed the phrasing. She continued, ignoring my snicker.

"I'll think, the worst has already happened and you survived it. You've wasted years of your life being a perfectionist."

I nodded *yes*, her hand still over my mouth. She shook her head slowly, deliberately *no*.

"It'll start off small. I'll only spend two hours instead of three preparing my topic for the comhrá and Múinteoir Nic Gabhann won't really notice because I already have excellent conversational Irish."

Her hand shifted slightly so it covered my nostrils, and

22

I tried to speak to tell her she was obstructing my breathing and I needed that to live, but her grip was clamped so tight that all I could do was lick her palm. She grimaced and snatched her hand away, wiping it on her skirt.

"Ew, don't lick my hand," she said, breaking the tension.

"What if there were tears on it?"

She didn't even smile. She continued her weird rant instead.

"Complacency will lead me to more failure. I'll start to think it's OK to doss off. It's only transition year, I'll tell myself. It doesn't count for anything. Then it becomes, It's only fifth year. The exams aren't till next year. It's only coursework. It's only a B. Hell, why not give myself a break and take ordinary-level Maths? I don't *need* to get the full six hundred and twenty-five points."

I didn't think anyone needed to get 625 points. But Meabh was the kind of person who'd probably engrave her Leaving Cert results on her tombstone, so I could see why she'd want them to be good. She took a few steps back from me then.

"Maybe after I've given up on higher-level Maths I'll think I have time to go to that party."

There was no party.

"Someone there offers me crack. And I think *hey, sure, I have a Biology lab to write up but I can do it in the morning.*"

"I feel like you've missed a step. Who do we know who brings crack to parties?"

"I've read *Go Ask Alice!*" she declared. Like that settled it. "Once you snort that meth, there's no going back."

I shook my head, realising that Meabh thought meth and crack were the same thing and she also had no idea how you took either of them.

"Years from now you'll wonder, what happened to that girl from school? She was going places once. Then one day you'll pass a person lying in the gutter, a needle sticking out of her arm and a glazed expression on her face. You'll think, that's so sad. I wonder what happened to her. She's so young. She's probably the same age as you are."

She trailed off, a faraway look in her eye.

"Is it you?" I asked.

She sighed, exasperated. "Yeah, *obviously* it's me. It'd be a pointless ending if it's just some random and I'm off finding a new renewable energy source or ending global capitalism."

I thought for a minute.

"There are a few holes in this," I said. "One: I guarantee I'm not going to be wondering what you're doing years from now."

I'd be too busy making love to my wife, Kristen Stewart, on a bed of Flubberygiblets™ money.

"Two: You clearly don't even know *how* to take meth and if you did, believe me, you're middle-class enough to end up in some country club rehab, not the gutter. And three: you'll die of a stress-induced coronary before any of this happens so I really wouldn't worry about it."

For a second she did nothing, and I thought she was considering my very reasonable points.

Then she burst into tears. Far too many tears for her to lick off her own face.

"FINE," I shouted over the wailing and rending of garments. "I'LL FIX IT!"

She paused in her dramatics and eyed me up and down. "How?"

"Well," I said thoughtfully, "what do you need?"

And that was how it started.

3

"Time," Meabh said hopelessly, "I need more time. I've worked out my schedule to an inch of its life." She pointed at some papers that were scattered across the room like she'd thrown them. "I simply can't do everything unless I give up sleep. And I've tried that before. It did *not* end well." She got a dark look on her face.

I had a mental image of her pacing a room with her hair on end. There was writing all over the walls and lots of red string connecting things. It felt very real.

"All right, weirdo. Give me your timetable. There's definitely somewhere you can cut back."

With great effort Meabh picked herself up off the floor and retrieved the timetable, handing it to me. It was blurry where it had got damp from being thrown near the showers and I had to gingerly remove a long blonde hair.

Meabh had a sensible dark brown bob and I had an explosion of brown curls that could not be tamed by either product or professional and simply had to be restrained for visibility purposes. So it was shower hair. I shuddered.

"OK, what about . . . cello lessons?"

"No, I can't quit those."

"Do you have to practise for two and a half hours a day though?"

"Yes."

"Two and a half hours? Come on, isn't, say, ninety minutes plenty?" I joked.

"Some studies show that two hours is the point of diminishing returns but I have it carefully planned, splitting time between scales, études, and repertoire, and I wouldn't call that research empirical, you know?"

I didn't understand any of that. But I guessed the cello was not something we were going to budge on.

"What about these classes here, what are they?" There was a yellow-coded ninety-minute block on Monday, Wednesday, and Friday.

Her face darkened. "Yoga."

"Ah yes, of course, you do seem the type, after all."

"Mum makes me. She says I need to relax."

"If she wants you to relax, maybe she should schedule some relaxation."

"If I schedule relaxation, all I'll do is think about all the things I need to do. Which is not relaxing."

"Well, you must be super flexible at least."

"I can barely touch my toes," she grumbled. "The instructor says I won't be able to be 'flexible in body until I am flexible in mind.' I tried explaining that that is not how hamstrings work."

"How long have you been doing it?"

"Since last year after the exams when all my eyelashes fell out."

"Huh . . . and you can't touch your toes yet?"

She demonstrated. She was *almost* there, but she did look exceptionally awkward.

"Your instructor might have a point, don't you think?"

"Mum won't let me quit yoga," Meabh said, and pursed her lips.

If my daughter's eyelashes had fallen out because of an exam I'd probably be crushing blues into her cereal every morning, but my family did tend to take the chemical route to our destination whenever possible.

"What's this?" Everything was acronyms and initials.

"The gym."

"You already go to yoga!" I protested.

"The gym is for working on strength and speed. For camogie."

I rolled my eyes. At least now it was obvious why Meabh was continually beating Holly for captain.

"That's Polish reading," Meabh continued, pointing to the schedule. "That's current affairs. What? I have to read about what's going on if I'm going to be in politics. That's showering."

"Your *showers* are scheduled?"

She shrugged. "I'm busy. That's kind of the problem."

"I know, but it's transition year. It's meant to be a doss."

Transition year is the best thing about our whole education

system. You do three years of studying to do your Junior Cert exams then you get transition year, which is meant to be for "personal development," before you do two years of study for the Leaving Cert exams. When adults remember their Leaving Cert year, they get this haunted look in their eyes, like they've been through shit you can't imagine, so the least they can do is give us a year of farting around.

"Transition year is an excellent opportunity to round out my skill set and get a head start on the senior curriculum."

Her lip wobbled and then tears filled her eyes. She pressed her fists into her eye sockets and pushed hard.

"All right, all right, that's probably how you lost your eyelashes," I said, pulling her fists away from her eyes by grabbing her wrists.

Meabh had always been a hectic mess, but I guess I'd assumed that was her personality and that she liked being like that. Now I was a bit worried about her. At the same time I was also mentally trying to tot up how much all of these lessons and instructors cost. Did principals make that much money? Or was Meabh's mam the one raking it in? I had no idea what a cello instructor charged or how much yoga class was. I knew for a fact there was free yoga on YouTube though.

"There are two options." I stroked my chin. "We can break your wrist *or* your ankle."

I waited for her to laugh. She didn't so I continued, "If you ask me, your wrist will free up way more time. No more cello, homework, or yoga!"

She stopped crying and sniffed up an escaping trail of snot. "You're right."

I wrinkled my nose. Upset Meabh was gross. "Huh?"

"I mean, not about the wrist thing, that's ridiculous. I can't break my wrist."

"Oh good. I was really worried you'd completely lost it there for a sec—"

"But my ankle definitely. I'd be able to stop taking PE, that's two doubles a week, and all my yoga classes and gym sessions . . ." She wasn't really talking to me any more. She was daydreaming about the free time she could fill with more work.

"Eh . . . I was joking, you know?" I said quickly. I could see she was deadly serious and I was a little alarmed. I wasn't sure if it was because I was concerned for her or because I didn't want to end up in trouble and having to explain how yes, it was all my idea but I didn't mean it.

She rounded on me. "No, you're brilliant! It's the only solution."

"You could talk to your parents," I said half-heartedly. I wouldn't talk to my parents either if it were me, and I was stupidly flattered by being called brilliant. Had anyone ever called me brilliant before? I felt like I would remember it if they had.

She laughed out loud for the first time. Maybe in her whole life. I tried to remember if I'd ever seen her laugh before.

"How, though?" she mumbled. "That's the question."

She began pacing the room and then walked out the door into the main hall. I followed her.

"We could get a hammer from the woodwork room." I shut my mouth. She'd probably do it. "I mean, no. Meabh. Seriously."

She looked around, ignoring me. Then she ran up the stairs and stood at the top. I stayed at the bottom.

"One, two, three . . . seventeen, eighteen, nineteen."

"Meabh, no."

"That's going to really bother me," she said. "Nineteen. Why nineteen? What kind of self-respecting architect puts an odd number of steps in a staircase?"

"Meabh, you can't jump down the stairs."

She clasped her hands together like she was going to dive into a pool, then took a few steps back and did a sort of mock run towards the stairs. She even turned around with her back to me and teetered precariously on the top step.

"Meabh, you'll crack your head open like that. You cannot do this."

"I can't do this," she agreed. "My brain is rejecting it. You know how you can't drown yourself either? Your body's instincts won't let you deliberately inhale water or stay submerged once the hypercapnia becomes overwhelming."

"How do you know that?" I was amazed that even as she contemplated injuring herself, she still found time to show off.

31

"I know everything," she said absently.

"Come downstairs and we'll think of something else."

"You come upstairs."

"You come downstairs."

"You come upstairs."

"No."

"Yes."

"You are so bossy," I said, giving up. It didn't seem wise to bicker with someone who was literally on the edge.

"So I'm thinking you could ask your dad if you could swap out doing cello for this term with doing your election stuff. The green whatsit and the application thingy."

"Oh no. That won't work. He can't know I'm struggling. No one can know. No. I'm going to need you to push me." She said it casually, as though it was the obvious solution. I guessed I counted as "no one."

She wriggled in front of me and braced herself as though she thought I was really going to just shove her down the stairs. Briefly I considered that we really needed Holly for this. Meabh annoyed me, sure, but I didn't have the edge it would take to maim her. Although Holly wouldn't push her archnemesis down a flight of stairs if she had any inkling that it would benefit Meabh.

"I am *not* going to do this. Get out of my way."

"Nope." She blocked the stairwell with both arms.

"This isn't going to work. I'll just go watch TV on my phone," I said, gesturing to the benches that lined the balcony.

"You can't stay there for ever. And Ms Devlin is going to come looking for you any minute now."

For a second it seemed as though she was going to fight back. And then her whole body just collapsed. Her shoulders drooped, her head flopped forwards, and her knees buckled. Silent tears sprang out of her eyes. How could one person cry so much?

"Please," she said. She grabbed the front of my jumper and pulled me so close I could smell her breath. It was still pepperminty from brushing her teeth that morning. No pre-class coffee for Meabh. She probably thought coffee was a gateway drug to cocaine.

"I know you think I'm losing my mind, but this is the only way I can get what I need. I'll owe you one. Anything you want. I will tutor you for the rest of the year!"

I frowned. That didn't sound like a reward.

This wasn't normal-person behaviour. Her parents were obviously way too hard on her. If I inspected her timetable closer I'd probably find three minutes for peeing twice a day. Meabh irritated the life out of everyone, but the girl had once rubbed all her own eyelashes out, for Christ's sake. If I didn't do this, she would keep trying to do everything on that timetable *and* the election on top of that. Then she really would lose it and I would know there was something I could have done.

Something absolutely bizarre and possibly illegal? Were you allowed to injure someone if they asked you to?

33

"Fine."

Her whole body perked up.

"Really?"

"Yes," I said, not quite believing I was saying it. "I guess I can push you down the stairs. But don't hold it against me if I enjoy it. Or if you injure something you don't want to injure. I cannot be held responsible if your brains leak out your head or something."

We both heard the bang of a door and exchanged a look. Meabh quickly ran downstairs and when she reappeared she shook her head. "No one there."

She returned to her position standing on the edge of the steps, elbows bent so her forearms protected her face but her hands would be spared from the impact. I stood behind her, raised my hands to around shoulder-blade level, and took a deep breath. I was a lot of things but I was not naturally a violent person. I closed my eyes. They stayed closed for a long time and I didn't move.

"JUST PUSH ME," she shouted finally.

"I can't."

"You can."

"I can't."

"You can."

"Aggggghhhhh!"

I pushed.

There was a clatter and a thump and a *thwack thwack*

thwack and a screech of pain. When my eyes sprang open, I saw Meabh in a ball at the bottom of the stairs.

"Are you OK?" I called.

"No! I definitely did something to my ankle," she groaned, but she sounded pleased. "Help me up."

Nothing like a please or thank you, eh? Wonder how much it costs for manners instructors.

I ran down the stairs but before I could reach her, I heard something that made my blood chill.

"Here, let me help." Kavi Thakrar crouched down beside Meabh and in one move scooped her into his arms.

4

For a moment none of us moved. I stalled on the bottom stair, Meabh was mute in Kavi's arms with a stricken expression, and he had a cheerful smile that I didn't quite get.

Kavi was a boy in our year, but he wasn't in our registration class. He was tall, with brown skin, curly black hair, and a sharp jawline. He seemed nice enough but I didn't know him well enough to tell if I could trust him.

"So," I said cagily, "I don't know what you think happened here—"

"I heard Meabh scream at you to push her and then I saw her tumble down the stairs and land in a heap." He grinned. "Which when you think about it is really weird, but you know, these things happen. When my brother was six he fell out of the tree house and didn't even hurt himself, so we were convinced he had superpowers and we decided to test it by doing something amazing. Skateboard off the garage roof. Then my dad found us up there and freaked out and tried to convince us to get down but we thought it was fine because of the powers and Dad ended up having to catch him as he slid off the roof, so like sometimes things that look weird on the surface make sense if you know the story."

"Right." I didn't know what to say to that.

Meabh and I locked eyes. I willed her to come up with a reasonable explanation. She was the smart one. Surely she could come up with something.

"Well, see, we were—"

"Oh no, it's OK. I heard your whole conversation before that, too," Kavi said, trying to wave the hand he had hooked under Meabh's legs.

"Oh." Meabh looked lost for words for the first time in her overly verbal life.

I got the impression Kavi wanted something – he was standing smiling at me and making no attempt to leave or do anything – but I didn't know what it was.

"There's nothing you can really do here," I warned. "If you tell a teacher what happened, Meabh will deny it. It's too stupid to be believable."

I wasn't sure that was true. If someone had a nosy at Meabh's schedule, they might think sabotaging herself for a break made a lot of sense.

But Kavi responded with wide eyes, "You think I want to get you in trouble?"

I exchanged another look with Meabh, who was squirming uncomfortably, like a kitten who didn't want to be held. I thought she'd rather be set down and hobble along on her banjaxed leg.

"Yeah? Why else are you being all *I saw what you did*."
I said the last part in my impression of a threatening scary-movie tone.

"I did not say that," he laughed, then he did a gruff impression of my threatening voice. "I saw what you did, grrrrrr."

"Why were you eavesdropping, then?"

"Ms Devlin told me to come find Meabh and then I heard you both talking and it sounded so interesting and then I realised there's a conspiracy afoot and so I listened to more and it all got very exciting and I'm sorry Meabh that your parents are so mean and your life is all busy and horrible and then I thought maybe *I* could push you off the stairs but then Aideen did it before I could offer and then you fell down here and then I picked you up so I could take you to the nurse and then you two were like *Kavi, why are you threatening us* and then I explained how I wasn't and then it's now."

I blinked.

"Well, let's go, then!" I said uncertainly. I had a bad feeling about this but right now Meabh needed actual medical attention. I'd deal with Kavi later.

Kavi jolted to attention and I followed him and Meabh out of the sports hall. We took the long way around the pitch. Ms Devlin was too engrossed in a fight between two of the girls to notice.

"THAT WAS AT LEAST SIX STEPS!" one was screaming at the other.

"IT WAS LESS THAN FOUR, YOU WAGON."

"Should we tell Ms Devlin about this?" Kavi bounced Meabh in his arms for emphasis. She looked deeply affronted.

"I'm not a *this*," she snapped.

"No," I said, "I think she needs to see someone right away."

The halls were empty and quiet but for the muffled sounds seeping from the classrooms. Kavi filled the silence with a cheerful monologue.

"This is so exciting. Nothing ever happens in school, does it? I mean no offence Meabh because I know you had to be injured in order for us to have this adventure but also it was your own choice of course. Remember the day the dog got into the halls and he was running up and down and everyone started leaving class and trying to catch him but he thought it was a game and kept running away and getting really excited?"

"Yeah," I said, wondering how many words he could fit in between here and the nurse's office.

"This is a bit like that. Like I did not chase the dog that day but I wish I did because it's nice to be involved, but now I'm involved, you know? I'm the guy who carried you to the sick bay. And then when you win the election you can remember that I was part of the whole conspiracy and we can have some kind of signal where when you say your speech you make an inside joke to me and Aideen about the injury and we'll know what you mean but no one else will know what you mean, know what I mean?"

"Uh . . ." Meabh struggled to find the words. She didn't have to though.

"And I think it's really great what you've done, Aideen. You know, you really helped out Meabh here. Everyone needs help sometimes and sure, you don't think help is going to look like pushing someone down the stairs and intentionally injuring them, but you just never know. It's actually really selfless of you because it must be hard to push someone down the stairs and not know if you're going to permanently disfigure them or something."

"Yes, I'm a regular teenage troubleshooter. Come to me with your stupid problem and I'll fix it, it'll only cost you a limb," I joked, relieved that Kavi didn't want to turn us in. If being part of a story was what was important to him, then that was fine. "Besides, it wasn't that hard. Are you saying you've never thought about pushing her down the stairs?"

I smiled serenely at Meabh. She narrowed her eyes.

"Oh my God, no. I have *never* thought of that." He looked down into her face. "I promise. I have never wanted to injure you."

Before Meabh could tell him she believed him, we were at the door to the sick bay.

"Whisht now," I said. "If the nurse hears one word about this, I swear I'll kill you." I suddenly realised that being part of a story was only useful if you got to *tell* the story. "No one hears anything about this, OK?"

I began to feel a little uneasy. The thought that I had literally pushed a girl down the stairs and seriously injured her was suddenly very real. The only thing standing between me and deep shit was one person with a bad case of verbal diarrhea and another who could turn on me at any point. We hadn't exactly been best friends before now, after all.

"I promise! No one will know," Kavi said earnestly.

Weirdly, I believed him.

And Meabh had no reason to double-cross me. Right?

"You can put her down and go," I said to Kavi. "She can make it in the door herself."

"Actually, I'm not sure I can." Meabh winced and pointed at her ankle.

I flinched. It had blown up and was turning purple and gross. It looked like a bloated corpse foot.

"Maybe we need to take your shoe off," I said, feeling queasy.

"OK, I'll hold her and you—"

"Oh my God, you two, we're literally at the office door, just bloody take me inside already."

I gave the door a rap. It's never open because they're afraid someone will break in while the old nun who acts as a "nurse" is having a nap and steal all the ibuprofen to sell on the streets.

The little nun unlocked the door and peered out

suspiciously. She was at least a hundred and fourteen. It was pretty obvious why we were there, but when we didn't offer any explanation, she asked.

"She's injured," I said. "We're not just carrying her around for the craic, you know."

Sister Dymphna frowned. "I don't like young ladies who are cheeky," she said.

I don't like old bats who are too senile to spot a pretty obvious problem.

I forced my lips into a tight smile and followed Kavi through the door, where he set Meabh down on the little single bed next to the wall.

"Off you go, young man," Sister Dymphna said. "It's not appropriate for you to be here with a young lady."

"But I brought her here," he said, pouting as though she'd said something mean instead of telling him to feck off back to class. Kavi was kind of an odd duck. I hadn't before appreciated his "I just escaped from a bunker" wide-eyed approach to life, but I was starting to enjoy it.

Sister Dymphna glared and Kavi scampered off, giving us a sad wave goodbye.

Meabh's groans drew my attention back to her. Her foot looked even worse somehow than it did a few seconds ago.

"Are you on your period, love?" Sister Dymphna asked gently.

Meabh's face contorted at the ridiculousness of this question, but I knew that Sister Dymphna asked this every time anyone came to the sick bay. She was obsessed. You could walk in with a pencil in your eye and she'd ask the same thing. I knew because I regularly skived off and no matter what I said was wrong with me, she looked at me like it was definitely my period and she knew that I wouldn't be having one if Satan hadn't tempted womankind with sin. I could tell Meabh had lost her ability to pretend to be the sweet, perfect student, so I saved her.

"She's sprained her ankle or something."

Sister Dymphna nodded like I'd told her something valuable that she couldn't have found out any other way.

"I'll be off, then," I said, and I gave Meabh a nod, but her eyes were squeezed tight shut. Then I felt a twinge. I think they call it guilt? Maybe I should not have agreed to throw her down a flight of stairs. You're probably not supposed to indulge people who are having actual breakdowns by encouraging their desperate impulses.

"Do you not want to stay here with your friend?" Sister D turned her face to me, pausing while unlacing Meabh's shoe.

I hesitated. Meabh was breathing hard, short breaths like she was in labour as Sister D eased the shoe off. I half expected her foot to come off with it.

I sighed. It was my doing, after all. The least I could do was hang around. Besides, I might have to remind her she'd begged me to do it in case she got any funny ideas about telling on me.

"Don't do me any favours," Meabh snapped as though my reluctance amazed her.

"I won't. Not again," I retorted, and threw myself into the chair that sat at the foot of the bed. I watched with my face scrunched up as Sister D held Meabh's foot and inspected it.

"I think it's sprained, love. But you'll have to get an X-ray just in case. I'll call your father."

Meabh groaned again. I couldn't tell if it was for the foot or her father.

Before she left to get Mr Kowalski, Sister D unlocked a cupboard that contained exactly one box of painkillers, took two out, and put the box back, locking the cupboard again. She gave these to Meabh with a glass of water and an ice pack from the small fridge-freezer that hummed in the corner.

"Good thing she locked that cupboard again, eh?" I said when she was gone. "Else she might come back to find us here absolutely off our tits, snorting lines of ibuprofen off the sink."

"You don't have to stay," Meabh said, not laughing. I suppose expecting her to appreciate my comic stylings was a bit much to ask under the circumstances.

"It's all right. I'm getting out of class, aren't I?"

Meabh made a face. "Do you think if I leave school early it'll count against my attendance record?"

"Probably. And then when you die Jesus will be like,

Go fuck yourself, Meabh. Down to hell with you. I know all about the day you missed double Maths because you went to A and E with a foot that looked like a purple cauliflower."

"Saint Peter," she said, wincing as she tried to shuffle into a more comfortable position.

"What?"

"It's Saint Peter who greets you when you die."

I rolled my eyes.

"Right, well, he'll be there too obviously. But when Jesus saw your name on the naughty list he was like, *Pete, I gotta come down and hang out with you at the gates and see this bitch for myself. Fuckin' chancer, she is."*

"He's not Santa. There's no list."

"Well, of course there's no list. It's all a load of bolloxology, but I'm not going to let that get in the way of making fun of you, am I?"

"Heaven forbid."

"They would if they could. They try and ban everything fun."

We both heard the footsteps at the same time and we both had the same reaction, where your shoulders slump and you resign yourself to being out of control of whatever happens next.

Mr Kowalski entered the room. He looked gentle and sweet. He looked like your friendly school principal, the kind from TV who tries really hard to understand the misunderstood. He was much older than most dads of people my age. He was an average height, average build white man with greying hair swept back in a style that has looked the exact same since the first time I met him. I half think if you reached up and touched it, you'd find it was actually moulded plastic like a Ken doll. He wore relaxed open-collar shirts and beige middle-aged trousers. No. Not trousers, *slacks*. He made embarrassing dad jokes and walked around the school smiling all the time like he was fucking delighted to be there. I didn't trust it one bit. I assumed he let the act drop at home and that's when he was horrible to Meabh.

"What did you do, angel?" he asked, his face pale and his voice concerned. He didn't even notice I was there, he was so worried.

Meabh burst into tears.

Christ, how had she anything left in the tank?

"I. Fell. Down. Stairs," she said through heaving sobs. He sat beside her on the bed and threw his arms around her and stroked her hair until she calmed down. When she got her breath back, she spoke again.

"I won't be able to play in the championship."

"Ah now, Meabh, you don't know that yet. It might be only be a minor twist."

Were his eyes closed? I was no sprainologist but it was definitely not minor.

"I don't think so, Daddy. It feels bad. I don't think it'll heal in time."

I almost choked when she called him "Daddy" but I

reined it in. There'd be time later to make fun of her for that.

"Don't worry, pet. I think if anyone's foot could make a miraculous recovery, it'll be yours."

I could see where she got her arrogance from. He thought even her ligaments were somehow better than everyone else's.

He looked at me then, his face shifting from worry to surprise.

"Aideen." He furrowed his brow.

"Sir."

He didn't know what to say when I didn't offer an explanation. I could tell he was trying to think of a polite way to ask what the hell I was doing with his daughter. I probably wasn't the kind of company he'd choose for her.

We wrestled with the silence for a few seconds, but I won.

"Meabh, do you think you can walk to the car if I get you crutches?" he asked, turning his attention back to her. "I don't think your old man is quite up to carrying you with my bad back. You didn't hurt your wrists or shoulders or anything?"

"My ribs feel a bit sore but I could use crutches." She smiled.

"That's my girl. Such a trooper. See, you'll be back on the pitch in no time. I know you, you won't let a thing like this get you down."

When he'd left the room, presumably to find Sister D

and locate crutches, Meabh's face dimmed. Like the sun that shone out of her arse, creating a halo effect, suddenly faded.

"He seems really worried about you," I said. But I was more than aware that someone could seem like one thing and be another.

"He'll accept it once he hears from the doctor. Maybe it will be broken after all."

"Fingers crossed," I said.

Meabh shifted so she was sitting on the edge of the bed. She looked forlornly at me.

"Can you help me get up?"

"It's just one thing after another with you, isn't it? 'Aideen, push me down the stairs. Aideen, take me to the nurse's office. Aideen, help me stand up.'"

"You're not as funny as you think you are."

"I am though," I said. But I got up and sat beside her so she could throw her arm around me, then hoisted her up to standing. She leaned on her good foot, but when she gingerly tried to put some weight on the other one, she winced.

"Your hair is in my mouth," I said, spitting it out. I resisted the urge to ask what shampoo she used because the scent was heavenly. Couldn't let her know that; her self-esteem was bloody dangerous as it was.

"Don't spit in my hair!"

"Don't get hair in my spit. That's my good saliva."

"You're exhausting."

"Says the girl who considered giving up sleep to take on more activities."

"That's different."

"I agree. It's very fucking different."

"You don't have to swear so much."

"I don't *have* to. But it makes me sound fucking cool."

She almost smiled.

"You can let me go now."

"I don't think I can. Unless you want to sit back down and wait for your crutches."

She eyed the bed.

"No, if I sit down again I won't be able to get up again. My ribs really do hurt."

"Sorry," I said automatically.

"No, don't be silly. You can't precision injure someone with a staircase."

We fell awkwardly silent, her hanging on to my neck. I hadn't realised there was a clock in the room, but suddenly it was ticking loudly.

"Look, seriously. Thank you for doing this." She caught my eye. It was hard not to when her face was almost stuck to my face. "I really do appreciate it. It's such a relief."

I wanted to shrug it off but I couldn't because my shoulders were in use, so I smiled instead and she smiled back. She really did look relieved. Like the stick up her arse had decreased in width or length. Whichever one would affect comfort more.

I felt a warmth in my stomach that I wasn't used to. Was this what good deeds felt like?

"All right, I give up. What is that? Papaya?"

Meabh gave me a blank look.

"Your hair or something. You smell amazing."

She immediately blushed, pink spreading across her slightly sallow cheeks.

"Mango body butter," she said. "From the Body Shop."

Great. I was standing there sniffing her skin. That wasn't weird at all.

Just as I was about to die of shame, the door opened again and I immediately rearranged my face into something more neutral, as though that could make me invisible to the principal.

"You should be resting with your leg elevated unless you absolutely have to be on your feet, Meabh. You want to bring down the swelling as quickly as possible."

"Yeah, Meabh," I said with an exaggerated sigh and a sly hint of a smile, "it's like you *want* to miss the whole season!"

She gave me a dirty look as I helped her into a pair of crutches. I beamed at her.

Then Mr Kowalski set his eyes on me, and I stood frozen while Meabh hobbled off down the corridor.

"Thank you for helping Meabh," Mr Kowalski said when she was out of earshot. "That was very kind."

I resisted the urge to roll my eyes. I wasn't falling for the nice guy bit.

"Now get yourself back to class. I know you're supposed to be in Maths right now and I don't want you missing any more than you have to. Those absences are starting to worry me again, Aideen."

"Yes, sir. Right back to class." I waved him off with a cheery goodbye and when the door swung closed I gave him the finger. It's the little things that keep me going.

5

If the principal wasn't staying the rest of the day, then I didn't see why I should either. I decided my bag would be fine in the sports hall overnight by itself. There was nothing in it anyway except a king-size Snickers. Which I would miss later, but it wasn't worth running into Ms Devlin and being downright bullied into remaining in class.

I took the long way home, looping round town and walking to the bus stop nearest Mam's work. As soon as I caught a glimpse of her laughing in between puffs of what I knew to be strawberry-flavoured vape, my heart slowed down for the first time since that morning when I realised she was gone. That's why I don't need to do PE. I get all my cardio from anxiety about what my mother is doing at any given moment. When I'm one hundred years old and using the Flubberygiblets cash to freeze my bod for whatever reason rich people do that, and they ask me how I survived this long on a diet of chocolate and TV, I'll be able to smile wryly and say it's all thanks to my mam and her parenting choices. I told myself she must have gone outside for a proper smoke that morning and I missed her.

On the bus I got some dirty looks from some middle-aged bore bags who took one look at me in my uniform and assumed I was mitching. People think it's old biddies who give teenagers a hard time but in my experience old biddies love me; it's people my mam's age who are uptight and look at me like I'm gonna burn their houses down. Somehow they can tell I'm poor just by looking at me. I don't know what it is that gives me away. The fact that my stop is a block of flats with graffiti and piles of rubbish dumped outside probably doesn't help. They look at me like I'm about to batter them round the head with a bottle of cider and steal their handbags.

I scowled back. I could be going to the dentist or the doctor or something. They didn't know. I thought about how I really needed to do that essay for Ms Devlin because I could sense today that I'd reached the limit of her patience and if I didn't do this one she'd lose the head.

When I got home the flat was so cold that I couldn't bear to get started on it, though, and instead I made myself three cups of tea in a row and watched daytime telly until it changed to early evening game shows and I heard Mam's key in the lock. She came in, threw her coat on the couch, and collapsed into it.

"Mam, we're trying to use the hooks, remember?" I grumbled, picking up her coat. I'd picked up these really pretty hooks in the charity shop that looked a bit like doorknobs but all colourful and painted. I'd hammered them into the wall myself with a shoe heel.

"Yes, love, sorry, habit of a lifetime."

You could say that again. If she came home and didn't leave everything lying at her arse I'd know the body snatchers had landed. I hugged her and she smiled. I don't hug her because I love her, although I do; I hug her to check. I didn't smell anything except a bit of her good perfume she got for Christmas last year. Not so much that it was trying to cover anything up though.

"Don't be giving me grief now," she said, wagging her finger at me. "I've had a long day and my feet are killing me. Do you know I basically did all of Margaret Burns's colour today, mixed it, applied it, washed it out, gave that old bat a head massage, the groans of her, like, obscene, and who does she tip? Bloody Nadine just because she's the one with the pair of scissors. And you'd think Nadine would maybe give me a euro or two because she knows I spent a lot longer on her than she did, but you know she wouldn't put her hand in her pocket to scratch her arse, that one."

"You're right, Mam. I don't know why you bother with her."

"Well, someone else did give a big tip. Little old Annie. And you know, if you look in my pocket you might find something to interest you."

I went back to Mam's coat and rifled through her pockets, extracting a small bottle.

"Ah, Mam, thank you so much!" I hugged her for real this time. It was fancy hair serum, the only one I'd ever tried that did anything to help the curls. It cost a bomb. We couldn't really afford to spend money on this. And yet, selfishly I was pleased she had without consulting me because I would have said no.

I felt bad for being suspicious of her all day when she was thinking of me and doing sweet things like this.

"Are you hungry?" I asked.

"Starving."

"I'll put something on," I said. "Go on, relax. And take that thing off. It's going to blow up someday." I meant the vape, which hung from a chain around her neck.

"It's grand, love. It's not one of those knockoff ones."

"Well, don't come crying to me when you've a massive hole in your tit," I said. "You'll be a quare sight then, walking round the town. *There goes Lisa Tit Hole*, they'll say as you pass by."

She rolled her eyes but she took the vape from around her neck and set it pointedly on the arm of the couch. Great. Now our couch could blow up and set our whole flat on fire. I didn't say that though because I'd done enough nagging.

The bread had a couple of tiny specks of mould on the crusts so I picked them off before popping them in the toaster.

"We need bread," I said, glancing over at Mam, who had put *Fair City* on.

"Oh right, sorry, love, you said that last night, didn't you? I totally forgot. I'll get it tomorrow, I promise."

I made a mental note to take a couple of euro from Mam's work tunic and stop at the shop on the way home.

We watched TV for a bit, but Mam was mostly on her phone. The only person who ever messaged me was Holly, but I kept glancing at my phone thinking I must have got a message and not heard it. Eventually I gave up and decided to message her. When I was mid-typing my phone buzzed in my hand and my heart did a little smile. Finally.

But it wasn't Holly.

The profile picture was of Hillary Clinton but I doubted she was getting in touch. Although I assumed if she did she would be disappointed with me for not living up to my potential, so it wasn't encouraging either way.

Unknown number
Hi! I only just got home.
We were there all day.
No breaks, just a sprain.

Aideen
Wrng #

Unknown number
No, it's not the wrong number.
I know perfectly well whose
number this is.

Aideen
R U actually sugestn there's no way
U cuda got a wrng numbr?

Meabh
Well, I didn't, did I? Besides,
that's not the point.
You know who this is.

Aideen
wel iz it sprained enuf 4 U 2 stay off
d team untl aftr d election?

Meabh
Genuinely cannot continue this
conversation if you're going to
type like that.

Aideen
K

I grinned to myself and waited. Mam's phone rang then; she got up and I heard it ringing all the way down the hall. She must have waited until her bedroom door was closed to answer it.

Meabh
Fine. Though I think translation of your messages
will soon be used alongside sudoku and crossword
puzzles to keep the minds of the elderly active.

Aideen
Wots ur prblm?

Meabh
I think you're contributing
to the downfall of the
English language.

Aideen
Not tht u snob. i fixd ur
lyf didnt i? sum ppl wud say thx

Meabh
I did say thanks. And I'm texting you because
I wanted to warn you. I shouldn't be telling you
this but Dad was asking after you on the way
to the hospital. He said that if you didn't pull
your socks up he'd have to pursue it. Then he
realised he shouldn't be saying it to me and
stopped talking.

Aideen
lol

This was actually bad news. I knew what "pursue it"
meant. With a horrible principal it would mean expulsion
or something. With a wannabe hero like Meabh's dad it
would mean education welfare, which was actually worse.
They were the social workers who came after you if you
didn't go to school often enough. Busybodies.

Meabh
You are hopeless.

Aideen
Ur welcome

Meabh
Thank you. I owe you.

Remember how I said this all started with Meabh and her tantrum? Well, it did. And she wouldn't like to hear this, but it's her fault it continued too. That text is important. It's gonna come back to bite her in the ass.

A couple of hours later, Mam got up to go to bed after spending the whole evening texting and I finally tore a few sheets of paper from a file block.

"Are you not going to bed?" she yawned.

"Homework."

"Right. Oh, by the way," she added with a kind of casualness that set my teeth on edge, "I'm going away with Bernie after work tomorrow. Just for a night."

I said nothing.

"She got a voucher for the spa at the Hillgrove and wants to take me!"

I can't stand Bernie. She's a bad influence. She gets Mam all worked up about the little things and stresses her out until Mam starts seeing problems where there are none. It's always my job to talk her down after that.

But that's not why I had that sick feeling in my stomach. Bernie didn't have an expensive voucher for two people to a fancy spa. And if she did, she wouldn't take Mam. I thought of her weird absence this morning, her secret phone call, the constant texting. This meant only one thing.

Dad was back.

After Mam went to bed, I tried to focus on my essay. I had to do *something*. I stared at the pages in my lap and tried flicking through the book. Having written ten lines that I had to squeeze out of me, I wanted to cry. How was anyone supposed to do this? Most of the words were easy, but they were in a jumbly, tumbly order so nothing made sense. I went to the chapter on the poem in our textbook and tried reading it, but concentrating on the long sentences made me feel like my eyes were crossed. I don't think I understood it all, but the first two paragraphs at least explained what the poem was about so I wrote them out in my own words. The whole time I was really thinking about Mam though. Why was Dad sniffing around again? What did he want this time? Maybe he'd give us some money. Maybe he'd stay. Maybe he'd realised that Mam was the love of his life and he wouldn't mess her around again.

Why did Mam always let him come back? Why was she such a doormat? Why was I the one who had to fix our life after she blew it to smithereens again and again? Was there something I could do this time *before* it all got fucked up instead of trying to mend it afterwards?

6

Even though I was up half the night and could *feel* the eye bags, I was early for school because around half six I simply gave up on trying to sleep. I got the early bus and figured I could spend the extra time with Holly, since she was always early. I texted her to let her know I'd be there. While I was walking up the hill towards the main entrance, Kavi appeared as if from nowhere, holding a set of three helium balloons. Each one had a single word of the phrase "Get Well Soon" printed on it.

"Please tell me those are not for Meabh," I said.

"But they are. Aren't they nice? I was going to stick them on her locker. I have tape in my bag. One time I was off school for three weeks with glandular fever and when I came back no one even noticed I was gone and I thought it would be nice for Meabh to feel like she was missed."

I rubbed the bridge of my nose. "Kavi, I don't think you should give her those."

"Why not?"

The truth was I didn't want it getting about that Kavi was a witness. My gut said he had no intention of telling this story, but if for any reason Mr K suspected anything

I didn't want him to grill Kavi. He seemed too good to outright lie to the principal.

I was wrong about that.

"They're plastic. Meabh won't like that."

"God, you're right. They're terrible for the environment. That's like getting Meabh a reverse gift. She loves the environment."

"Right, Kavi, we all love the environment. Just stick them in your locker or something."

He nodded seriously and began sprinting up the hill without another word, the balloons trailing behind him in the air.

No one was in the sports hall when I arrived early for registration, except Holly. Mostly people hung out by the lockers until the first bell. I imagined Kavi there now and realised I had not made the most inconspicuous suggestion. The thought of him wrestling balloons into his locker made me want to laugh and bury my face in my hands at the same time.

Holly smiled and patted a bouncy ball beside her when she saw me. I took a wobbly seat and she handed me a coffee cup from the school café. She was shivering in the huge hall, which hadn't quite heated up yet, because she refused to wear the puffy coat her mam had bought. Actually she'd given it to me and I was wearing it and it was super warm.

I took my cup and sniffed. Steamed milk with cinnamon. My favourite. "Thanks."

63

"Anytime, hun. Why are you so early? What happened to you yesterday? Did you hear Queen Meabh broke her ankle? I saw her this morning by the lockers, and she was wearing some kind of special boot."

I ignored her first questions. Normally I would tell Holly I suspected my dad was back in our lives, but saying it out loud made it more real and I wanted to pretend for another little while. "She didn't break it, it's sprained."

"How do you know?" Holly said, shocked. I never knew the gossip from school unless I heard it from her. I quite enjoyed having information she didn't. Even if I had to lie about it.

"I was there when she fell."

"WHAT? Oh my God. Tell me everything. How'd she do it? Did she trip over her own ego? Did her head swell up so much that she couldn't stay balanced and she fell over? Did she simply collapse under the weight of her own arrogance?"

I laughed.

"I think she just tripped like a regular person," I said. "She was actually pretty hurt. Her foot swelled up and looked really weird."

"Is that it?" she said, clearly disappointed that I didn't have a more embarrassing story for her.

"That's it." I shrugged. I obviously wasn't telling her the real story. It occurred to me that maybe this was the first time I'd ever kept anything from Holly, and I felt a terrible urge to spill it all. But it just felt wrong. Like I'd be handing her the perfect way to take Meabh down, and even if I didn't like Meabh, I had agreed to help her. I couldn't stab her in the back now.

Holly looked annoyed for a second. Then she rearranged her face into something more neutral and sighed.

"I'm only sorry I won't get the chance to be chosen as captain over her. She'll think the only reason she didn't get it is because she *can't* get it."

"Who cares what she thinks?" I said. "She wasn't going to get it anyway. You were. At least this way you don't have to deal with her on the team at all."

"I suppose," Holly said, but she didn't seem comforted. "You don't get it though – you don't have a *thing*. You don't know what it's like to be the best at something and then have someone else continually try and take it from you. She doesn't even deserve it. She only got captain last year because her dad's the principal and Ms Devlin was being a lick arse."

Oh yeah, it must be so hard for you being great at things, and it's so easy for me being rubbish at everything.

That wasn't fair. I shouldn't think that. She didn't mean it like that. I brushed off the prickly pin feelings.

The rest of the class began arriving. A few grumpy, crumpled morning faces staring blankly, a lot more loud chatter and laughing.

"Will you do my eyes?" Holly produced a liquid eyeliner

pen from her pocket. "I spent twenty minutes on it this morning and I couldn't get them even," she pouted.

Eyeliner is my one great skill. So in fact, I am the best at that. My expertise in perfectly equal lines and delicate flicks is mostly useless but definitely unparalleled.

Holly's face relaxed as she closed her eyes and her cheek was soft where I rested my hand to steady it as I applied the black liquid in one single swift motion.

She checked it in her phone camera.

"Perfect, even while bouncing," she said, and smooched the air in my general direction.

I took a sip of my coffee, feeling unreasonably pleased with myself. Holly was my best friend and I liked making her happy. Some days, like today, it was easy.

"I really shouldn't have wasted my morning on make-up anyway because I didn't do that English homework. Did you?" Holly seemed hopeful that we would at least both be in the same boat. Although she didn't have two strikes already.

"I did for a change," I said, and she slumped a little so I added, "But it's terrible."

"Ms Devlin is going to kill me."

"Why didn't you do it last night?"

"Oh. Last-minute thing. I met up with someone and went to see a film. When I got back I was too tired. Meant to get up early, but you know what I'm like."

I didn't say anything. Holly joined the paper last year and made new friends. She introduced them to me and they were nice enough but they never became *my* friends. Since she got editor in September she'd been spending more and more time with them. Especially Jill. I couldn't help but feel a little jealous even though I knew she was entitled to friendships outside of ours. She'd always had a lot of friends. But until Jill, there hadn't been anyone she was really close to. That was me. I was the one she went places with and told her secrets to. Like the time she saw balls for the first time and was surprised to find out they weren't separate on the outside. We had both pictured them as being a bit like a Newton's cradle. No one else knew that. Holly admitted to me the thoughts and feelings that made her sound stupid. We had always trusted each other with those things.

Meabh finally hobbled in and stood in front of a ball. I watched her glare at it as though the rubber sphere was telling her she couldn't possibly manoeuvre herself onto it with that boot. Her eyes said *challenge accepted*. Gingerly she lifted her bad foot and in a sort of one-legged squat lowered herself onto it. A few people laughed. Meabh didn't seem at all embarrassed and when she landed without incident her face said *I told you so*. Then she noticed me watching and our eyes met for the briefest second before I looked away. What were the rules now? Were we meant to say hello to each other?

Ms Devlin strode in and distracted me by pointing at both Holly and me. She didn't even have to tell us to leave the coffee cups outside. I downed as much of mine as I could while slinking slowly to the door and setting the cup on the windowsill. Meabh's eyes followed us, probably because she was worried we'd leave our litter behind when we left.

Ms Devlin called names and reminded people to check the bottoms of their shoes for gum because she'd found some stuck to the BRAND-NEW sports hall floor (which presumably she personally inspected each night and lovingly caressed) and she would rather assume carelessness than outright sabotage at this early stage.

"Any more takers for student council president?" Ms Devlin said, and she looked disappointed in us all when no one said anything. "There's still time. All you have to do is submit a few proposals. It's only a few pages."

I could feel Meabh's energy humming from the corner of the room. She really believed someone was dying to snatch her new crown away before she could polish it.

On our way out I made a point of looking directly at her as I picked up our used coffee cups and took them with me. Holly didn't seem to notice. She was babbling about something else.

"We don't have any classes together for the rest of the day," she pouted. "Have lunch with me at the restaurant."

Transition years were allowed to go off school grounds to this café down the street. People called it the restaurant to differentiate it from the school café. Holly noticed me hesitating.

I really wanted to go for lunch with Holly. I hadn't got to spend much quality time with her lately.

"It's my treat," she said pleadingly.

"You already bought me coffee this morning," I said.

"And you did my eyeliner. Those are professional-grade skills. We're even," she replied.

We were never even. But I smiled anyway. I could never say no to her.

When the lunch bell rang I waited for Holly at the front steps of the main entrance. I stuck my headphones in and played my Creepy Vibes and Spooky Beats playlist through my covert Wi-Fi access and leaned my head back to soak up a rare ray of January sun. Dozens of students milled past me and I felt like I was in a music video. One of the ones where the singer stands still and everyone moves really fast around them. Then someone touched me and I jumped. I expected to see Holly when I opened my eyes. But the figure standing over me was blocking the sun. A feat Holly was not capable of.

"Kavi?"

So I know I said it all started with Meabh and her nonsense. But there was Kavi. Where would I be without him? Maybe it would have been a very short story about how I once pushed a girl downstairs and then carried on with the rest of my life as normal.

"I have been looking all over for you," he said, exasperated.

I was skeptical. "What do you want?"

"I need you to come with me," he said urgently.

"I need to get lunch. I'm starving."

"Don't you even want to know why?"

I shrugged and closed my eyes again.

"Are you tired? Did you not sleep last night? Sometimes I don't sleep well. You know those nights where you go to bed and you lie there and you're like, ah, I really need to go to sleep right now because I have to wake up really early but then the weird thoughts come into your head and you get sucked into the weird thought place and forget that you're meant to be sleeping until you're like, oh no, I'm supposed to be trying to sleep, so you close your eyes again but then like ten minutes later you realise you've done it again. I don't know why that happens some nights, you know?"

"You should try mixing sugar into your coffee during the day instead of cocaine, Kavi."

"What do you mean? I don't drink coffee. You know my mam says that you shouldn't drink coffee until you're twenty-one because it stunts your growth and I don't want to stunt my growth. I'm six feet but I'd like to be six foot one because my brother said if you're over six feet you get more dates on Tinder. Even though I can't go on Tinder yet, I'm thinking I will when I'm eighteen, and I want to be able to maximize my chances at finding true love."

Pulling my earphones out, I opened my eyes and took a long look at him. He was tall. Though to me everyone was tall. He had soft-looking skin and black hair with cute curls; his eyes were big, dark brown, and framed by long thick lashes I'd kill for. He was very good-looking, but I wasn't sure Tinder's USP was long-lasting matches.

"Kavi, I feel confident you will not lose out on the love of your life because you're *only* six foot tall," I said, not adding that he'd have to find a good fucking listener. "But tell me, and I cannot stress this enough, in *one sentence*, why are you here?"

He frowned. His tongue started to peek out of his mouth and I knew he was struggling to fit everything he wanted to say into one sentence.

"I brought you a new client," he said finally, clearly proud of his restraint.

I pinched the bridge of my nose. "What are you talking about?"

"Come with me," he insisted.

I had to admit I was curious. Then I saw Holly approaching. Jill was beside her. They were laughing at some probably very smart joke. I looked at Kavi. He looked so hopeful.

"Hey, Jill's going to join us, OK?" Holly asked. She didn't even notice Kavi at first, until I glanced at him and she realised she'd interrupted our conversation. Confusion settled in the furrows of her brow.

Oblivious, Jill looked brightly at me. "I thought we could go to this café near the cinema. We had the most amazing Malteser squares there last night."

Oh, we did, did we?

My stomach turned.

"I'm sorry," I said airily. "I need to skip. I promised Kavi we'd do a thing and I totally forgot."

Jill smiled at Kavi. Holly's frown deepened.

"What thing are you two doing?" She caught herself mid-sentence and tried to end on a pleasantly curious note rather than the deeply suspicious one she'd started on.

I glanced at Kavi. Without a second of hesitation he chimed in.

"Irish Oral. My teacher asked if I could do a demonstration of a conversation for the Junior Cert classes and I asked Aideen because she's basically fluent."

I felt a weird flush of pride that Kavi even knew I was a good speaker. Holly always did better than me at essays and stuff but it wasn't because of the language. I speak English fluently too and it has never helped me write about symbolism in Emily Dickinson either.

Holly smiled a tight smile. "Text me later?"

I nodded and waved her off feeling a pang as she and Jill erupted into giggles a second later.

Kavi took me to a spot I often hung out in, especially if Holly was doing paper stuff at lunch or she was off sick. It's a prefab building at the back of the school that for some reason has been planted in the wrong direction. Instead of the doors facing towards the school, they are at the back, facing the wall that surrounds the whole grounds. I would sit on the steps, where I could be pretty sheltered from anyone noticing me. The odd couple came round to try and get the shift where no one could see them, but they would mosey on pretty quickly when they saw I was there. It was peaceful and although the view wasn't great, I felt like I could relax because no one was looking at me.

"I arranged to meet her here because I've seen you here before," Kavi said.

So much for privacy.

"That one time. Do you remember? I came here to kiss Jessica Ashley and you were already here and I don't know if you were waiting to kiss someone too although it didn't look like it because you were eating a sandwich and that doesn't seem like a thing people do before kissing but you just never know. And a week later Jessica and I broke up, so it's a pretty bad memory."

Then a girl appeared. I recognised her; her name was Orla. She was Black, with dark skin, long hair, and a normally beaming smile. There were four paid and much coveted student jobs in our school, one of which was office aide, and Orla had snagged that post this year. They had to give up lunchtimes and stay the night before the paper's publication to help with printing. I'd noticed her a couple of weeks ago when I went with Holly to watch. She'd been sitting in the corner smiling at her phone and ignoring

Holly scanning the proofs and having an absolute conniption over a split infinitive she hadn't caught.

"This is Orla," Kavi said. She wasn't smiling her normal smile. She looked nervous.

"I know."

"It's OK. She's nice," Kavi said to her.

Did I seem not nice?

"Orla has a problem," Kavi explained.

"And?" I said, definitely not committing to anything. I never said I would fix everyone's problems for them.

"And you said you were a troubleshooter. That you fix people's problems."

I stared at him. Apparently I had kind of said it.

"Kavi . . . that was a joke."

His face fell. He looked crushed. Like Santa himself had descended from heaven and told him he was a bad boy and he wasn't getting any presents for Christmas. Weirdly, I didn't want to be the one who'd made him look like that. But what was I supposed to do?

"Just listen," he said pleadingly.

Well, I guessed that was what I was supposed to do.

I sighed as though this was the world's biggest inconvenience.

"I'm not saying I can do anything about it," I warned. "And I'm not maiming anyone either. That was a one-time deal."

"Did she say *maim*?" Orla said faintly.

"What can I supposedly do for you, Orla?"

She looked at Kavi. He nodded encouragingly. She looked at me.

"I need my phone," she whispered, and she looked over her shoulder like someone would be dying to listen to this conversation.

I was unimpressed. How much could you really *need* a phone?

"Seriously?"

"It's in Mr Kowalski's office."

"So it was confiscated? You'll get it back tomorrow."

She shook her head, eyes wide. "You don't understand. It's the fourth time it's been confiscated and he's going to call my dads in."

"I can't really do anything about that. I don't think stealing your phone back will make him forget. If anything, you'll be in more trouble."

I didn't get this girl. She had to be at least seventeen, if not eighteen, and she was worried about being told off by her parents? Get in trouble, suck it up. Life goes on.

"I don't want to steal it. I just need to delete some stuff on it before they get it, in case my dads see it. They'll read the messages when Mr Kowalski gives them the phone."

Kavi mouthed the word *sexts* and pointed at his nipples.

"Don't you have a passcode on it?"

"Yes, but they'll make me enter it."

"So, when you're putting in the code, delete the messages?"

"I might not have time to do that. I can't risk it."

"So let me get this straight. You want me to break into the principal's office and delete your sensitive material off your phone and put it back clean?"

"NO!" she shouted, as though my words could magically make it happen. "Sorry. I mean *I* need to delete them. I don't want you to see them any more than I want my parents to see them." She rubbed the back of her neck. "I'd pay you but I don't have any money," she added, biting her lip.

"Yeah, same," I said.

Kavi looked hopefully at me. Orla looked miserable.

Was this even something I could do? How was I supposed to get into his office when he wasn't there? Confiscated phones were in a locked drawer. Mine had found its way in there more than once. But I wasn't fucking Nancy Drew, I didn't carry a lock-picking kit with me at all times.

And then it hit me. I didn't need one.

I needed a favour.

Remember how I said Meabh was going to regret that text?

7

Meabh
I can't do it.

Aideen
U sed u owe me 1.
U sed those xact wrds.

I sent her a screenshot of her own text like it was a legally binding agreement.

Meabh
I keep thinking about how you
must have made your autocorrect
recognise these halfwords and I don't
understand why you'd go to that kind
of effort.

Aideen
You'r avoidin th questio.

Meabh
Oh my God. You'er just doing it
to annoy me, aren't you?

Aideen

Ha ha u spelled you're wrng.

Aideen

Also u owe me.

I sent the screenshot again and hoped the message radiated the same smug satisfaction I felt.

Meabh

You'll get in trouble. You'll get caught.

Aideen

Will I tho? Wen I hve keys + door code? I no u no wat it is. How will ne1 no I've even been there?

Aideen

Hello?

Meabh

You promise it's for a good cause?

Aideen

I sed dat alreddy

Meabh

Yeah, but how do I know your idea of a good cause matches with my idea of a good cause?

I waited ten full minutes.

Meabh
1:00 a.m. The front entrance.

Mam wasn't home when I left the house in Holly's puffy coat. She'd left for her trip with "Bernie" before I'd even got home from school that day. Honestly, it was kind of a relief. I'd had a sick feeling in my stomach on the bus home worrying that I'd run into Dad. I didn't want to see them getting into his car, or even catch a glimpse of it turning the corner. She'd left me two twenties on the fridge door, stuck by a magnet. Definitely Dad's money.

I wanted to be a person who had so much integrity that they wouldn't spend it, but integrity is for people with other income streams, so I'd gone to the corner shop, bought a few essentials, and put the rest in the back of my pants drawer. I always tried to siphon off a bit of cash here and there and stash it for when a bill came. Even though Dad being around was bad news, at least it would help me build up my little safety net of cash. But as soon as I had the thought, I felt guilty. It wasn't worth it.

That night my coat didn't quite keep out the bite of the night air and my heart hammered as I walked out of my building past a car with its lights on, illuminating a group of boys maybe a bit older than me. I trained my eyes straight in front of me. I didn't even want to notice what colour the car was. The pub at the end of the street had people standing outside smoking and laughing with drinks in their hands. I thought one guy was pissing up the side wall but I tried not to look. No one said anything to me as I passed on the other side. I tensed up anyway. I didn't want to put my earbuds in until I was in a quieter neighborhood. If someone got near me I wanted to hear them.

The buses don't run at night, so I had to walk the whole way, but thankfully the closer I got to school, the less stressful the journey was. Streetlights were broken up with trees, flats turned into houses with leafy gardens, and drunk people were replaced with blissful silence. I took the opportunity to fill it with Taylor Swift. I know it's basic to love Tay, but the girl knows how to write a bop. I've never even had a girlfriend, yet somehow I listen to one of her albums and I end up thinking wistfully of all my lost loves and feeling hope that I'll find love again somehow.

When I got to the school gate I let the earbuds dangle round my neck and considered how to tackle the problem I hadn't seen coming. The giant wrought-iron gates were locked with a chain and padlock. The sight of them made me realise what I was doing. I wasn't sneaking into the kitchen for a midnight snack. I was breaking and entering. I tried to reach the padlock but the gaps between the bars of the gate weren't wide enough to let me get my arms in and reach round. Even if Meabh thought to bring this key too, and let's face it, she obviously would, I wouldn't be able to open it.

I looked around. The gates were bordered on either side by half a stone wall topped off with wrought-iron fencing. If I could get on the wall bit, I'd be able to get over the fence, but I wasn't going to be able to make it that far in the first place. It was almost as if the gate and wall were designed to keep people out.

Oh well, too bad. Better go home to bed and start my criminal career another time.

I took my phone out to text Meabh and tell her the plan was off. I couldn't text Orla, for obvious reasons, but hopefully she'd figure it out when she arrived and I wasn't here.

But what if she waited around in the dark for me? That didn't sound safe. What if she waited for ages and something happened to her? I'm not saying it would be my fault – it's not like I'd be the one who jumped out of the bushes and kidnapped her to sacrifice her to Satan – but I'd feel bad if it happened all the same. It was better that none of us were loitering alone in the dead of night, even if it was in a nice area. I'd just have to loiter alone in the dead of night until she turned up.

Aideen
Plans off.

As soon as the whoosh of the message sounded, I heard a tut in reply. I looked up and Meabh was standing there with her phone screen lighting up her face. That meant I could see the disapproval clearly. I could also see that her sharp bob had been ruffled by sleep, or at least pretending to sleep before she snuck out. It suited her. She looked softer, less like a scary teacher.

"There's an apostrophe in 'plan's off.' It's a contraction. *The plan is off.*"

So much for that.

"How is it that you live a life of scheduled pee breaks and yet you still somehow manage to find the time and energy to correct my grammar?"

"I have loads more free time now though," she said, and she jiggled her foot, showing off the space boot the doctor had given her.

"Well, you need to hobble back to the mother ship," I said. "The gates are locked. From the inside."

"I have the key."

Of course you do.

"I can't reach the lock, I already tried," I said, feeling my cheeks heat up. I was glad she couldn't see that in the dark. "You must think I'm really stupid."

"I never said that." She sounded surprised.

"You didn't have to. Look, never mind that. How do these gates get open in the morning?"

"The caretaker uses the side gate, which you can only

82

get into with a key card, and then he opens the front gates from the inside."

"And you have the key card?"

"No, there's only one. The caretaker has it, not Dad."

"So we're going home!" I checked my phone. I could get home and have a mug of hot milk instead of going to jail.

"I didn't say that either. You need to go over the fence and then you can unlock the padlock."

"And if my legs were six foot long, I would totally climb up there and do that. But you're seeing the problem, right?" I said, waving an arm down the length of my body. There was no way Meabh could get around *that*.

"I brought assistance." She shrugged off her backpack and opened it up, pulling out a plastic fold-up footstool.

I stared at it.

"If I'm going to do something criminal I'm going to make sure I do it right." Meabh *tsked*. "Fail to prepare—"

"Don't finish that." I pointed my finger at her. "The last time you said that to me I almost killed you. Don't tempt me."

"What are you talking about?"

I could still hear her snotty little voice and I imitated it. *"Fail to prepare."* When she didn't seem to get it, I added, "The audition?"

Her eyes were blank for a second and then I watched as the memory came back.

"For the sixth-class play?" she asked slowly.

The last year of primary school, our whole class did a play in Irish and entered a national competition for Irish-language school drama. I'd memorised the whole audition monologue for the part I wanted: the narrator. The best part, because it had the most lines and you didn't have to make a dick of yourself prancing around the stage. The day of the audition, the teacher gave us all a consent form that said if we got through to the finals we'd have to pay €30 to go to Galway and perform. I didn't think Mam would be able to afford that. I didn't throw the audition but I remember my heart was so heavy I couldn't perform. I forgot a few lines and stuttered over the ones I remembered. When I sat down, Holly asked me what had happened and I whispered back that I didn't have time to practise the night before. I told her the truth later. She said she would have paid for me out of her credit union savings. But Meabh overheard me anyway. "Fail to prepare, prepare to fail," she said, flouncing up to the stage to deliver her flawless audition.

"I forgot about that," Meabh said, looking uncomfortable. "Hey! Is that why you put rose hips in my costume the first night?"

We had not got through to the finals. Some blamed Meabh's itchy performance as the narrator.

"I forgot about that," I said, grinning.

If Meabh was willing to go through with this, then I certainly could. Then I looked at the gate again and stopped grinning. Why hadn't I thought of how to get over it? I should have known there'd be a lock and it didn't take a genius to see how hard it would be to climb over the rails. Some help I was, if I didn't even think of the basics.

I took the stool from her and tested my weight on it. It looked flimsy but it held out. With the extra height, my hands could reach the top of the wall, but I didn't have the strength to pull myself up.

"Come on," Meabh said in a Ms Devlin tone of voice. "Use all of your upper-body strength, not just your arms."

"I'm trying," I said through gritted teeth. "But I don't have upper-body strength. I'd like to see you do it!"

"I could do it!" Meabh rolled up her sleeves. "I can do five reps of close-grip pull-ups."

"Stop saying words that don't mean anything," I said, but I did at least understand with her sleeves rolled up that Meabh had proper guns. They were kind of impressive. Not that I'd tell her that.

She pushed me out of the way and tried to get on the footstool. The thing was, her boot was bigger than the whole step and when she tried to stand on it, it didn't look remotely safe.

"You can't get on that," I said. Then I sighed. "Let me try again."

"Maybe I could give you a boost?" she said, though she didn't look convinced.

"You can't put that much weight on your foot. You're not steady as it is."

"Maybe when Orla gets here she'll be able to do it?"

"I don't know. I didn't ask her how many reps she can do." Orla hadn't struck me as a pull-ups kind of girl.

Meabh pursed her lips.

"I could give you a boost," Kavi said brightly.

"What the actual fuck?" I clutched my heart.

"Why are *you* here?" Meabh demanded.

Kavi looked bewildered at our mixture of confusion and shock.

"Why is *she* here?" another voice chimed in. It was Orla this time and she was pointing at Meabh.

Meabh *hmphed* and drew herself up, apparently finding it galling that anyone would question her presence at anything, even a midnight break-in.

"I am the only reason you're even getting in here for your little mission," she said.

Orla rounded on me.

"You told *her*?" she asked, disbelieving. "Is this some kind of trap? She's the principal's daughter!"

"You're Principal Kowalski's daughter?" Kavi asked, seemingly surprised by this information.

Meabh rolled her eyes. "Kowalska is just the feminine version of Kowalski."

"I know that. I don't want to assume that just because you have a Polish name and Mr Kowalski has the same

Polish name that you're related. I don't want people assuming every Indian kid in school is related to me. I mean, that's really offensive, and I don't want to offend you."

"The only other Indian kid in school is your brother," Meabh pointed out.

"For now." He shrugged. "Maybe next year there'll be loads, and I don't want people going round thinking they're all my brother. Aren't you the one who said the other day that Ireland is a country that has entered a period of racial and cultural diversification and that now is the time to address the issues of systemic racism and xenophobia embedded in our society? And then you spent like ten minutes giving out about that lady politician who keeps posting pictures of brown kids and Eastern European kids and complaining about there being no 'Irish' people left, until Mr McCann promised that he would not use the words Celtic and Irish interchangeably again?"

Meabh's mouth dropped open ever so slightly.

"I mean. Yes. I did say that. *Exactly* that."

Kavi grinned broadly. Not an I-caught-you-out-with-your-own-words kind of grin. He looked genuinely pleased that he'd repeated word for word what she'd said and now they were on the same page.

Meabh eyed Kavi with new respect, even if he wasn't smug enough to rub "winning" their exchange in her face the way she would.

Then her face lit up. "By the way, don't say *lady* politician. She's just a politician. And a dickhead."

"Not a lady dickhead," I added.

Orla huffed loudly, deliberately. The three of us looked at her. She was standing with her hands on her hips and tapping her foot.

"That was all very fun and everything, but you still haven't explained to me why the hell you told Meabh Kowalska about my . . . problem. Or what on earth she's doing here."

"Chill your tits," I said. "I have not told her what your problem is. But do I look like feckin' Columbo to you? You wanted into the school. I needed a way in. And Meabh here owes me a little favour."

Something occurred to me then. Call it divine inspiration. Call it a sudden spurt of genius. Call it the stupid idea that set me further down a path that had started with Meabh's tantrum and would end up being either the best or worst thing that ever happened to me.

In the moment all I thought was that it had sure come in handy having Meabh owe me one. And Orla worked in the school office. Maybe she'd be able to doctor my attendance record. Or my grades.

"And so do you," I said.

"What do you mean?" Orla asked suspiciously, glancing at Kavi. He was the one who'd brought her to me, after all.

"I mean, I do this for you, then you owe me a favour. Get it?"

"What about tickets to my modern dance class performance? We're doing a Britney retrospective next month."

"Uh . . . no. I pick the favour."

"What if I can't do it? What if you, like, ask me for a kidney or something?"

"I don't need a kidney. And I'm not going to ask you for something you can't do. What good is that to me?"

She bit her lip. Then she nodded.

"Do you want to buy tickets to the Britney thing, then? They're only fifteen euros a head."

"All right then." I clapped my hands together, pretending I hadn't heard that. "Let's do this."

"So you do want me to give you a boost, then?" Kavi asked, clasping his hands together in preparation.

"Are you kidding me? Kavi, you're six foot ten. Climb the fuck over the wall and let us in," I said, and threw the keys at him.

8

Meabh insisted that there was no high-tech security, but I kept imagining invisible sensors crisscrossing the grounds and having to do an elaborate gymnastics routine to get through them. Or worse.

"Don't you think if there were school attack dogs, A, that would be terribly unsafe for a building full of children, and B, you'd have seen some sign of them before? Where do you think they keep these imaginary dogs of yours?" Meabh rolled her eyes.

I answered by shrugging and leading our distinctly unstealthy group around the perimeter and up a grassy hill to the side entrance.

"My feet are getting wet," Meabh moaned. "Can we not go up the path?"

"Liar. Only one foot is getting wet. You'll live."

The path was lined with solar lamps that were fading already, but I wasn't going to take any chances. When we reached the building's side entrance my heart was pounding, and only partly because I'd had to walk all the way up a hill. There was a keypad with a flashing red light.

Meabh caught my eye for the briefest moment. Hers

shone in the dark. I could tell she was having a feeling, a moment of pause. I didn't know her well enough to read what it meant though. It crossed my mind that this really *was* a trap. That she was so offended that I'd do something as morally outrageous as break into this hallowed institution after hours that she had arranged a sting operation. Was her hesitation a sign that she felt bad about her forthcoming betrayal after I'd helped her? Or did it just mean she'd never done anything like this before and was concerned that it was some kind of stain on her soul that she couldn't take back?

"Hurry up to fuck," Orla said, rubbing her arms. "This cold is going to seize up my muscles and I have a rehearsal in the morning."

I locked eyes with Meabh again, trying to tell her that it would be OK. She sucked in a breath and pulled her gaze from mine to focus on the keypad. Watching her, the thought occurred to me that when Meabh had her moment of doubt, her eyes had found mine. Like she trusted me or something?

The light turned green and I stopped wondering about Meabh. A simultaneous four-person sigh of relief made us giggle.

"Shhhh," I said, pushing the door open. I motioned for Orla to stick behind me. Then I turned and put my hand out to Meabh for the keys to her dad's office. She didn't give them to me.

Kavi tried to follow me and Orla into the building but I blocked his way. Sort of. I mean, he was twice my size.

We had a silent standoff.

"Lads," I said after a second. "Youse can't come in? We can't have a fucking parade down the hall."

"Why not? There's no one here," Meabh hissed. "And it's freezing out."

Kavi's face fell. "I came all this way and I only got to go over the gate and now I'm being killed off?"

"It's not a film," I said, bemused. "You're not dying. You can go home, actually, Kavi."

"No he can't," Meabh said. "We need to get back out the gate, and then Kavi needs to lock it and climb back over. And before you say it, I'm not leaving the keys with you. I'm staying with you until you give them back. I need to replace them tonight and I don't trust you on your own. How do I know you won't ransack the office or something?"

"What would I do that for?" I asked, offended.

"I don't know. For kicks. For all I know this is some kind of ruse to get in and make a mess and do whip-its and poppers and spray-paint the walls with rude words."

A loud "HA" escaped from my mouth. "For someone so smart, you have no idea what you're saying, do you? What *are* whip-its?" I challenged her with a smirk on my face.

"I know what they are. I don't have to tell you."

"You don't know."

"I do."

"You definitely don't."

"I—"

Meabh cut herself off. I followed her gaze. Kavi and Orla were watching us bicker. Orla was trying unsuccessfully to smother a laugh.

"I guess if you can't take standing outside for a few short minutes," I gave in with pointed resignation.

After about three steps in, I realised each time Meabh's hard plastic boot hit the tile, there was a loud click. My shoulders tensed up. There might not have been anyone in the building, but there was something about breaking and entering that made you want to be quiet. I swung around and Meabh stopped walking and looked around herself like she didn't know where that sound was coming from.

Our extremely conspicuous group made its way down the hall and around the corner. One more hallway, past the lockers, and through a set of double doors that would open up onto the atrium where the principal's office was. Meabh clicked loudly the whole way. I pushed open the door into the atrium and the others followed me towards the office.

It took about five seconds for the alarm to start ringing.

It took zero seconds for our group to go from hushed voices and held breath to a loud argument in the middle of the atrium. OK, not the group, me and Meabh.

"What the fuck, Meabh?" I rounded on her, yelling over the blaring alarm.

"Don't shout at me!" she yelled back.

"I have to shout, because there's a fucking security alarm going off!"

"Well, obviously I didn't know about that, did I?"

"I don't know. Did you?"

"Oh yes, I've always longed to have breaking and entering on my school record. Written up by my own father."

"Meabh, breaking and entering doesn't go on your school record, it gets you a criminal one."

She turned pale, realising the same thing that had occurred to me earlier. If we did get caught, of all of us, Meabh had the least to worry about. She would obviously get away with it, even though I'm sure her dad would have a full-on breakdown at the thought of her doing anything that didn't further her greater ambitions. I was on my last chance of last chances and would definitely be expelled if we were caught. Sure, finishing up school and doing my exams, especially in this bloody prison, was not exactly high on my list of priorities, but I was scared that if I really fucked up, it would make things harder on Mam. It would alert the social and they'd blame her for not being there for me and she'd have a spiral and then . . . better not to think of that. I just couldn't get caught. I eyed Kavi and Orla. I had no idea how this would work out for them.

Kavi put one hand over each of our mouths. "Maybe we should stop arguing and Meabh could try turning off the alarm."

Meabh and I exchanged a look. Both our faces were still half covered with Kavi's hands. Orla was biting her lip and hopping from one foot to another like she was getting ready to do one of her dances, or maybe just sprint home. I pointed at a panel near the door, assuming it was the one connected to the alarm system. As a group, we approached the panel and stared at it.

"Do you think if I put in the wrong number something worse will happen?" Meabh said, and I wondered if she was picturing a net falling from the sky to trap us, like I was.

Orla rolled her eyes. "What could be worse than this? My dads can probably hear this alarm and we live six streets over."

Meabh began entering her PIN.

"Wait! Stop!"

Everyone looked at me like I was losing it.

"If we turn that off, won't it show it's been disabled? Which means someone who has the code broke in. If we just leave now then it could be anyone. It could even be a malfunction."

Meabh pulled her hand away from the panel.

"Do you think it's, like, connected to the police or something?" I asked, imagining a red wire running from the school all the way to a red flashing light in the middle of the police station.

Meabh inspected the panel and shook her head. "I think it'll be connected to a security company."

"They'll probably ring your dad," Orla said, looking nervous. Meabh nodded, agreeing.

"How long do think it would take him to get here?" I asked.

Meabh thought, shaking her head slightly. "Fifteen minutes?" she guessed. "We better go."

I glanced at Orla, who looked sick and pleading.

"You cannot be thinking about still going to get your phone," Meabh said with constricted breath, as though she couldn't imagine anything more stupid.

Orla was close to tears. "No, we have to leave, I know."

I squeezed my eyes shut for a second. We'd come this far.

"Fuck it. We can do it," I said. "But you two should go." I pointed to Meabh and Kavi. "We'll be quicker on our own."

"I'm not leaving," Kavi pouted. "This is the exciting part."

I groaned. "It won't be exciting if we get caught, Kavi. I'll be expelled at best, and you three will be in serious trouble at the very least."

"Then you need a lookout," he said. "And we're wasting time."

He made a good point. A lookout would be helpful. It might stop us all from getting caught.

"Well, fine. You go, Meabh."

She looked affronted. "I'm not going to be the only one who goes. How would that look? That you three end up in a jail cell and I walk free because I bailed on you?"

"It'll look great on your university application," I pointed out. "You know, when you're not a criminal?"

"I have a very strong ethical code," Meabh sniffed. She looked around. "Clearly I have extended it to include breaking and entering for this evening, but if I get caught then at least it's honest. I will have a clear conscience. You know, Sartre's conception of freedom was based on—"

I exchanged an exasperated look with Kavi. He put his hand back over Meabh's mouth.

"We don't have time for Sartre," he said when the visible part of her face scrunched up in protest.

"You can stay, but it's your funeral." I shook my head at her like I thought she was being silly.

Secretly I was kind of impressed that she'd stick with us. But she didn't need to know that.

I took the key ring dangling from Meabh's pocket while both of her hands were prying Kavi's hand from her face. He let go easily but she jumped when she felt my hand sweep over her hip. Her hand reached out on instinct and grasped my fingers. The second it took her to realise I was just reaching for the keys was the longest second of the night. It was like for a moment every sense I had homed in on her hand clutching my fingers. When it passed, it felt like time sped up again. She blushed and we both did that smile you do when you're trying to pass someone in the street but you keep stepping the same way. The "oops, aren't we silly" smile. I had to shake off the feeling as Orla grabbed me and dragged me towards the door, while Meabh and Kavi stayed in the atrium as lookouts.

Orla and I hurried over to the cabinet. The bottom drawer was where Mr K kept confiscated items. I knew this from when he took my phone. And the time he took my vagina embroidery that I'd made for Home Ec. And the time he took my plastic ruler that I'd spent ages filing down into a point because he said it was now a weapon and "shivs are against school rules."

I was five foot nothing, what did he think I was going to do? Poke someone hard in the knee? It had just been something to do instead of conjuring French verbs. I tossed the key ring to Orla and let her try each of the approximately four million keys in the lock. I couldn't watch her going through each one knowing we had maybe three minutes to get out of here. How long had that stupid argument in the atrium taken? One minute? Two? More?

But I wasn't going to waste my one opportunity to look around. This was the enemy's lair and I would be unlikely to ever have unfettered access again. I tried the desk drawers but they were locked too. Were two security alarms and a door key not enough for this man? Who did he think he was? Fuckin' Jack Reacher or something. On the desk was a framed photo of Meabh, her mum, and a dog that looked like an old lady. For real, this dog looked like its name should have been Mildred. Meabh looked a bit younger than she was now, maybe thirteen? They were at a lake and there were snowy mountains in the background. It didn't look like it was in Ireland. It looked like what I thought the Alps probably looked like, but I'd never googled them so I couldn't be sure.

"Thank God." Orla sighed with relief as the bottom drawer slid open, revealing four phones and a bottle of nail polish. Relief flooded over me. I checked the time. We'd taken another three minutes. I began chewing on the inside of my cheek.

Orla pressed down on the phone's on button and mumbled a prayer under her breath.

"Please, God, don't be out of battery, you piece of shit, please, God."

One of the lesser-known prayers. You heard it around, sure, but only if you stuck it out to the end of the rosary.

Orla tapped her foot as she waited for the phone to boot up. It was taking an absurdly long time. I popped my head out the door and Kavi shook his head. No one coming yet. Maybe the alarm wasn't connected to anything?

The electronic bleep of Orla's phone pulled me back into the room. Orla blessed herself, as though God really did have a vested interest in her deleting some sexts.

"You know what I don't get," I said, trying not to show I was getting seriously antsy.

"Hmm?" Orla barely heard me, but she was furiously tapping her screen.

"I'm amazed you could feel all sexty in the middle of

Geography. I know all it does for me is put me to sleep, but to each their own or whatever."

"We weren't really sexting," Orla admitted. "Believe it or not, Ms Kavanagh's droning doesn't do it for me either."

"So then why are we here deleting your messages?"

She seemed like she was considering something when I heard a noise coming from her phone.

"Are you calling someone?" I hissed, finally reaching the breaking point.

Orla ignored me and held the phone up to her ear.

"This is not really the time? We are all going to get in deep shit and you want to make a phone call?" My screeching alerted Kavi, whose face appeared in the door frame. I gestured at Orla holding the phone to her ear and my eyes bugged. I didn't even have words.

The person on the other end picked up. A deep voice said Orla's name. He sounded confused. I'd also be confused if someone called me at – I checked the clock on the wall – 1:30 a.m. Actually I wouldn't be confused. It would be Holly and she'd be drunk and crying about whoever her latest crush was and all I'd have to do would be to murmur "mmmm" over and over until she calmed down.

"Babe, do not text me again until I text you."

His response was a low muffled noise.

"No, I'm not breaking up with you. I don't have my phone. No, I know I'm talking to you on the phone now. Just listen. I'm not going to have my phone for a few days.

You can't text me or call me, OK? Don't forget to come to the Britney show but don't approach me, OK, babe? It's only fifteen euros. No, you can't talk to me, but you'll see my dancing, isn't that enough? OK, bring friends. Love you more."

Just as I was about to have a coronary, Kavi took the phone from her hand and hung up.

"Come on," he said, sounding annoyed for the first time. Orla had the decency to look sorry. Kavi threw the phone into the drawer and Orla locked the cabinet back up. When we emerged from the room, I turned to lock the office and Meabh shrieked. I jumped out of my skin.

"Meabh!" I shouted, ready to tell her she was this close to killing me, but then I saw what she saw. I reached out and found Kavi's arm. He was already looking at the same thing I was looking at. A car had driven around the side of the building and parked right outside the window.

9

"That's my dad and Gerry, the caretaker," Meabh said. I weighed up the options as fast as I could.

Kavi tried to send me a signal like he was a baseball coach. I didn't roll my eyes, to save time. I just looked at Orla, Kavi, and Meabh, and said one word.

"Hide."

Someone had to take the fall for this. If Mr Kowalski came up here and found nothing, he'd search the school. If he came up and found me, he'd have no reason to think anyone else was involved. I wasn't exactly known for my vast circle of friends. He'd have no reason to think I wasn't alone.

"You'll be expelled," Meabh said, noticing I wasn't moving.

"I'll be fine," I lied. This had been my stupid idea, after all. If one of us was going down, it should be me.

None of them moved. The car was almost at the front of the building. If the headlights hit the right place, they would show all four of us, frozen in the atrium.

"I have an idea," Kavi said. "I'll create a distraction. Hide in the office. Run when the coast is clear."

"What about—"

It was too late for me to ask about him. He'd already taken off down the corridor towards the lockers. There was nothing else I could do now. The three of us dove into Mr Kowalski's office and I locked the door behind us. Meabh gave me a quizzical look. Seconds later I heard the *beep beep* of Mr Kowalski disabling the alarm on the front door. After a second there was blessed peace from the noise but the echo of it still rang through my head.

"It's likely nothing," a man's voice said. I assumed that was Gerry. "But we'll have a look around just to be sure. Should we call the Gardaí?"

"No, I think that would be overkill. It's probably the same as last time the alarm went off. Kids messing around," Mr Kowalski said. "Sorry for getting you up. We need to get that card copied or something."

I could barely hear him over the sound of my own heart pounding in my ears. Orla was hiding behind the cabinet, as though that would help if he actually came in here. Meabh was slumped over in her dad's chair, her forehead flat to the desk. I stood directly in front of the door. Even though I knew if he came in, we'd all be caught, I still felt vulnerable, like I was the first in the line of fire. I don't think anyone was breathing. And then I saw the handle move, heard the door rattle slightly in its frame.

"Office is still locked," Mr Kowalski said.

Meabh brought her legs up to her chest and buried her face in her knees. Orla scrunched her eyes shut tight.

BANG.

I flinched.

BANG.

Two sets of footsteps took off, away from the direction of the office.

I could breathe again. Quick, short breaths, but still oxygen in the lungs.

"That's Kavi's distraction, guys. We need to get out of here."

Orla and Meabh huddled up behind me as I put the key in the lock.

"Wait, where are we going?" Meabh whispered. "We can't go out there without a plan."

"The front door?" Orla said, like it was obvious. "Mr Kowalski just disarmed it. It's the closest to us."

Meabh and I both nodded in response and I turned the key slowly. The click of the lock tumbling over was deafening.

I half expected when I creaked the door open to find Mr Kowalski standing there with a thundering expression on his face and a pair of handcuffs or something.

He wasn't. But the lights were on in the atrium and I felt terribly exposed putting a toe out into the open space. Meabh was clutching on to the back of my jacket. I could smell her mango lotion again, she was so close. If the wafting scent of the Body Shop gave us away I was going to kill her. We took a few tentative steps out into the atrium, a weird conga line. I stopped almost immediately and turned on my two limpets.

Meabh winced and pointed at her foot, apparently thinking I was annoyed about the clicking of her boot on the tiles.

I shook my head and nodded towards the doors. The glass atrium looked out on the front drive, which was now completely lit up. It would take us at least ten minutes to get down to the gate with Meabh's foot slowing us down, and if Mr K or Gerry came back to the atrium, all they'd have to do would be to glance out the window and we'd be there, fully illuminated, trying to hobble down the hill.

I mean, Orla and I could get down there in three minutes and sprint home. But that didn't seem in the spirit of Meabh's Sartre speech, wherever that had been going.

Orla pointed towards the hallway we'd come down to begin with, through the doors that had started this whole mess. I looked around, wondering which direction Mr Kowalski, Gerry, and Kavi had gone. I hoped he had escaped by now, but if he had, that meant Mr K might reappear any second.

I shrugged at them both and we altered our course towards the corridor. I winced each time I heard the deafening click of Meabh's boot and prayed it wasn't really as loud as it seemed. We turned down one corridor as quickly and as quietly as we could. Then I heard a muffled voice and stopped dead, my procession bumping into each other and then me. I strained my ears and realised it was Kavi's voice, coming from the corridor with the lockers in it. Then I heard Mr Kowalski's voice.

Kavi had been caught. My heart sank. Would he be in a lot of trouble? I gestured for Orla and Meabh to stay put as I crept forward towards the junction in the hallway. Holding my breath, I peeked around the corner. Mr Kowalski was standing with his back to me; Kavi, taller than the principal, was trying to shrink into himself and look small and helpless. He held one of the bloody Get Well Soon balloons which bobbed absurdly by his face, the other two were on the floor, burst.

"Kavi, this is extremely serious."

"I'm really sorry, Mr Kowalski, I didn't think. I wasn't going to do anything bad. I swear I was just putting the balloons on her locker. I thought it would be a nice surprise. You know, one time my nan surprised me by putting balloons on my bedroom door on my birthday because it was a school day and my dad made me go even though it was my birthday so she wanted to cheer me up, so I wanted to cheer Meabh up."

Kavi caught my eye. At least I thought he did. But his hangdog expression didn't flicker. I realised in that second that he had meant to get caught. This *was* his plan.

"I wasn't aware you were even friends with my daughter."

"I'm not really. But I just . . . I haven't told anyone this.

I haven't told her. Please, sir, you can't tell her what I'm about to tell you."

"Kavi, I'm not sure this is relevant. Let's go back to my office, please."

Shit.

"Oh, sir, it is relevant though," Kavi wailed, and he slumped to the floor. Mr Kowalski sighed but I could tell he wasn't truly angry. There was something about Kavi that made him seem so harmless that you couldn't really be mad at him. I had no idea what Kavi was about to say to explain what he was doing.

"Kavi, please stand up. We can talk about this in my office."

I thought quickly. We couldn't go back in the direction of the atrium. Even if we made it to the door before Mr Kowalski got there, he would definitely spot us outside. The only choice was to get to the side door and get down the hill in the darkness.

I glanced back at Meabh and Orla. They hadn't moved. Not even shifting their weight. I shuffled back to them as quickly as I could without being noisy and prayed Kavi could keep Mr Kowalski in the hallway for another few minutes.

"We have to go this way." I gestured to the door at the end of the long, long hallway.

Meabh's expression said, *Are you fucking kidding me*, but her mouth said nothing. My eyes met Orla's. I looked to

Meabh's foot. Orla nodded. I put my finger to my lips, indicating for Meabh to be quiet, and for a second she looked confused. Then Orla grasped her under her arms and I picked her up by the feet. Meabh's eyes bugged but to her credit she didn't let out a peep. We carried her down the hall towards the junction, her expression mutinous the whole time.

"Sir, the problem is so huge."

I edged backwards, letting him spot me behind Mr Kowalski's back.

"I just need to tell you about it but I don't know how to say the words." Kavi sounded deeply upset.

Kavi began sobbing loudly and we used the cover of the noise to scurry past.

"What is it, son? Tell me," Mr K said gently.

We reached the door and I thanked myself for leaving it ajar earlier. I nudged it open with my shoulder and as the door swung shut behind me, I heard a loud, strangled yell.

"I'M IN LOVE WITH MEABH KOWALSKA."

Out on the grass, Orla and I locked eyes and we both burst out laughing, dropping Meabh on the damp grass.

It took a moment for us to recover while Meabh scowled and struggled to get up.

"Come on." Orla held out her hand. "We need to go."

I stood up and dusted dirt off my bum but I shook my head.

"I'm not going until I see what happened to Kavi," I said. "He got in deep shit for us."

"Yeah, and I don't think he'd want us to waste it by getting caught out here."

"We won't get caught out here. But you go on."

"I'm staying if you're staying," Meabh said.

"Actually," I said, "you're the one who really needs to go."

"Oh yeah, why's that?" Meabh had her hands on her hips. I think that was just her neutral stance at this stage, after spending all her life in confrontation mode.

"Don't you think your dad is going to look for his keys when he gets home again? You need to put them back before he realises you're gone or he'll put two and two together."

"What about locking the gate?" Meabh countered.

"We need Kavi for that anyway and that's not happening tonight. We just have to hope your dad thinks he forgot to lock up when he sees it in the morning."

Meabh wanted to argue. I could see the urge bubbling on her lips, but she couldn't come up with anything. She made a *hmphing* noise and threw her hands up in the air. Without another word to us, she started down the hill towards the gate.

I gave Orla a sidelong glance. "Maybe we should help her down, she's going to—"

We watched Meabh slip on the wet grass and slide at least four feet before coming to a stop. I had to stuff my fist in my mouth. Orla clapped both hands over hers. Meabh stood, shoulders tensed around her ears and fists clenched, and very determinedly did not look around. She simply kept walking as if nothing had happened. However, after a few seconds, she raised one hand high and give us both the finger while we shook with silent laughter.

When we'd calmed down enough to speak in whispers again, I told Orla she should go.

"Nah," she said. "The least I can do is wait with you."

I smiled at my shoes. It was nice of her but I didn't know how to say so without sounding like a total mush, so I pivoted back to our mission.

"You could tell me why we did this if all your photos are fully clothed."

"Would it count as me paying you back if I do?" she asked hopefully.

"Dream on," I scoffed.

She started talking anyway.

"My dads are just really ... let's be nice and say overprotective? When I was younger, these girls bullied me but it was all through texts and stuff and not at school so no one noticed, and it wasn't until I went to secondary school that I told them what happened. I think they felt guilty for not noticing and it made them weird. They always want to check my phone and where I'm going and what I'm doing and who I'm with. They threw a party for the whole dance class once so they could meet everyone who was in it." Orla rolled her eyes. "God forbid I hang out with someone they haven't seen before."

I couldn't imagine Mam being like that. She loved

Holly. She knew how hard things had been before Holly was my friend and I think she doted on Holly for saving me from hundreds of lunches eaten alone.

"When I started seeing Kyle, they went into overdrive," Orla continued. "They put a tracking app on my phone. They were convinced he was going to pressure me into doing something I didn't want to do. I get it. I know they care, but I am so sick of them looking in on every aspect of my life. So I told them me and Kyle broke up and I delete all my messages and get my friends to text me fake ones. You know, about homework and stuff."

I tried to process all that information.

"OK, so you're thinking that with your phone confiscated they're going to think that you were getting texts in class? Being bullied again?"

"Right," she said, rolling her eyes. "And they'll insist on looking at my messages, which I hadn't deleted yet."

"But what they'll actually find is that you are still tipping at Kyle and you lied."

"Exactly. And I want a bit of freedom. If that means lying to them then it's their own fault for being so intrusive."

She looked miserable and I felt a rush of pity. I wondered if that's what Mam felt like when I was always snooping and checking up on her.

"You could have told me all this earlier," I said. "Then you wouldn't have had to come here. I'd have deleted everything for you." I tried giving her a reassuring pat on the arm but I felt silly so I stopped. She didn't seem to notice and she smiled at me.

"I didn't want to explain everything about my life to someone I didn't know. I'm sick of always being asked about everything I do. I guess I'm used to coming up with excuses too."

She seemed to realise what I was thinking, which was that she didn't know me any better right now than she did this afternoon, so why was she telling me now?

"But you seem really sound," she said. "I don't know anyone else who would help me do something like this, especially if I'd told them what I told you. Most people would say it was my own fault for sending sexts in the first place and to accept the punishment. My friends said it was my fault for lying and I should be honest about it. They don't get it."

I felt uncomfortable hearing nice things. I didn't really deserve it just for *not* being a total arsehole.

"Kavi's your friend. He didn't say that to you."

Orla's brow knitted in confusion.

"Kavi's not my friend. I mean, he seems lovely and all, but I don't know him. He overheard me talking to Anna and he pulled me aside. He said he thought he knew someone who could help." She looked at me curiously. "Why *did* you help?"

"I didn't think it was fair for you to get in trouble when you didn't really do anything wrong. Whomst among us hasn't sent a dirty message?" I waved my arms grandly like the priest does in Mass when he gets going. "Let he who is without sexts cast the first stone."

I hadn't sent any sexts. But only because no one wanted to see them.

"I haven't sent any dirty messages. I told you that," Orla said stoutly.

"Sure. OK. In all those messages there isn't one that would make your da blush? I believe you." I crossed my heart and winked at Orla, who looked away and pretended not to hear me.

10

Mam texted me the next morning to let me know she was going straight to work from her "spa night", so at least I didn't have to worry about her and Dad coming home in the middle of the day; but she added that she'd had a brilliant time, so I knew she couldn't be far off bringing him home again. She could only ever keep it a secret for so long.

It had been two thirty before I got home from our escapade so I decided to take a wee half day and I rolled into school around twelve. At least I only had fifty minutes to go before lunch. My sole plan for the day was to find out what had happened to Kavi. Orla and I had waited until we saw his parents drive up and then we left while the gate was still open.

I really hoped he was OK. I tried to find him on social media to ask but I didn't get an answer from any of the accounts I could find. I suspected his parents had confiscated his devices. I'd even resorted to texting Meabh to ask her if she knew anything. She hadn't heard. Her dad was apparently more discreet when he was talking about other students. I was looking for Kavi when Ms Devlin accosted me at the door to her English room.

"Miss Cleary," she said sharply. "I *know* you weren't in registration this morning. What time did you get in?"

"Just got here, miss."

"And is there a reason why you missed the whole morning?"

I swung my schoolbag round in front of me and rummaged in it. Looking up at Ms Devlin, I grinned.

"I have a note here. Don't worry."

She groaned and I handed her a crumpled-up piece of paper torn from my Maths homework copy.

She read it out loud.

"Aideen has permission to be absent this morning. She is attending treatment for an imbalance in her humours. She has an excess of yellow bile."

I nodded seriously. "Yellow bile, miss. It causes aggression and liver derangement."

Ms Devlin pinched the bridge of her nose. "I could call your mother to verify this. What do you think would happen then?"

"I'm sure she'd love to hear from you, miss. You can talk about how I'm your favourite student and how upset you'll be when I die of humours."

The phone number the school had for my mother was my own mobile number. I'd filled in the registration forms myself way back when and I put down my phone number because at the time Mum was always losing hers or breaking her phone or leaving it in a taxi and just buying another cheap pay-as-you-go. I realised what a gift I'd given myself the first time my first-year form tutor, Mr McCann, had phoned Mam to give out about something I'd done wrong (turned up to World Book Day without a costume. GASP).

Ms Devlin looked at me with an uncertain expression. After a long moment she sighed and shooed me into the classroom.

"You better have your homework," she muttered, casting me a mutinous glance.

I smiled broadly. "Will I? Won't I?" I said with mock anticipation. "It's a thrilling time to be alive, isn't it?"

Thankfully I did actually have *something*. It wasn't anything that was going to blow her mind, but I'd tried. It had been too long since I'd handed something in and I had to avoid raising too much concern.

I scanned the room for Kavi and didn't see him. The English room had tables that fit two people, instead of individual desks, and Holly was sitting beside Sinead O'Brien. I tried to smother the spark of jealousy. Holly didn't look at me and I got the creeping sensation of realising she was annoyed with me. What did I do?

Right. Ditched her at lunch yesterday. Somehow with all the drama about Orla I'd completely forgotten to text Holly all night. That had never happened before.

Choosing a seat in the corner, I wondered if I could position my hand over my ear in a way that would hide my earphones and then I could listen to my Culchie Wedding Classics playlist while Ms Devlin droned on. Maybe it would be one of those days she got us to sit and write a story or something. When that happened she usually let us listen to music if we wanted to. Sure, I'd have to write an essay, but there were no rules about how good it would be. I mean, unless you count "grades" as rules. I'm not bound by such conventions. The last time we did "creative writing" I basically wrote a recap of the first episode of my favourite TV show.

Ms Devlin perched on the end of her desk. Perched is not the right word. Perched sounds prim. Ms Devlin was not prim. She was sturdy and she spread her legs and gestured wildly like she was determined to take up as much space as possible.

"Right, lads," she said, clapping her hands together, "in light of our upcoming election, I thought we would start a unit on persuasive writing. Unfortunately, no one else has signed up to run for student council president. YET. There's still time. Maybe this task will inspire you to give Meabh a run for her money. Not that you aren't an ideal candidate, Ms Kowalska, but choice is the root of democracy."

Meabh smiled tightly. I wasn't sure she believed in democracy as much as she believed in being a benevolent dictator.

"So, to stretch our critical-thinking muscles, I would like us to engage in some spirited debate."

The class groaned. Meabh beamed. Holly was also looking at Meabh, and I saw her roll her eyes and then whisper something to Sinead that made her snicker.

117

"I will give you a topic and a position, and in groups—"

Groups.

I loathed group work. Everyone staring at each other waiting for someone to speak. The pressure to say something, make some kind of contribution mounting. The bit at the end where the teacher always asked someone to share the group's work and everyone exchanged glances, a game of presentation chicken. It was only bearable if you got someone in your group who *wanted* to do all the work. Like Holly or Meabh.

Kris raised her hand.

"No, you can't choose your own groups," Ms Devlin said without bothering to call on her. "Do I look stupid?"

She pointed at each of us in turn and said, "A, B, C, D, E, A, B, C, D, E," and so on until we'd been sorted into groups of five.

"As up here, Bs here . . ." she barked, pointing at various tables. I got lucky not having to move. Group E had to come to me.

Within seconds, Mícheál and Bonnie appeared at my table. So did Holly. Which would have been great – I could have got a chance to clear the air about yesterday – except the last member of our group, frowning at the desk with her hands on her hips, was Meabh.

We exchanged the briefest glance and in that second we agreed to pretend as though nothing had happened. As though I wasn't dying to ask her if she'd seen Kavi this

118

morning or convince her to pry some details from her dad about what had happened to him.

Holly opened her mouth to speak but Meabh got there first.

"We're going to have to sort this into a more manageable configuration. Pull the table out two feet from the wall and one foot back and we can arrange the chairs around it so that everyone can see everyone. I'll sit here where there's more space because I'm going to take notes."

She said all this in one breath while Holly glowered.

I hoped Holly wouldn't start anything. Meabh was being her usual obnoxious self, but this could descend into chaos quickly if the two of them got going at each other. To my relief, Holly contented herself with a meaningful look at me, so I rolled my eyes, hoping that would satisfy her. Meabh noticed and for a second a hurt look flashed across her face. She immediately averted her eyes and pulled the table out to the "correct" position. My cheeks were on fire. I'd rolled my eyes at Meabh at least once a week for ten years, but suddenly I felt like a huge arsehole.

The only thing worse than doing group work with no one who wants to do anything is doing group work with two people who want to do everything. It becomes a battle of wills that everyone else at the table has to endure.

Meabh took out her folder, which also had a clipboard on the front, and Holly snorted. Holly took out her own notepad and pen. Meabh raised her eyebrows.

"I said I'd take notes," Meabh said.

"Don't worry, I'll take them," Holly said sweetly.

"I'll present then," Meabh replied.

"I think it makes more sense if the person who takes notes presents. Otherwise you'll have to read my messy handwriting."

Meabh and Holly glared at each other. Mícheál and Bonnie exchanged glances. Bonnie leaned back in her seat, realising she wouldn't have to contribute anything.

"Hey, Mícheál, I heard Angela Berry is having a party at her house when her mum is away on some work trip. You going?"

Mícheál shrugged. "When is it?"

"Not this Saturday; next one, I think."

Ms Devlin came to our table with a scrap of paper.

"We have two pro groups and two anti groups, so I'm going to give you the option. Whichever you want." She set a tablet down on the table too, for us to do research. "I'll be checking the history," she sang as she walked away.

Meabh snatched the paper quickly as though Holly was going to take it from her. Holly didn't move, she just smirked, and Meabh blushed.

"Consuming meat should be illegal," she read in as dignified a tone as she could manage.

"Pro!" Holly said quickly. "We'll be pro. We'll discuss impact on climate change, trauma to the labour force. It's easy. I did a piece on it for the paper."

Meabh shook her head. "Anti," she said.

"Aren't you a vegan?" Holly asked.

"Yes, but this is a state paternalism issue. We can argue much more effectively on a liberty and autonomy stance."

"Wrong! We can rebut those arguments by arguing that a libertarian state agenda fails society."

All I could think was that there was no way anyone else in our class even knew half the words they were using. They would win no matter what they chose.

"There are race and class issues here too," Meabh said through gritted teeth. "You wanna talk about labour? Let's discuss the exploitation of farmers in the global south so that white girls can get mass-produced quinoa in Tesco."

"You mean like you do?" Holly said with exasperated disbelief.

"NOBODY'S PERFECT," Meabh roared. The entire class turned around to stare at our group. Ms Devlin didn't even look up.

It was going to be a long class.

"I hate her," Holly said as we walked out of class. Me and the rest of the class had been traumatised by the last fifty minutes of our lives. I didn't think Mícheál was ever going to be able to talk about it. At one point he tried to intervene and . . . well, at least he'd escaped with his life, if not his dignity. That was something.

"I know you do. Although sometimes I think if the

121

two of you were friends, you could plot to take over the world."

It was a chilling thought actually. On the one hand I had no doubt they'd quickly sort out all the world's problems. On the other they would inevitably disagree on some minor detail and blow us all up rather than compromise.

Holly wrinkled her nose. "I could never be friends with her. Don't you think she's just the worst possible human being on the face of the planet?"

I didn't know what to say. Meabh was annoying. She was arrogant and a know-it-all and self-righteous and a craicuum. But the worst possible human?

"Yeah, probably."

That gnawing feeling of guilt came over me again, though, and I looked over my shoulder to make sure she wasn't walking right behind us or something.

"I would love to take her down a peg or two. I wanted to beat her out for captain fair and square, but she took that away from me."

"She sprained her ankle. I don't think that was about you."

Holly cut her eyes to me and gave me an icy look that made my stomach roll over.

"Sorry. That came out wrong. I just meant . . ." I didn't know how to end that. What else could I have meant?

Holly didn't let me off the hook. She waited. My heart pounded as I grasped for some words that would smooth things over. I hated when she was mad at me. I hated when anyone was mad at me, but especially Holly. Then, as though she'd just remembered, she snapped at me again.

"What was that yesterday, anyway? You were helping Kavi with a presentation? Seriously?"

What's that supposed to mean?

Stop. She's annoyed with you. Understandably annoyed. She doesn't mean anything by it.

"Yeah. I. Just Irish. I know he should ask someone else but he asked me. I felt bad."

"You ditched me for lunch. It was so rude."

"I'm sorry," I said, meaning it. "I wouldn't have done it if you were going to be left alone, but you had Jill."

Holly seemed to weigh up whether I was making a point about Jill or not.

"Here, you know what I remembered last night?" I said, changing the subject. "The time we put rose hips from your garden in Meabh's costume for the play."

Holly laughed and my heart felt safe enough to slow down again. "Oh my God. I had completely forgotten that. We ruined the whole play. Totally worth it though."

I spent the rest of the day trying to make it up to her and get us back to normal. I completely forgot about finding out what happened to Kavi. I couldn't explain it. Whenever things were weird between us I felt like I couldn't live with it. It was a black hole sucking the life out of me and I needed it to go away.

I'd do anything to make it go away.

11

By the time I left school that afternoon, Holly seemed grand with me.

I walked her over to the office so she could oversee the paper printing. Orla was behind the desk with earphones on and she was clearly running through the steps of her dance. I tried to guess which Britney song it was.

She looked up and saw me. I waved and she took her earbuds out and grinned.

"'Toxic'?" I guessed.

"How did you know?!" she laughed.

Holly glanced between us, confused. A crease formed between her eyebrows.

"Do you wanna stay? Hang out?" Holly asked me.

Just then Jill arrived, literally rolling up her sleeves, and said hi to everyone.

Part of me wanted to stay. I wanted to make sure things were OK with us, and also watching Holly in her element was kind of nice. The paper came out every other Thursday, and Holly always spent most of the evening before in the school office, tweaking the final layout and making last-minute edits. I'd gone with her before and watched her work.

Which I know sounds boring, but it wasn't. She got this super intense look on her face and she'd roll up her sleeves and put her hair in a ponytail. She'd take it out an hour later when she was yelling that there were six typos that the copy editor hadn't noticed in one article and did she have to go through the whole thing herself?! She'd tie it back up when she realised there was a blank space where a photo should be and she had to call up the photographer and give out. It was cute, though.

By the end of the night her hair would be greasy and she'd be five minutes from a coronary, but as much as she complained, I knew that she loved it. Becoming editor in chief this year had been her crowning achievement. I knew it meant much more to her than captain of the camogie team, which I suspected she only wanted because Meabh had it all three junior years. This was the thing she actually loved.

But I didn't like being stuck with Holly's newspaper friends. I could never relax around them. I was always thinking of whether I was acting right or if the thing I was going to say was stupid. So I told Holly I didn't want to get in the way at the office and hugged her goodbye. I waved goodbye to Orla too and she waved back, mid-spin.

On my way out I finally spotted Kavi sitting on the couch in the atrium. I instantly felt horrible for forgetting about him all afternoon. I sidled up, worried he was going to be really annoyed, but when he saw it was me, he grinned, so I sat beside him.

"Well, what do I owe you?" I said, trying to make a

125

joke out of it. When Kavi looked confused, I continued, "That was not a *plan*. That was a full-on martyr mission. Did you get in much trouble?"

Kavi waved me off. "Not as much trouble as the time I swung a golf club into my little brother's face – even though that was an accident, my parents were still really, really mad at me. Maybe they are just as mad this time. I'm not sure. They took my phone away for a week and I have in-school suspension."

"In-school suspension?" I asked dubiously.

"For the rest of the week. I sit in a classroom by myself. Just me and Mr Kowalski. He said he didn't want me missing class and that I was normally a really good student and that he didn't think that I 'fully understood the gravity of my misdemeanour' at the time. He is letting me off easy because he doesn't want me to have a criminal record over a mistake. It was kind of tricky when he asked how I got in."

I hadn't thought of that and I winced, but Kavi had thought of everything.

"But I just played stupid. Said the gate was unlocked, I figured there was no way you guys could have relocked it, and I said I climbed in through an open window and accidentally set off the alarm. He seemed a bit suspicious so I need to be extra good I think. And of course now he thinks I'm in love with his daughter so that's a bit awkward. He had a long talk with me today about the difference between love and infatuation and about consent."

I grimaced.

"It was nice!"

How was Mr Kowalski such a hippie at school and yet such a demon parent with Meabh?

"Well, that's amazing," I said. I felt horribly guilty. It should have been me. It felt wrong to have someone protect me like that. Selfish. "But you took a massive risk."

He smiled like it was no big deal, which made me feel worse.

"Thank you," I said, though it didn't really feel like enough. I couldn't work out what he was getting from all this. Just another story he couldn't tell anyone?

At that moment Mr Kowalski stepped out of his office. Immediately Kavi flopped onto my shoulder and began wailing at the top of his lungs.

"SHE'S THE MOST BEAUTIFUL GIRL IN THE WHOLE WORLD BUT SHE DOESN'T EVEN KNOW I EXIST." He flailed backwards and collapsed on the sofa with a hand over his forehead like an old movie star dying of consumption.

I waved at Mr Kowalski with one hand and patted Kavi's knee with the other.

Mam was already home when I got there. I tensed, on the lookout for signs of Dad. Nothing. My shoulders dropped. I should have realised he wasn't there when I didn't see the mark of Satan hovering over the building. Mam was hanging laundry in the windows. There wasn't anywhere to dry clothes in our flat so I'd stuck a nail in either side of the wall beside the window and hung my own makeshift washing line. It was very effective but Mam always complained that you could see our laundry from the ground outside since the blind broke and the landlord wouldn't replace it. Apparently, the fact that the cord on a twenty-year-old blind snapped was due to misuse and not normal wear and tear and so it wasn't his responsibility.

"You're back early," I said, a tight squeeze in my throat as I tried to sound casual. It's not even humanly possible to sound casual if you're not. It's like licking your elbow: it seems like it should be possible but it isn't.

I squeezed up beside her and began helping to put the laundry out. She smelled like strawberry mist.

"Oh, crashed around lunchtime. I was wrecked. Nadine let me go home."

Great. It wasn't like we needed the money. And obviously she was irreplaceable at work. Mam unballed a pair of socks and hung them across the radiator.

"We stayed up all night chatting."

"You and Bernie?" I asked.

"Yeah, obviously, love. How did you get on?"

"Nothing exciting." I wondered how she'd react if I said I'd enlisted a ragtag bunch of misfits to break into school in the middle of the night and got a boy suspended.

She stood absently with a pair of pants in her hand

that had nowhere to go. There was no room on my makeshift washing line and no more room on the radiator. She hung them off the door handle and threw her arms round me.

"I'm sorry I left you alone, love. I'll make it up to you. Do you want to watch a movie and have a crisp bowl tonight?"

I breathed her in, relaxing. She seemed fine. Maybe everything was OK. Maybe I was only imagining the worst, thinking Dad was around.

"Sounds good," I said.

"Good. Because I already bought these." She broke away from me and went to the cupboard, pulling out three sharing bags of different pickled-onion-flavoured crisps. The greatest and most underrated crisp flavour.

We put on our favourite film, *Dating Amber*, and put all the crisps in a mixing bowl. We pulled throws around us for the cosy factor. Mine was the red one, worn but so soft. Hers was the green-and-blue one, bobbly but toasty.

However, even before Amber and Eddie started fake dating Mam was back texting. I tried giving her a few pointed looks and loud sighs. It's no fun watching a film when the person you're with is on their phone. You might as well be watching it on your own. Holly did it all the time and I hated it.

"I'm going to the loo. You don't have to pause it though," I said about half an hour in.

"All right, love."

Mam's room was dark and I knew she'd see the light

if I turned it on, so I used the flashlight on my phone. Her red sports bag was on her bed, along with three folded tops that she must not have worn when she was away. I shone the light into the bag. It was empty except for half a pack of gum and a crumpled-up receipt. I flattened it out and sighed when I saw she'd spent €5.10 on a garage coffee and the pack of gum. What a waste of money. I looked around, wanting some other clue to jump out at me. I had my suspicions, but I needed confirmation.

I'd just given up on finding anything incriminating when I spotted it. In a ceramic dish I'd made her in primary school. It was painted red and said *Best Mam EVER* in clumsy handwriting. You couldn't see the words now, though; they were obscured by the pile of tangled-up necklaces and silver rings from eBay that turned your finger green.

But on top of it all, glinting in the torch light, a gold ring. My heart sank. I knew that ring and I knew it lived in the back of my mam's sock drawer in a little gauzy pouch most of the time. I picked it up and inspected it, somehow hoping it was an identical but different ring. One that didn't have the engraving I saw when I picked it up and held it to the light.

Lisa & Aidan ♡

I spent the next two days on high alert. After school I'd walk the whole length of the street, past our flat, and double back again before I went upstairs. I didn't know what I'd do if I saw his car. I had imaginary conversations with him in my head, where I'd take him aside and tell him clearly and firmly that his presence was unwanted and that he should go back to his real wife or I'd tell her that he was coming around here again. In reality, if I did see his car I probably wouldn't go home. I'd turn right around, turn off my phone, and find a cave to live in instead.

Mam always worked late on Thursday, but then she said she was also going to stay late on Friday because the other girl who normally did Friday night was sick. A fine story. Friday evening, I pulled a pile of cushions over to the windowsill, draped myself in my red blanket, and watched for her to come home. If she was really working she'd leave around eight. I only relaxed when I saw her walking up the street around eight forty.

Unless she knew I'd be watching and she got him to drop her one street over.

Well, as long as he wasn't coming up here, that was something for now. Still, I wondered how I could get Mam to see that he wasn't worth having around. If she dumped *him* for a change then surely she wouldn't be so badly affected. On TV the characters are always having deep realisations about their own lives when they perform in the school play. I couldn't sign Mam up for a local drama group, but maybe I could find her a different kind of narrative kick up the bum?

Saturday night I could feel some kind of calm. Mam stayed in with me and Holly came round and I made us all watch a really awful film called *The Other Woman* about three women who team up to get revenge on the same cheating man. I kept giving Mam side glances through the first ten minutes, but then Holly and Mam began talking about hairstyles for curly hair, and halfway through Mam started giving Holly a bloody updo and going on about how Holly could probably go blonde if she wanted to but why would you ruin your gorgeous red hair for that. I huffed and stuffed Oreos into my mouth and made very relevant remarks about the film. Like, "People who cheat are just really selfish. They only want to have their cake and eat it too." Both of them ignored me and I realised I should have told Holly what was going on so she could have been in on it. I didn't know why I hadn't told her yet. I felt embarrassed.

Sunday morning I made Mam breakfast in bed. I bet Dad never did that. He never could because he would never live with us. Because he would never leave his wife.

I climbed into Mam's bed with her and sipped on a cup of tea.

"This is nice, isn't it? The two of us on a Sunday morning," I said cheerfully. "How's your eggs?"

"Perfect, love. What's brought this on?" she asked, with a mouthful of toast.

"Just wanted to spend some time with my favourite . . . mother." I almost said *parent*, but I thought that would be

132

a bit too pointed. "Remember the time we went on holidays to Galway?"

If anyone ever asked me a time in my life when I was really happy, that's what I'd pick. It was hazy, but I remember me and Mam washing sand from between our toes and skin that smelled like coconut sunscreen. I remember feeling peaceful. There was no drinking that week, she didn't need it. And I wasn't worried; it was back when I believed her when she said there'd be no drinking ever again.

"I don't know if staying in your auntie Jacinta's house while she was in Spain really counts as a holiday." She gave me an apologetic smile. "I promise I'll take you on a proper holiday someday."

"It *was* proper," I protested. "We went to the beach. We got ice cream. We had barbecues. Just the two of us. It was brilliant."

"I remember getting you ice cream from the corner shop because the ice-cream van on the beach was twice the price. And you cried because you really wanted to get one from the van."

This was not going the way I'd envisioned. I tried not to show my hurt that she kept batting away my good memories like they were nothing. I needed to keep things upbeat. Mam was always so blue whenever Dad was gone and she didn't appreciate that we could be happy, just the two of us. If she'd only see how much we already had.

"We don't need money to be happy, Mam. I cried

because I saw a dead crab, too. Like let's not put too much emphasis on what an eight-year-old cries about."

"You're right, love, money doesn't buy happiness." She pulled my head towards her and kissed my temple and I could smell a faint whiff of her perfume. Her Mam smell. "Family is what's important."

"And we're a perfect family," I said. "Just the way we are."

There. I'd said it. I'd let her know I knew, without saying the words. Maybe we could at least talk about it. It was up to her now. If she said anything, even if she just asked me why I was being weird, I'd take it as a sign to tell her how I felt.

She didn't meet my eyes. Instead she took a long sip of her tea. Then she frowned and opened her mouth. I held my breath.

"Did you forget my sweetener?"

12

Somehow only a week had passed since the day I'd pushed Meabh Kowalska down the stairs. On my way into school on Monday morning I saw Orla get out of her dad's car. There was a beat between when she saw me and when she waved. I waved back.

"Who's that?" her dad asked. He was a handsome man with a shaved head and dark skin like Orla. "I've not seen her before. Did she join your dance class?"

Orla sighed and cut her eyes to me as if to say, *See what I mean?* It made me feel like I'd done the right thing, even if Kavi had had to sacrifice his phone for a few days. A bit of pride swelled in my chest like a balloon inflating. I wasn't used to that, but I'd helped her and it felt great.

She made a "come here" gesture at me and I actually did that thing where you look around to see if the person is gesturing at someone else. She wasn't.

"Uh, hi," I said meekly when I reached the car. I never knew how to act around parents. Holly's mam thought I was bad news and I wondered if there was something about me that gave that impression.

"This is my friend Aideen. Aideen, this is my dad."

For some reason I blushed.

"Hi, Mr . . ." I trailed off, realising I didn't know Orla's surname.

"Nice to meet you, Aideen," he said, his lips quirking. "You must be new friends?"

"Yes, Dad, new friends. And now we have to go to class." Orla pulled me away by the elbow and I waved goodbye to her dad, feeling a pang, wishing just for a second that it was real.

Holly and I bounced on our exercise balls during registration. I would have abs of steel soon. You wouldn't be able to see them because of the comfortable layer of squish on top, but that was fine with me.

"Do you think if you were rich and famous and you gave loads of cash to charity, you'd tell everyone, or would you keep it a secret because then everyone would ask and you'd have to say no to some people?" I asked Holly seriously.

"I'd definitely tell everyone," she said without missing a beat. "And I'd say I was telling them to 'raise awareness' and encourage other people to donate. Win-win."

"Good point. So you don't think there's any secret philanderers?"

Holly stared at me for a minute.

"I think you mean philanthropists," she said.

"Oh, what did I say?"

"Philanderer."

"What's that mean, then?"

"Someone who does loads of affairs."

"Definitely not the same as doing loads of good deeds, then."

"Not unless they're really good at it," Holly said.

"Like they want to make sure as many people as possible get to experience their mind-blowing moves."

We both laughed and Ms Devlin *hmphed.*

"Anything you'd like to share with the class?"

"We were wondering," I started. Holly elbowed me to tell me to shut up. "How good you'd have to be at sex for it to be considered a public service to bag as many people as possible?"

There was a ripple of laughter.

"If that level of talent exists, girls, I haven't yet encountered it," Ms Devlin drawled, neither scandalised nor particularly annoyed.

Ronan shuddered. "Miss, you cannot be telling us you've had sex."

"There are a few nuns wandering the halls of this place, Ronan. I am not one of them. I'm sorry that comes as a surprise to you."

Before he could reply, Ms Devlin clapped her hands together and pressed on. I heard him mutter, "Devlin has the clap," to the boy next to him. I really judged Holly's friend Jill for going out with him. He was handsome, in a bland-white-guy-with-blond-hair-and-blue-eyes kind of way, but he was such a knob. There was a moment when the whole class realised that Ms Devlin had heard him say it. I think every single person held their breath.

Ms Devlin looked at Ronan like he was a spider and she was considering whether or not to squish him.

"Ronan. My sexual health is none of your business. However, chlamydia is a serious infection with long-term consequences, and is often undetectable. If any of you are concerned about sexually transmitted infections, I advise you to visit your doctor for regular testing. There's no shame in that and you can talk to me anytime."

We all exhaled. Ronan's shoulders relaxed. He'd gotten away with it. I was a little disappointed. I knew Ms Devlin liked to make things into a teachable moment, but still. Ronan was a worm.

Ms Devlin smiled, and then added, as though she'd forgotten, "Oh and Ronan, go to Mr Kowalski's office and tell him what you said, please." Ronan paled.

Ms Devlin clapped her hands together. "Now, anyone in Mr Walker's Geography class first period, you're in luck. He is not in this morning and there was no sub available at short notice. So! You're with me in PE with the third years."

"Aideen cannot take part in PE today because she is suffering from hysteria." Ms Devlin sighed. "Aideen, tell me, what is hysteria?"

"Um, you know, when bitches be crazy?" I said.

"This is your most offensive illness yet."

"Tell me about it." I nodded my head vigorously. "Of course my doctor is a *man*. He was all like, you should stop reading and having opinions. So maybe I shouldn't do any homework either?" I tried to look simply curious about her thoughts on the matter.

"Unfortunately, this note only covers PE. Perhaps you could use the time to get some homework done? I believe the cure for hysteria is overthrowing the patriarchy, and you won't get much of that done if you're held back a year."

We both knew I couldn't be held back in transition year, but I saluted her anyway and skipped off to the balcony.

Meabh had dragged her leg up the same stairs that had aided in her deliberate downfall, and she was sitting on the floor of my balcony surrounded by papers, highlighters, and an expensive laptop. She wore a strained expression. Her booted foot was stretched out to one side, which looked very uncomfortable. I couldn't help but notice how in her awkward position her skirt had ridden up her thighs. She was wearing tights, of course, but they were sheer, and I felt strange about even noticing such things about Meabh. She was not my type, after all. My type was . . . I didn't know, but it wasn't Meabh. Her face was scrunched up in concentration. It was kind of sweet.

Not a word I'd normally use for the likes of Meabh Kowalska.

"How are you tits deep in work and it's only nine fifteen?"

"I'm always tits deep," she said absently. "I walk around brushing my work off my nipples on a twenty-four seven basis."

"Sounds chafey," I said.

She murmured an affirmative noise and I took to the far corner of the bench that ran the perimeter of the balcony. I leaned against the wall and opened my Maths book. Might as well start with the thing I was failing most, if there were degrees of failing, and go from there.

We worked in near silence for half an hour, except for her exuberant typing and the sound of me gnawing the inside of my cheek hoping that my mouth would fill with blood and drown me because nothing in this book made the slightest bit of sense.

"Do you mind?" Meabh said after a while, sounding irritated.

"What's your problem?"

"You keep sighing."

"Do I?"

"Every thirty seconds. It's distracting. What are you working on?"

"Maths."

"I can see that," she snapped. "I mean what topic specifically."

"Trigonometry."

She lugged herself off the floor with exactly zero grace

and lumbered over to me. The boot was throwing her off balance.

"Are you gonna do it for me?" I said, brightening. "That would really help."

She gave me one of her Meabh stares. The one that was half teacher, half international despot.

"That would solve your problem for five minutes. Would it help you actually improve in Maths?"

That felt like a rhetorical question.

She scanned my work with a frown on her face that deepened as she turned the pages.

"This doesn't make any sense," she said, looking up.

"Right? That's what I've been saying."

"No, I mean, I think you've missed something somewhere. Were you off sick at the start of this unit?"

How to answer that? No, I was not off sick. Yes, I was often off and had definitely missed something. Multiple somethings.

"Wow, I'm offended you don't keep track of my attendance."

Meabh and I hadn't actually shared a lot of classes since we were in primary school. It didn't surprise me at all that she didn't notice if I was absent a lot, but I sort of assumed Mr Kowalski had my photo stuck to a dartboard in his home office and maybe she'd have asked about that. So self-involved of her not to have bothered.

"All right, come on, then. We find the hole, we fill it up."

"Yeo," I said.

"Fill the hole in your *knowledge*, you degenerate."

"With the fingers of information?"

She closed her eyes and pressed her lips together. And then I saw it. She wasn't exasperated. She was trying to *look* exasperated, but she wanted to laugh.

"Hah! You think I'm hilarious," I said, poking her in the side.

"I do not." She swatted my hand away.

"You do."

"I absolutely don't."

"You do. You do. You do."

"I do not. I think you need help with Maths, so let me give it to you."

I opened my mouth but she cut me off before I could say what I was going to say.

"—Don't even dare." She pointed an accusing finger.

"I was *going* to say thank you," I lied. "Get your mind out of the gutter. Jeez."

Meabh looked skeptical.

Just as I had budged up to make room for Meabh beside me, a girl I recognised from the choir, Laura, appeared at the top of the stairs. She had long, wispy blonde hair and pale skin. Her eyebrows were so white they almost disappeared on her face.

Laura glanced awkwardly between me and Meabh. I'd barely ever spoken to her so I assumed she wanted to talk to Meabh and I wondered if I was meant to give them privacy. Laura hesitated before striding over purposefully and then seeming to lose her nerve again. She began wringing her hands.

"Do you want me to go?" I said finally, unable to bear this a second longer.

Meabh looked confused.

"No. I wanted to talk to *you*," Laura said tightly, as though if she said the words through gritted teeth Meabh wouldn't hear them.

Bewildered, I shrugged. "OK . . . ?"

Her eyes flickered over to Meabh again.

"Well, I can't leave!" Meabh pouted. "Do you know how much effort it took me to get up here?" She shook her boot at us.

There were several games of badminton going on in the hall below us. It was cold outside. I contemplated the options and then with purpose I marched over to the supply cupboard, opened it, and kicked aside a basketball. With a flourish I gestured Laura into the dark cupboard and gave Meabh a mystified look as I closed the door behind me.

"What brings you to my office?" I joked. It was pitch-black and only the crack from the door frame let any light in. Someday I would look back on this part of my life as a period when I spent more time than usual in dark cupboards.

"This is good," Laura said, her voice wavering.

"It smells like rubber and sweaty hands," I said, "but whatever tingles your jingles."

"No, I mean it's dark. Then I don't have to look you in the eye when I say this."

She was nervous and it was making me nervous.

"OK . . ." I said warily. "Spit it out."

"I need a favour," she said.

I closed my eyes to gather patience. My "agent" was out there hustling on my behalf again, but it was just as dark with my eyes open as closed so it didn't work.

"Oh, for God's sake. Did Kavi send you to me?"

"Kavi? No, I heard from my sister that you had done some kind of favour for her friend Orla, and all you wanted in return was a favour back."

So much for being sworn to secrecy.

"Well, that was . . . you know, a favour to a friend," I said, smudging the details. I mean, initially I had thought she was Kavi's friend, after all. Not that I owed him any favours either, but it was only a fib.

"But it's true?"

"Yeah, I guess," I said uneasily. It had been an interesting week. Meabh's drama. The break-in. It was all kind of fun and exciting. So why did I feel unsure about doing it again?

"Would you do one for me?" she asked, a pleading note in her voice.

I thought about how happy Orla had been to see me

this morning. Because she'd been desperate and I fixed it. But she'd deserved help. She was really stuck.

"Depends what it is," I said finally. There had to be limits. If I was going to do this, and it looked like I was, then I couldn't help everyone who asked. There'd need to be some boundaries. Though I didn't know what they were yet.

"You can't tell anyone," she said.

"All right." I shrugged, though she couldn't see it in the dark. It made no odds to me. I already hadn't been able to tell people about my great . . . what was it? Philanthropy! My philanthropy had all been secret so far and I was good at keeping secrets for people. I'd been practising my whole life. What was one more?

"No, I mean it," she said, sounding very bossy for someone who wanted me to do her a favour.

"I offer a fully confidential service. Seal of the fuckin' confessional right here," I said. Then I thought of something else. "Unless you, like, murdered someone. I can't be helping you move a dead body or anything. I do not have the upper-body strength. Trust me, I can't even climb up a wall."

"What has that got to do . . . Never mind. I didn't murder someone."

"Go on, then. Tell me your sins, child," I said in my most priestly voice.

"If you're not going to take this seriously—"

"No, I'm sorry, I am," I apologised. I was dead serious in this room in the dark surrounded by deflated balls.

She took a deep breath. "I need you to get the morning-after pill for me."

I waited.

That was it, apparently.

"Is that it?"

"Yes," she said testily.

"And you're willing to owe me a favour if I do this?" I said. One of us was getting the short end of the stick here and I needed to make sure she realised that for my own conscience. "A favour I can collect at *any* time."

"That's fine."

"Why, though? I mean . . . OK, it's a *bit* embarrassing. Like when you go in with a yeast infection and some nosy old biddie doesn't give you space to say it privately to yer one behind the counter. But you'd get over it."

"My dad is the chemist," she said. "At Crossan's."

It was starting to make slightly more sense now.

"Well, he's not every chemist, is he, though?"

"No, but he knows them all. It's a small town. What if they recognise me?"

Far be it from me to question someone's paranoia.

"Why don't you get a friend to do it?" I asked.

"I don't want to tell them!" she said, scandalised. "It's awful enough as it is without everyone I know talking about it."

"What's so awful about you getting the ride?" I said. I hadn't got the ride yet but I really wanted to get

146

some practice in before I married Kristen and moved to Hawaii.

"Will you keep your voice down?" she said, though I was speaking at a perfectly low level and the only eavesdropper was a pile of gym mats covered in decades of teenage foot sweat.

"It was with my ex-boyfriend," she went on. "They're going to judge me for the backslide."

"I don't think you can get pregnant that way."

"That's not what that means," she said, and I could practically feel the heat from her blush. "He broke up with me and broke my heart and then I slept with him the second he showed any interest again. I thought it meant he wanted to get back with me but it didn't. It's embarrassing. I should be less pathetic."

She sounded really sad and I had an urge to hug her. I didn't though because I was basically a stranger. I heard a sniff in the dark.

"Look," I said in my softest voice. "You got your heart pulped. You missed someone and then you wanted to feel like they loved you again. That's not pathetic. It's your heart, it's soft and mushy and it's supposed to be and I'm sorry he thought it was OK to mess with it but that's his mistake, not yours."

She sniffed again. Then quite alarmingly, as I couldn't see it coming, I felt a pair of arms flung round me. When I recovered from the surprise, I hugged her back.

*

147

I agreed to go to the chemist at lunchtime and Laura insisted on staying in the cupboard for a bit to sort herself out. Meabh gave me a curious look when I exited.

"Don't ask," I said.

"Another favour?" she guessed.

"I couldn't possibly comment."

I thought she might be nosy about it but she just nodded.

"All right, then. Trigonometry."

Half an hour later my brain was burning. I clutched my head in my hands.

"Oh God, is this what knowledge feels like?"

"You are such a drama queen. You're doing fine. You're lucky you're near the start of the unit. You didn't miss too much." Meabh was standing behind me, resting her forearm on my shoulder. "Don't forget the unit of measurement or your answer means nothing."

"Yes, miss," I said, looking up at her. I noticed then, when she was so close to me, how long and dark her eyelashes were. At least they'd grown back after the exam stress. You'd probably look quite weird close up if you had none.

She'd have an absolute heart attack if she knew how behind I was on everything. We might have been at the start of trigonometry, but there were at least three other units I had struggled through without picking up any new knowledge. In fact, aside from Irish, trigonometry was now officially my best subject, and believe me when I say the gap was wide. But I did manage to get through today's homework at least, and when we closed the book, I felt this weird sense of lightness. Knowing that there was at least one class today where I wouldn't disappoint or anger the teacher was kind of nice.

Meabh looked forlornly at her own stack of work. She sat down beside me, stretching her leg out on the bench, and it was her turn to sigh. My lightness turned to stone and I felt horribly guilty all of a sudden. She had actual important stuff to be at and I'd taken up her time with my stupid homework.

"I'm sorry," I said, really meaning it.

"What for?" she said, surprised.

"I'm wasting your time. What's the point of me helping you get extra time to do your work if I end up using it for myself?"

She looked taken aback, but I wasn't sure why. Maybe she expected me to be selfish as well as stupid.

"You didn't do anything wrong," she said slowly. "I offered to help you. That's not the problem anyway. It's just . . ." She gestured limply at the carnage of her work area.

"Can't be fucked?" I said knowingly.

She laughed. "Kind of the opposite. There's so much I want to do, I don't know where to start. We have to submit a brief paper for each policy we're proposing. They have to be approved by the staff. After last year."

Last year the only senior who ran for student council president had attempted exactly one change to the school: a free nacho bar for the café. Needless to say his term in office was not considered a success.

"Start with the most important," I said, thinking of my own homework strategy.

"They're all important," she said, rubbing her eyes.

"Hey, watch that or you'll ruin the Disney princess eyelashes again."

"Disney princess eyelashes?" Meabh said, sounding like she was trying to figure out where the insult was.

"How about you start with the easiest one then?" I asked.

Meabh cleared her throat. "Why the easiest one?" Her cheeks had turned slightly pink.

I didn't think *because it's the easiest* would satisfy her as well reasoned, so I thought quickly.

"Because when you finish it, you'll feel accomplished, and then you'll have momentum for getting the rest done."

"That's a good idea," she said thoughtfully. "I could submit a simple one right away. It will show the voters that I'm serious about getting things done and I have workable plans."

"I wouldn't worry about the voters too much. They don't have anyone else to vote for."

"Thank God," she said. Then she realised what she'd said and backtracked. "I mean, not because I don't believe in the democratic process. I'd just hate for it to be one of those popularity things. Can you imagine Ronan running against me? He'd win because everyone hates me but his big input to the school would be, I don't know, jelly-wrestling Wednesdays."

She wasn't wrong.

"Hey." I shrugged. "I don't care if you want to take control of the student council by force and declare yourself emperor. It makes no odds to me."

I believed that Meabh really did want to use her power to do good things and God knows the people in our school were not smart enough to see that. It was like Holly had said, you had to tell them what they wanted to hear even if it wasn't going to do anyone any good.

"Empress," she corrected me immediately. She couldn't help herself.

"So what's the easiest one, then?" I said, ignoring her.

"I had an idea for a green initiative. It can be implemented with zero cost and zero labour. In fact it will save the school time and money. Really I'm surprised it didn't happen years ago."

"Go get 'em, Emperor."

"Empress."

I rolled my eyes.

The door to the storage cupboard creaked open and Laura emerged, looking calm and collected. Apart from the streaky mascara on her face. She gave us both a dignified nod and walked downstairs without another word, as though nothing had happened.

13

Ronan was trying to huff the next morning. But it's hard to really take someone's bad mood seriously when they're sitting on a bouncy ball with their arms folded and their bottom lip pouting.

"His mam was disgusted with him," Holly whispered to me. "She said that next time he stepped out of line she would pull him from the Gaelic team."

"Whoa. Just over back talk?" I said. I mean, I was pleased, but surprised she'd go for such a strong punishment.

"Well, apparently she's super religious, so I think the whole STD thing set her off. She thinks he's an altar boy who shouldn't even know what that is. Jill wasn't happy with him either."

Every now and then I had to believe karma was real.

Ms Devlin cleared her throat. "Friday is the last day to sign up for student council elections, and while you'd think I would be beaten down enough by your indifference at this stage, inexplicably I'm still hopeful for a volunteer." She'd been reminding us daily and yet there were no takers. The bell rang and Ms Devlin dismissed us with a weary hand wave. "Meabh, can you hold on a moment? I read your policy paper."

Holly rolled her eyes at me. I pretended not to notice and gave Ms Devlin a wave as we walked past instead. She nodded, but then her expression changed.

"Aideen," she said sharply. "Go and wash your face, please. You know you're not allowed to wear make-up to school."

It was true. I hadn't been able to sleep because Mam had come home late "from work" again and I spent most of the night thinking of insults I could casually lob at Dad if he dared show his face. Around six, puffy eyed, I gave up and put on a YouTube tutorial for something to do.

"What are you talking about?" I said with my most beamingest smile. "This is my natural face."

"Your eyelids are rainbow coloured," she said.

"That's one of my diseases, miss. Kind of insensitive of you to make fun of me."

"Miss Cleary, you are wearing a full face of make-up. If I dragged my finger down your face there'd be a groove in your cheek."

I sighed dramatically.

"OK, I'm going to level with you," I said conspiratorially. "I am wearing *some* make-up. But you and I both know that you don't really give a fuck so let's pretend you didn't see me this morning and we'll both go about our day."

Ms Devlin's eyes bugged. "I am going to pretend I didn't hear that."

"Exactly, Eileen," I said, and I winked.

"That's not what . . . My name isn't Eileen." She threw

153

her hands up and waved me away, clearly having given up the fight. Meabh was waiting impatiently by her side, desperate to hear what Ms D thought of her paper. I slowed down as we walked out of the hall, hoping to hear some of the feedback, and Holly trailed behind with me. As we reached the door, Ms Devlin's voice echoed across the hall.

"Your paper was beautifully written, Meabh, succinct and persuasive. Making the school paper digital would save money and energy."

Making the paper digital. My brain practically shrugged from lack of interest. Then it hit me. Just as the words hit Holly too. Without thinking I threw both arms around her waist and dragged her out of the hall, letting the fire doors slam behind us. She struggled against me.

"Let. Me. Go."

I dragged her down to the girls' changing room. She screeched the whole way like she was being murdered and I could only assume Ms Devlin didn't have it in her to come and investigate a murder. I only let Holly go when we were safe inside the changing room. Then, panting and sweaty, I blocked the door.

Holly stood in front of me, eyes on fire.

"Let me out. Now," she said, sounding dangerous.

I shook my head. "I can't do that."

"She wants to make my paper *dig–i–tal*." Holly enunciated each syllable as though it were some disgusting creature she was inspecting.

"I heard." I held both hands up, the way you do when you're faced with a wild animal. Totally useless gesture, but based on the misguided instinct to reason with it. "But if you go out there now and start screaming about it, that isn't going to help. You'll only piss off Ms D. She won't take you seriously."

Holly snorted and folded her arms. She began pacing the changing room with quick, aggressive steps. It took a full minute for her to slow down. After a second she let out a shriek of frustration so sudden it made me jump.

I'd only ever heard one other person over the age of two make a noise like that, and weirdly it was in the exact same room. I made a mental note that if I ever wanted to try some therapeutic screaming, the acoustics in here were great.

"You're right," she said finally, although it came out resentful rather than grateful.

I sighed with relief and sat down to let my heart return to its normal rhythm.

"How on earth did you manage to drag me down here?" Holly asked, and she laughed. I was bent over and sucking in deep breaths. When I surfaced, I said, "Adrenaline. Like those mams who lift cars off their babies."

"Am I the car or the baby?" she asked, and although she was smiling, there was a hint of sarcasm I didn't understand.

"You're my baby, baby," I said, giving her a light punch on the arm.

The door to the changing room swung open then and

fifteen first years barrelled in, giving us dirty looks. I ignored them.

"So what are you going to do?" I tried not to sound too nervous.

"I can't reason with the likes of Meabh," she said. "I'm going to have to beat her at her own game."

"What do you mean?" I asked warily. But Holly had already swept past me and out the door. I cursed myself for letting my guard down too quickly as I tried to keep up with her long, quick strides.

We reached the door to the sports hall. She closed her eyes and took one more deep, calming breath. When she opened them she had a perfectly neutral expression. The kind serial killers probably used when they wanted to look "normal".

It did not look normal.

Ms Devlin was still talking with Meabh, and they looked up at us, confused, when Holly burst into the hall, throwing open both doors like she was a celebrity arriving at a party.

"Ms Devlin," Holly said in an oddly formal voice. The anxiety was making me feel nauseous. I took a few steps to the side, towards the back of the room. I didn't even know what I was anxious about yet. It was like a primal threat response. Something bad was about to happen.

"Holly?" Ms Devlin asked, squeezing *Why are you behaving in this dramatic fashion* into one word.

Holly smiled and I saw her eyes flicker to Meabh. From the way her shoulders tensed, she was expecting something bad too. They stared each other down.

"I would like to run for president."

I hurried to keep up with Holly as she headed in the direction of her next class. Ms Devlin had been thrilled to have a new candidate. I couldn't figure out whether she didn't notice that Meabh had been struck speechless for the first time in her life or that Holly had been possessed by a demon, giving her red demon eyes when she spoke. Maybe Ms D mistook that look for enthusiasm, but I knew it was homicidal rage. Perhaps Ms Devlin enjoyed the prospect of the drama a real rivalry would bring to the occasion. What's an election without a little hair pulling and back biting and literal stabbings in the playground?

"Holly, slow down. My legs are half the length of yours."

She relaxed her pace and seemed to shake herself out of her thoughts. "Sorry. I was thinking about what I should do."

"So you think you might *not* run?"

"No. I am definitely running. She's not getting away with that stupid policy. No, I was thinking about how to win. I'm gonna debate her. Ms Devlin will love it if I suggest a debate. And I'm going to make posters. I'm going to knock on people's doors if I have to." She clenched her jaw and then added, "Not that I think I will have to because hello, everyone hates her. But I'm going to make sure that people

157

vote and I'm going to make sure that they all vote for me so that when she loses, she knows that she lost because *I* made it happen."

When did you turn into such an arsehole?

That wasn't fair. She was angry. She was venting to her best friend. I shouldn't be so judgemental.

"Come on," I wheedled. "That sounds like a lot of work. Can you really be arsed?"

She stopped dead in the hallway, causing a mini pileup of students behind her. She ignored them as they sidestepped and gave us dirty looks.

"Yes, I can. I'm sick of her taking everything and acting like she deserves it. The only reason she would win otherwise is because no one else bothered running. I'm sick of her telling everyone what to do."

"OK. I get it. But maybe there's another way to get her to change her mind about the paper. I mean, do you really want to be school council president? Or do you just want to beat Meabh?"

"I want to beat Meabh," Holly said like she didn't get my point.

How do you argue with that?

"It looks like so much work."

"She *makes* it so much work." Holly waved me off and started walking again. "It doesn't have to be like that. You hand in a couple of proposals, you do some student-staff consultations, you argue for your stupid ideas, they say no, you put it all down on your CV or something. It'll look good when I apply for Oxbridge and Trinity."

"You have the paper to look good," I pointed out. "You don't need this."

"I won't have the paper if it goes digital," she snapped.

"You will. It'll just be . . . online," I said meekly, not really seeing the massive problem.

"One of the reasons the paper is so popular is because it's in print. We can hand it out. We leave it in common areas. People pick it up and look through it and articles or photos catch their eye." Holly was explaining this in a tone that implied I was really stupid and she was really patient. "But if you're sitting on your phone, you're not going to go to the school website and look it up. Not when you can watch scenes from musicals performed by a cast of old mops on TikTok."

I couldn't argue with that. I had an overpowering urge to see *The Sound of Music* with Captain von Trapp played by a Swiffer. And all the von Trapp kids could be dustpans with googly eyes.

Holly narrowed her eyes and a sudden coldness startled me out of contemplating how I could monetise Evan Hansen the feather duster for Flubberygiblets.

"Why do you care if I want to be student council president or not?" Holly asked. "When did you become Meabh's little helper and start fighting her battles for her?"

That was a bit close for comfort.

"I'm not her helper," I protested. "It just seems like you're getting into a fight that isn't worth it."

"It's worth it to me. You know that. You know how I feel about her and if you had any loyalty you'd have my back. If you hated someone, I'd hate them too. That's part of being someone's best friend."

Not if it's based on petty bullshit.

No, that wasn't fair either. She was only asking for loyalty, wasn't she? Maybe I *was* the one being a bad friend.

"I do—" I said. I meant to finish the sentence and say *I do hate her*, but the memory of her hurt expression when she saw me roll my eyes at her in English class cut me off. Holly didn't seem to notice. We'd reached her classroom door, and she paused.

"Stop trying to undermine me, then, and support me instead."

I didn't have a chance to reply. She entered her class and left me behind, looking at the door. Why was I always upsetting her? Holly had been my best friend my whole life and I couldn't even get on her side. Was she right? Was I betraying her? But when I thought of Meabh, she didn't seem like the person we'd hated all these years. That person was a myth we'd built up around her. Holly would never see that. My guts churned and I tried to fight back tears. It didn't work. I locked myself in the nearest toilet stall and let them come for exactly two minutes. Then I washed my face and went to French.

When I entered, Miss Sullivan rounded on me.

"The class started ten minutes ago," she snapped, and pointed me back towards the door. Six, but whatever. Miss Sullivan wasn't like Ms Devlin. She wouldn't brush off my cheek. She was more the type who'd scream me into a puddle and then scrape me off the floor and into a bucket.

Sighing, I turned around and waited outside the room for a minute as I heard Miss Sullivan tell the class to read the newspaper article and find examples of *le conditionel*.

"Miss Cleary," she said in clipped tones, when she'd followed me out and closed the door behind her.

"Yes, miss?" I said, trying to look abashed when what I really felt was tired and fed up.

"Your behaviour is becoming untenable."

I gave her a blank look.

"You're often late. When you turn up, that is. You don't put any effort in to your homework. Your Junior Cert results were very poor. You hand in your written work on what appears to be a whim. It's not good enough."

"I'm sorry, miss."

She heaved a sigh. "I'm sure. But if I don't see a major improvement this term, I'm going to have to take disciplinary action. I want every. Single. Assignment."

The only good part of the rest of the day was catching up with Laura after lunch. Sure, I'd had to answer some embarrassing questions at the chemist.

"Have you had unprotected sex in the last seventy-two hours?"

"Yep. With a boy. And his bare penis. My bad."

But that was fine.

I saw her standing picking her nails and biting her lip by the prefab building, waiting for me. I sidled up to her as quickly as possible and spoke in my best old-timey gangster voice.

"I got the goods, mugsy."

She jumped out of her skin and screamed.

When she calmed down and I stopped laughing I passed off the pill in a covert handshake. I insisted on that part. It was silly but when she squeezed my hand and thanked me I felt all warm and fuzzy. I could fix things. It was so easy to make her happy.

The rest of the day lived up to the beginning though. My History teacher gave me extra homework for failing the last test. I burned my scones in Home Economics. I couldn't concentrate because I couldn't stop thinking about Holly. Actually, thinking wasn't the right word. I didn't have thoughts, just a heavy, thick layer of grimy self-loathing that everything else got stuck in. Of course I failed the test. I was stupid. Of course I burned the scones, I was useless. Of course I was a bad friend.

I barely noticed how I got home. I was thinking about ways I could make it up to her. How I could show her I was on her side. Always. Part of me thought the best thing

I could do would be to stop talking to Meabh. But I kept searching for other ideas. After all, Holly didn't know I *was* talking to Meabh, so how would that help?

When I reached the flat, still running on autopilot, I shouted hi to my mother and went straight to my room. I badly needed a nap. Or a shower. Or a lobotomy. Something to shake the day off.

"Aideen, would you come in here, please?" Mam called out.

Had Mam noticed my mood from one "hi"? I rubbed my face and thought that actually maybe I could talk to her. She knew Holly almost as well as I did. Maybe she could help. We could have a cup of tea and I would tell her the whole story. Oh, all right, not the whole story. Just the "Holly is mad at me what do I do?" part. I slunk into the kitchen, hoping she'd break out the biscuits if she saw how bad things were.

"Hello, love."

I wanted to turn around and walk out again.

"Hi, Dad."

14

He sat on our sofa with a stupid smile on his stupid face and his fancy stupid shoes on our footrest. The footrest was one million years old and manky as fuck but I still felt the heat of fury rise up in me when I noticed. Who the fuck was he to be putting his dirty shoes on our stuff? Dickhead.

"Mind getting your shoes off the fucking furniture?" I said coldly.

"Aideen!"

Mam sounded shocked at my language, which was entirely for his benefit as every second word out of her mouth usually had asterisks in it. She was standing holding the kettle over three mugs. Did she really think we were all going to sit down and have a cup of tea?

Dad stood up. "I should go."

"Aidan, no." She looked at me, pleading. "Aideen."

A whole storm raged inside me. Everything about him made me sick. There had been a time when I was little when I didn't feel that way, but it was because I didn't really understand what was going on. I didn't think it was strange that my dad only came round now and then. Or that he would disappear for months on end. I knew kids whose parents were divorced and I knew that sometimes dads didn't live with you. That wasn't strange. I didn't think it was weird that sometimes I saw them kissing either. I understood that when he went away, Mam was sad and that made her drink.

From overheard smoky conversations that my mam had in the kitchen with her friends I gradually put the past together. Dad had married this woman, Sarah, a year or two before he met Mam. Dad had an affair with Mam and then I arrived. At some point he asked Mam to marry him, even though he was still with Sarah. She waited for him to leave for years, but he never did. For some reason there was this part of Mam that wanted to believe he would, so badly that she just couldn't give up hope. Sometimes he'd come back to her and he'd claim that she was the one he really loved. Sometimes he'd disappear and I'd see pictures of him celebrating an anniversary or a new baby online. He had four kids with Sarah now. One of them was older than me.

He didn't know I followed him. I'd friended him with a random picture of a hot woman and figured he'd accept. Thankfully he'd never slid into my DMs. I knew Mam must see those pictures too, although if she was friends with him it was also under a fake profile.

A couple of years after I figured all this out, something else occurred to me and I rang the records office. I asked about my birth certificate. There was no father listed.

No trail. I wondered sometimes if Mam named me

after him to make a point. *You can't pretend she's not yours.* But from what I'd seen she was just that obsessed with him.

She looked so happy every time he came around. And so devastated every time he left. Was it worth it? The moments of joy paid for with days when she couldn't even get out of bed? If I made it worse for her, was I taking away the only thing that made her smile? Was being happy for a little while better than never being happy? It didn't feel like that. It felt like ruining your life for the same scrap of affection over and over because you didn't think you deserved any more than that.

"Sorry," I said, trying my best to squash the bitterness in my voice. Mam smiled, a real smile, and I saw how her eyes lit up when she handed him a cup of tea and he said, "Thanks, love." For a second I thought I was right to let her have this moment. But he never had the same spark when *he* looked at *her.*

I forced myself to sip on my tea. I sat at the table though, and not on the sofa near them. Dad had to turn around and crane his neck to look at me.

"How's school going?" he asked.

Don't you get a report? You pay for it, after all. Or do you not bother to open it?

The fees for my school were not huge and they were meant to be a "voluntary donation" but I know they helped me get in because my entrance exam was abysmal. I was dying to go to St Louise's because it was where Holly was

166

going. I felt like I'd compromised myself by accepting his money. I should have told him to shove it up his arse and gone to St Rose's instead, which was closer to where I lived and not as obsessed with exams. But there was no Holly there. I sold myself out for her.

"It's grand," I said.

"You still knocking about with that wee girl with the red hair?"

I have one friend and you can't even remember her name. Classic. Can you remember the names of Rachel, Thomas, Christopher, and James's friends?

"Yeah."

Mam gave me a meaningful look over her mug.

What's happened that you're here again? Fight with Sarah? A lull in the relationship? Is she not in the mood lately? Did you fancy fucking someone different and knew you wouldn't have to make any effort with Mam?

"How's work or whatever?"

Dad perked up. Of course he did, it was about him. He launched into a full explanation about what was going on at his company and I didn't even pretend to listen. Imagine being so up your own hole that you don't realise when someone is only asking a question to be polite and instead you think a sixteen-year-old girl is actually interested in your shite company.

"Cool," I said when he finally stopped talking. "I have loads of homework."

Have I done my penance?

Mam nodded to let me go and I resisted the urge to slam my door behind me.

My bag was full of books when I kicked it and it hurt my toe but it reminded me that I really did have to do homework. I put my earbuds in and opened the French file and tried to focus. I held my pen in my hand over a pad of paper and tried to ignore the pounding in my head. I played the same few lines over and over again but the meaning didn't come. I knew some of the words, but there were too many that didn't mean anything to me. A few loud laughs penetrated past the deep voice of the French fella in my head and it made me tense up. How could she sit in there laughing with him? The paper in front of me became blurry and a tear dropped out and splashed on the page. I blinked really fast so no more could get out and I opened up my messages.

Aideen
He's back.

Holly
Come over.

I threw a big hoodie on and slipped out the front door. Mam didn't notice and I suspected she wouldn't for some time. I walked to the bus stop and waited. It was two buses to get to Holly's and by the time I got to the first changeover

I thought I'd calmed down. The whole of my Sad Ladies of the Nineties playlist had played through and smushed down the churny awful thoughts of Mam and Dad. Or Aidan rather. Why did I even still call him Dad? He didn't deserve it. He didn't *want* it! I was just another unfortunate consequence of his "complicated" relationship status. He liked to swoop in, wreak havoc, and then disappear with no thought for what was left behind. I wondered if he thought about us when he wasn't here. Did we cease to exist for him when he wasn't looking directly at us?

Holly was waiting for me at the bus stop. She had a tea in a to-go mug, which she held out to me.

"You didn't have to meet me here," I said.

"Come here," she said, and she held her arms wide. I sank into them and cried into the soft fluffy collar of her coat.

15

I stayed at Holly's that night even though her mam made one of those sucking-lemon faces. I heard her and Holly whispering in strained voices outside her room. Holly's mam did not like me. She thought I was bad news. But I'd rather look at her sour puss over breakfast than go home and have to face Dad spending the night. There weren't songs loud enough to drown out the trauma of hearing your mam getting the ride.

I set my alarm for six but put it on vibrate under my pillow so it wouldn't wake Holly up. We'd been up late talking and it had been really nice. Like old times. She told me about the time Jason Keyes asked her to rub him on the bum and she said no. We laughed about that for a while. She played footsie with my bare feet under the covers.

When the alarm went off, all I wanted to do was put the pillow over my face, but I still had that homework and ignoring it was not an option. As I rummaged through my bag, trying my best to be quiet, Holly startled me.

"What are you doing?" she groaned.

"I have to do this homework or I'm going to legit be expelled," I said. "Go back to sleep."

She rolled over and looked at her phone. "It's six a.m."

"I know, that's why I said go back to sleep."

"What subject is it? Maths?"

"French. I got the Maths done the other day. Your nemesis helped me actually." I don't know why I told her that. Especially after I'd resolved not to defend Meabh in front of Holly. It felt like a confession.

She was silent for a second.

"Come back to bed and I'll do it for you in a bit." She patted the space beside her. "I'm cold."

I climbed back into bed beside her but she didn't go back to sleep. We lay facing each other and she pouted.

"Why was she helping you with Maths?"

"You know what she's like. I was doing it in PE and she just couldn't help herself."

"So what, you're, like, friends now?"

"No, of course not. It's just she's not in PE any more because of her foot so she sits up in the balcony with me and does her student council plan stuff. I mean, not with me. Just there. And I'm there."

I tried not to sound guilty. Why did I even feel guilty? I hadn't done anything. I hadn't told Holly about the favour I'd done Meabh. Or the favour she'd done me. Or that I'd told her to start with her green initiative, even though I hadn't known what it was at the time. But then she'd never asked me specifically, *Aideen, did you push Meabh down the stairs in order to give her more time to work on her student council plans and then did she help you break into the school in*

171

the middle of the night and then did you inadvertently advise her to kill the hard copy of my beloved school newspaper?

So, like, it hadn't come up.

"Is there anything you want to tell me?" Holly said.

My heart went from zero to sixty. Or whatever the heart equivalent numbers are.

"Like what?"

I thought about Meabh's long, dark eyelashes and strong arms and the way her skirt rode up when she sat on the bench. My throat felt hot.

Holly appeared to think about it for a moment, but I knew she wasn't really thinking. She knew whatever she wanted to say next. But she wanted it to seem like it was off the top of her head.

That, or she's deliberately trying to make you anxious.

That was silly. Why would she want to do that?

"Did you know she was going to kill the paper?" Holly asked finally.

"What? No, of course I didn't." I was surprised that she'd even thought that. I might not be being 100 per cent honest with Holly, but I loved her and if I knew about something that was going to hurt her, I would have prepared her.

She should know that about you.

Before I opened my mouth to say so though, I caught myself. Holly was angry and she was upset and she didn't mean to be hurtful. If she didn't mean it then I shouldn't be annoyed with her. I swallowed my indignation.

"If I'd known, I would have told you. She had her laptop and papers and graphs and stuff spread out but she never said anything about exactly what she was planning."

"Yeah, OK," Holly sighed. Almost immediately she perked up again. "Now that we're going to be campaigning against each other, she's probably going to work on that during PE too."

"I mean, she also does things at home, I'm sure," I said, not liking how excited Holly suddenly was.

"But you said she spread out all her papers and she had her laptop?"

"I mean—"

"You can be my spy! If she says anything about her plans. Any tiny thing she says or you overhear, tell me, OK?" She leaned her face so close to mine, the tips of our noses touched.

My stomach gurgled, and it wasn't because I hadn't had dinner last night.

"I don't . . ." My words got lost on the way out of my mouth.

"Let's get some sleep." Holly rolled over. "I have to get up in an hour to do your homework."

"You don't have to, I can do it," I said. I hadn't asked her to do it and somehow I felt guilty anyway.

"Don't be silly," she said, and I could hear in her voice that she was already falling asleep again. "It's only ordinary level. It'll take you an hour and it'll take me ten minutes.

That's not an efficient use of time. Keep me warm." She yawned and pulled my arm around her waist and she snuggled into me.

After that, I might as well have got up because I didn't get back to sleep. I lay awake looking at the back of Holly's head and wondering why I felt good and terrible at the same time.

A few hours later, Ms Devlin was wrapping up registration and I could see Meabh was bouncing nervously on her ball. She had the same kind of expression as when she knew the answer to something and could barely contain herself long enough for the teacher to finish asking the question. As soon as the bell went for the first class, she launched herself off her exercise ball, utilising the momentum provided by its bouncy surface. With surprising speed for someone wearing a space boot, she accosted Holly.

"We need to speak to Ms Devlin," she said.

"Why?" Holly said suspiciously. She was clearly caught off guard by Meabh speaking to her.

"We need to discuss the election. There are issues."

"What issues?"

"I'd rather discuss it with Ms Devlin present as an arbitrator."

Holly rolled her eyes at me but relented.

I followed Holly and Meabh up to Ms Devlin, feeling very much like this was my business, but Ms Devlin disagreed for some reason, citing that I was neither on the school paper nor part of the election.

"You could always sign up to run," she added as I huffed out of the room, walking a little quicker away from that suggestion.

I pretended to walk off into the distance, towards the main building, while the door slowly closed itself, but as soon as it shut, I hurried back to it and pressed my ear against it.

"What are we doing?" Kavi said. I jumped.

"How do you do that?"

"Do what?" he asked, confused.

"Never mind."

I paused, expecting Kavi to tell me why he was waiting for me. I assumed he'd heard of a new client and unexpectedly I was excited about what we might do next. I was kind of killing it in the favour business so far. *Client* made me sound like a fancy businessperson though, which I wasn't. Beneficiary? Made me sound like the Queen or something. We were distracted almost immediately by a loud, high-pitched scream of, "Are you fucking kidding me?!"

Kavi and I both put our ears to the door, facing each other. We sent silent facial expression messages that I'm pretty sure followed the line of *Do you think what we're doing is wrong? OK, good, me neither.*

"Holly. I realise you're upset, but Meabh makes a valid point here. I know you're smart enough to see that."

175

That was Ms Devlin.

"She's just doing it to get me to stop running."

I mouthed Holly's name at Kavi.

"I am not. Run if you want but I genuinely think it would be unfair for you to keep working in the press and running for public office at the same time." Meabh's voice was unmistakeable. It had that I'm-right-and-you're-wrong tone even when she *wasn't* arguing about something.

Kavi widened his eyes at me. My heart sank.

"Public office? The press? It's a school newspaper and student council."

"The paper will be open to accusations of bias even if you leave, so this is the very least you can do."

"Miss, come on."

"I'm sorry, Holly, you're going to have to choose."

There was silence then for what felt like a long time. When Holly finally spoke, her voice was steely.

"I am going to run for student council. And I'm going to win. And then I will go back to being editor of a paper that is still printed on *paper*."

Kavi bared his teeth in an anxious grimace.

"They're gonna kill each other," he said in a stage whisper.

"Yes," I agreed. This was not good.

"You don't even want to be president," Meabh shrieked.

"I really, really do," Holly replied.

I felt sick. I didn't want to listen to any more.

"I'm going to class," I said dully. "You should too."

"I'm so late," Kavi said anxiously. "Mr Kowalski will be so mad at me if I get in trouble again."

He was ten minutes late. At most. I resisted the urge to strangle him.

"You'll be grand. Go over to the nurse's office and ask for a painkiller. You can say that's why you're late. Don't be surprised if Sister D asks you if you're on your period though."

"I don't get periods," he said seriously.

"You don't say."

I started off towards my own class, heading in the opposite direction.

"Will you meet me for lunch?" Kavi said across the growing space between us.

Right. He was bringing me a new client.

"Sure. The prefab?" I suggested.

"Our usual place." He winked.

"Uh, yeah. Sure." I shook my head to myself. Strange boy.

I muddled through French, with actual completed homework that Miss Sullivan held up to the light as though she would be able to spot the counterfeit. She was not. Or rather she had so few examples of my own handwriting that this could plausibly be it. I tried to arrange my face into pleasant befuddlement, as though I had no idea what she could possibly be doing.

I didn't text Holly. I knew it was selfish but she was going to be so angry about being basically forced off the paper and when she got like that, nothing I could say was right. I did pass Meabh in the hall between French and Biology and she gave me a small smile. She looked a little bit confused when I didn't smile back. But what did she expect? That she could help me with one set of Maths problems and I'd ignore that she was waging war on my best friend?

I hated that this was escalating. They both assumed the worst in each other and were both totally convinced that they were right to do so.

Besides, I reasoned, if I did message Holly, then she'd know I'd been listening in. She didn't know I knew. And she hadn't found me. She hadn't sent an expletive-laden text about Meabh's treachery. I know you might think, well, it had only been a couple of hours – but Holly had texted me three and a half minutes after she had her first kiss. She was still with the guy at the time. Was I self-absorbed for feeling hurt now just because she didn't need me, especially when I was deliberately avoiding her?

I felt even worse when I thought about the French homework I'd just handed in. If she hadn't done it, I would have got in trouble again. The guilt gnawed at me until I finally fired off a message, trying to sound merely curious about what had happened with Ms Devlin. Holly could be annoyed with me because I didn't ask, after all. When I realised that, I felt a flood of relief. Of course. She was annoyed that I hadn't been thoughtful enough to ask her what happened.

Bet she messaged Jill.

Jill was on the paper. It only made sense. It didn't mean anything. I didn't even know if that was true.

Aideen
What happened with Ms D?

I waited for an answer and kept checking my phone through the morning classes but got nothing. I went on Instagram and saw she'd been active since I sent the message. So she'd looked at her phone but she hadn't opened my message on purpose. I tried not to dwell on why that made me feel so terrible. I was being stupid as usual.

When the lunch bell rang, it took all my willpower to go and meet Kavi instead of going to find Holly.

He was sitting on my steps at the back of the prefab and he had a lunch box.

"Well?" I said, expectant.

"Do you want a samosa?" he asked, removing the lid and holding out his lunch box to display his wares. They smelled amazing.

"No. I'm good, thanks. What's up?"

"Well, I had a good morning after I saw you. The trick

about going to get a painkiller worked, although Sister Dymphna did give me a suspicious look when she was taking the ibuprofen out of the cupboard. I think she was onto me."

"No, she thought you were drug seeking. She thinks everyone is. Don't worry about it. I meant more like, what's up with the . . . the business? Has someone else been seeking my very special services?"

He shrugged with a mouthful of samosa and made an *I dunno* noise.

Was he doing this on purpose to annoy me? Why make me meet him if he didn't have something to tell me?

Kavi swallowed. "It's not a really a business," he said. "I guess it's not a charity either . . . it's more like a social enterprise!"

"What's a social enterprise?" I said, unable to hide my annoyance. Though it didn't seem like Kavi even noticed.

"It's *like* a business but instead of keeping the profits you do something good with it."

I liked the sound of that.

"Are you OK?" he asked. So he had noticed. I felt bad for being grumpy with him when he was always nice to me.

"Yeah, I'm fine. Just. You know. Life."

He nodded seriously.

"You sure you don't want one?" He waved his food under my nose.

"Oh all right then, budge up," I said, and Kavi scooted

along the step and made a space for me. I bit into one of the samosas.

"Christ alive. Did you make this?" I said. Kavi was a food genius.

"I helped. But my dad did most of the work. He spent like four hours doing these yesterday and I'm surprised there were any leftovers."

Mam's cooking was more the fish fingers and beans school of culinary delights, and if we got a takeaway, it was a chippy. I'd never even been to a restaurant. But I didn't say any of that. I didn't want Kavi to think I was uncultured or sheltered because I'd never had proper Indian food. I didn't think Patak's curry in a jar was really the same thing. "Does your mam cook too?"

"Mam can't make cheese on toast, never mind samosas. Try the sauce."

I was about to when I heard the crackle of the tannoy system and with a jolt realised it was my name they were calling.

Could Aideen Cleary please come to the school office. Aideen Cleary to the school office, please.

My heart sank. That couldn't be anything good. Had something happened to Mam? I checked my phone in case I had a missed call but there was nothing.

Maybe I was just being expelled.

16

There was another student sitting in the office when I got there. A Black girl with light brown skin and braids. Angela Berry. She was the kind of gorgeous that made people slow down when she walked past. And she was older, a sixth year. Social media influencer. School play star. She had her own car supposedly paid for with endorsement money. Rumour had it though she'd crashed it twice already.

Everyone knew her.

She was tapping her foot nervously but there was no principal, teacher, or social worker waiting for me. Orla was behind the counter. She smiled, relieved, when she saw me.

"Thank God. I was afraid to call for you again in case anyone noticed. I thought one wee quick callout wouldn't be suspicious."

"What's going on?" I asked. "I thought my mam had died or something."

Orla appeared stricken by this. "Why? Is she ill? I'm so sorry."

"No. I was exaggerating. I mean, I thought something serious had happened."

She cringed. "I didn't think of that. Sorry. But look, I really need your help."

"Again?"

She nodded. Then she shook her head.

"Not me." She waved Angela over from where she was sitting chewing her fingernails and tapping her foot.

Angela sprang up and walked towards us, giving me a once-over.

"Her? Really?" She narrowed her eyes at me. I suppose I didn't look like the kind of person who could fix things, seeing as I just about grazed her shoulders.

Orla reassured her, "I told you she helped me. You can trust her."

"What did she do for you?" Angela asked. Orla hesitated.

That was when Kavi made his presence known.

"Oh my God, such a good story," Kavi said excitedly.

Everyone jumped. Including me. I didn't realise he'd followed me, but I was beginning to think he simply had the ability to materialise out of thin air.

I cut him off. "All transactions are confidential," I said.

"I wasn't going to *tell* the story," he said indignantly. "I was just saying it was a good one."

Angela nodded approvingly. "Well, that's good business," she said.

She seemed to consider us for another second.

"OK, I'll tell you," Angela said finally.

I waited. When she didn't say anything I gave her my best *go on then* face.

"Out here? Where anyone can walk in on us?" Angela frowned.

"You can go in here." Orla unlocked the supply cupboard and the three of us squeezed in. More dark closets, less breathing room. Kavi sat on a box of printer paper and I flattened myself against the wall. Angela somehow managed to look confident and at ease even here. That must be what self-esteem does for you.

"Why is he here too?" Angela eyed Kavi.

Kavi and I exchanged a look. Mine said, *why* are *you here?* His said, *why* wouldn't *I be here?*

"Whatever, I don't have time for this." Angela waved off our hesitation. "So you know Mr Walker? Super strict, minus craic, face like a slapped arse?"

I nodded. I had him for Geography. We did not get along. Surprise surprise.

"Well, I had him last period and I may or may not have written some kinda rude comments about him on a sheet of paper for my friend to read."

I nodded. We'd all been there.

"Well, I also had to hand in a long essay. I borrowed my friend's stapler to keep the sheets together and—"

I cringed. Kavi clapped his hand over his mouth.

"Exactly," Angela groaned. "I handed in the essay and

then realised I'd also included the sheet with the, um . . . comments."

"How bad are these comments?" I asked, barely able to breathe from secondhand cringe.

"Uh . . . I suppose they span the range from mildly rude to a suggestion that he's a case for post-birth abortion?"

I couldn't help but snort.

"In my defence," Angela declared, "he shouted at me for not participating in a discussion when loads of other people weren't and he said he saw me in the last play and said, 'If only you had so little to say then.' I'm not going to take that kind of attack on my performance, you know?"

"Right . . ." I nodded. "So what we're looking at here is you getting detention, right? And you'll be in deep shit with your parents, obviously."

"It's not my parents." She shook her head. "Getting in trouble with them is fine. Yeah, they'd be annoyed and I'd have my phone taken off me or whatever but that doesn't matter. It's the detention. I can't stay after school."

No one *wanted* to stay after school.

"You know my dad isn't well, right?"

I exchanged a look with Kavi. His expression implied he did know.

"I didn't. Sorry."

"He is. It's fine. He's going to be OK." Angela's jaw twitched and I wondered if he was really going to be OK

185

or if this was something she had to tell herself. "If I get detention I miss visiting hours. My mam is out of town all week so he'd be all alone."

"That's right," I said, a memory of what Mícheál had said in English last week coming back to me. I assumed he too often had flashbacks of that class but for different reasons. "You're having a party on Saturday."

"Yeah," she said uneasily. "You can come if you want? I guess."

I shook my head. "You're all right. I'll do it," I said. You didn't get a much better cause than this one. You had to really love someone to sit around eating grapes and catching MRSA and Angela clearly loved her dad a lot.

Angela let out a huge sigh. "Thank you so much."

"Where is the offending item now, do you know?"

"It's in his room. But I think he's marking those papers as we speak."

"So he might have already seen it?"

"I don't think I'd be standing here talking to you if he had. But there isn't much time."

"We need a distraction," I said. I gave the door of the store room a light nudge with my toe and it swung open.

I signalled to Orla.

"Would you be able to get away for ten minutes? We need to distract Mr Walker."

She checked the time on her phone. "If I'm not here when the secretary gets back, I'll be in deep shit. But I

186

know I owe you. Oh!" she exclaimed, suddenly excited. "What if I get the whole dance troupe to practise in the hall? He'd definitely come out and look at the racket. And let me tell you, our 'Baby One More Time' routine is so tight right now."

"I appreciate the offer but I don't want you to get fired."

There was no point calling in a favour from someone only to get them in trouble.

"I could fall down outside and pretend to be hurt," Angela said. "See what he thinks of my acting skills then," she added, muttering under her breath.

I shook my head. "I don't want you anywhere near this. Plausible deniability."

Kavi and I exchanged a look. His look said *I got this.* My look said *I don't know about this.*

"I did great last time," he protested. "Very distracting."

There was no other option that I could think of and we were running out of time.

"OK, I need that same energy, but like . . . where you don't get caught and get suspended. That part is vital. Can you do that?"

He nodded. Kavi in business mode was a quiet Kavi.

"Do you know what you're going to do?" I asked.

He grinned. "I'll improvise."

Upstairs, I indicated for Kavi to stay put for a second. I slunk past Mr Walker's room. The door was closed but there was a small window you could look through. There was one student in there. A white boy with dark hair that curled around his ears. I could handle one boy. I recognised him from the year below me. Daniel something. He was one of the techy boys who did things with computers that I didn't understand. He was bent over a piece of work but he was surreptitiously trying to pick his nose. I could just about see Mr Walker at his desk with a pile of papers.

He didn't look enraged yet. That was a good sign. I slipped into the classroom next door, which was empty, and sent a signal to Kavi. From where I was standing, I watched him begin panting excessively and then he ran really fast and burst into Mr Walker's room. I closed the door to my classroom and slid to the floor, crouching awkwardly so I couldn't be spotted through the window, but I could hear Kavi through the wall.

"Sir! Sir! Come quick. I think I saw someone breaking into your car!"

"What?!"

I heard a scramble of chair legs against the wooden floor.

"Did you call the police?" Mr Walker said urgently.

"Uh . . . yes. I did," Kavi lied.

I shook my head. He could have come up with a thousand less dramatic stories, but Kavi loved a good story, after all. I briefly wondered if Mr K still thought he was pining for Meabh.

I waited for them to leave and Mr Walker gave a threatening "Don't move" order to Daniel Something.

I stole into Mr Walker's room, feeling very covert, and gave Daniel Something a glare.

"Not a word," I said.

He furrowed his brow. He had no idea what I was talking about.

I sat in Mr Walker's chair and marvelled at how comfortable it was. Why did teachers get comfy chairs when we were the ones who had to sit down all day? There was a stack of papers on the desk in front of me and I flicked through them, looking for Angela's name. It wasn't there. I snatched the stack of marked papers, praying it wasn't in those. It wasn't.

"He put a bunch of homework in the bottom drawer," Daniel Something said.

I opened the drawer. It was one of those deep ones. It was piled high with about a hundred papers. Ugh, being a teacher was so grim. I thought about some of the papers I handed in and had a tiny sliver of sympathy for my teachers. Imagine having to read that crap all day. Actually, wasn't I really doing them a favour when I *didn't* do my homework? Lightening their load?

I dropped to my knees and began flicking through the papers in the drawer. I didn't recognise enough names to know if I had the right year group so I couldn't even skip past any.

"What're you at, anyway?" Daniel Something said, like it was only mildly curious that I was doing what I was doing.

"I'm doing someone a favour," I said brusquely.

"Why though?"

"Because I do that," I said. Seána O'Brien. Nope. Seamus Keegan. Nope. Lina Jankauskas. Nope.

"But why, though?"

"Ughhhh, because I do!"

Then, finally thinking, I popped my head over the desk.

"Why? Do you need something?"

When I thought about it later, I realised that Meabh might have started this whole thing. Kavi took that one favour and snowballed it into another. But at some point, maybe this exact point, I was the one who picked up the snowball and started chucking it in every direction.

"Like what?" Daniel asked.

"I don't know. Like a favour. Something you need done that you can't get done for yourself."

I was going to have to come up with a better elevator pitch.

I didn't know him well enough to know if he had tattling tendencies, but I figured if I did a favour for him, he'd be less inclined to rat me out. As Daniel appeared to muse on this, I returned to my papers. At least it kept him quiet.

Dylan Cheung. Nope. Conor Quinn. Natasha Farrell. Nope.

"There is one thing," Daniel Something said.

I popped my head up again and rested my arms, folded, on the desk.

"What can I do for you, Daniel?" I asked, amiably and not at all like I was on the fucking clock. How much time had passed? How much time would it take Mr Walker to get to the car park and realise his car was fine?

"You know Angela Berry?"

Shit. Did he somehow know what I was doing?

"Uh, yeah . . ."

"Her party is on Saturday."

Thank God.

"Yeah, I know."

"Well, I want to go."

"And you're not invited?" I said, thinking of Angela's reluctant invitation to have me at her party. It seemed unlikely she'd want this random boy three years below her.

"No, that's not it. Angela said I could go. Her cousin is my best friend."

OK, just me then.

"So what's the problem?"

"There's no way my mum will let me go. She is so strict and my grandparents are visiting."

I felt unmoved. Although having a techy person owe me a favour would undoubtedly come in handy.

Daniel fiddled with his pencil. "I've never been to a party or anything. She thinks parties are all drinking and sex and so she won't ever let me go. I get left out of everything. On Monday all anyone's going to be talking about is this stupid party and I'll be the only one who didn't get to go and I'll be the loser *again*."

I didn't care about being invited to things everyone was doing, but I did know how it felt to feel like everyone had something you didn't. That you were the odd one out. His face was so pained and so pathetic, he reminded me of something that was so gross it was endearing. Like one of those really ugly dogs that look like they're inside out but they still deserve love.

"All right," I said, sighing heavily, like this was a huge ask. Getting to a party would be a piece of cake compared to breaking into school and trying to break bones, but Daniel needed to feel indebted to me. "But you owe me one, OK?"

He pumped his fist and uttered a very intense, "YES!"

I looked back at my papers and there it was. I pulled the offending sheet off and stuffed the essay back in the pile.

"There you are, you wee bugger," I muttered, looking over the comments with a smile.

"I could say the same thing to you," Ms Devlin said.

17

I looked from the paper in my hand to the open drawer, up to Ms Devlin's face. I'd seen her angry before, but this was something special.

She held her hand out for the sheet and I stood up. I contemplated whether it would fit in my mouth if I scrunched it up. I wouldn't put it past her to fish it out of my mouth, if I was honest. I handed the sheet over. She inspected it. I watched her take in whatever Angela had written on it, knowing that there was nothing identifiable on the paper now that it was detached from Angela's homework.

She folded it and put it in her pocket. "Come with me," she said.

I followed behind her in silence, through the halls, across the field, into the sports complex, and down the hall to her office.

Ms Devlin sat and gestured to a chair opposite her desk. She didn't say anything. I wondered if she was waiting for an explanation, and that felt like a trap. I took in the office. There wasn't much to it, except for a stack of cones in the corner and a succulent on the desk. I hadn't been in it before. Seeing as Ms Devlin loved to have private chats with me, I figured she kept her office for only the most serious infractions.

"I like what you've done with the place," I said.

"This isn't the time, Aideen," she said. I hadn't heard her use that tone before. The one that didn't have any humour in it.

She took the piece of paper from her pocket. "Did you write this?"

I nodded. Somehow I couldn't bring myself to say yes to her face.

"And what were you doing in Mr Walker's drawers?"

I resisted every urge to say that I would never, ever go near Mr Walker's drawers; I didn't think she'd appreciate the double entendre.

"I didn't want him to see it. I accidentally handed it in with homework."

Thank God I actually had Mr Walker for Geography or I don't know how I'd have explained that.

Ms Devlin narrowed her eyes. Then she wiggled her mouse and typed in the password on her computer. I tried to follow what it was. You never know when you might need these things. It started with *S4*, but unfortunately that was all I got.

Ms Devlin peered at her screen, typing in a few things, scrolling, and eventually reading something.

"You haven't had Geography today. And from what I

can see here, you haven't handed in homework in at least two weeks."

"I . . . I had Geography on Monday, I handed it in then. I only realised today I lost this sheet. I waited for Mr Walker to go to the toilet during lunch and snuck in and got it. I know it was wrong but I didn't want him to read what I wrote. I was only thinking of his feelings, you know."

I tried to apply some of my charm and smiled innocently. It didn't work.

"I spoke to Miss Sullivan yesterday," she said.

Shit.

"She said you've handed in three assignments since the start of term?" Her brows were knitted together and she seemed more worried than her usual gruff self.

"I knew you were struggling in English and Maths, but French too?" She looked at her screen. "And Geography, evidently."

And Business Studies, Home Ec, and Biology.

"Miss, I got one A, four Cs, and five Ds in my junior. It can't really be a surprise that I'm not good at school."

"How *could* you be good?" she said, exasperated. "You don't try!"

"I'm not academic," I said, thinking of what Mam had said when I'd got my results. She said I had other abilities, but she didn't elaborate on what they were.

"You're a bright girl. I'm not asking you to get all As. I'm asking you to live up to your potential," she said.

Here it came. An inspirational speech. I'd heard them before. They came right before whatever do-gooder had seized on you completely gave up because you didn't turn your life around based on their sage wisdom.

"You're unfocused. And I know that you've had a difficult time in the past with your mother. There's been social work involvement? How are things now?"

I sighed, annoyed.

"I am so sick of hearing about potential," I said, sidestepping the social work bits. No way was I going into that. "What if this is my potential? What if this is the best I can do – what then? Look at my first year and you'll see I was getting Ds back then too. You might see the odd C. Why would I work my arse off when that's the best I can do anyway? Some people are never going to be able to do better! As much as you want to have your inspiring teacher moment, I'm only going to disappoint you!"

Ms Devlin looked taken aback at my sudden serious outburst and I regretted it only slightly.

"You won't disappoint me if you try," she said. She was so earnest I felt sad for her. She needed a life of her own to worry about.

"You *need* me to be terrible," I said. "If everyone can get As if they only try hard enough, then As become totally meaningless. It's not designed for everyone to succeed. A few people will be exceptional. Everyone else is getting by in the middle. But you need me at the bottom. I'm the low bar everyone else can jump over."

Ms Devlin seemed to be trying to think of something she could say. I could tell I'd surprised her. I'd surprised myself with how true those words sounded. It had taken me ages to work out that feeling and I'd never said it out loud. I'd wrestled with this thorny, tangledy mess and somehow over the years managed to sort it into an idea that rang as true as a bell inside me.

"If that's true," she said finally, "and I'm not saying it is. But if it is true, I want you to game the system. Don't let it beat you."

There was a part of me that wanted to say, *Yes, I'll do what you want and work really hard and then you'll be happy.* I didn't blame her. She was only doing her job, and she was new to being my form tutor so she hadn't been worn into the ground by my perpetual failure yet. But I knew I couldn't give her the thing she wanted. She wanted me to buck up and get a B and then she could be proud that I achieved something. Then she could feel like she'd helped the bad student blossom.

I'd give her that moment if I could. She probably deserved it. But I didn't have it in me. In first year I thought maybe, just maybe it would be different in secondary school. People would be my friend and I wouldn't feel lost every time I tried to follow what was going on in class. And I tried. I tried so, so hard for a while. But nothing ever clicked. Maths felt like someone was trying to teach me a foreign language by speaking another foreign language. English was some kind of riddle where people said things but meant other things and I was supposed to be the author's therapist and analyse it all. And everything else required some kind of photographic memory. I couldn't remember what happened on *Fair City* last week, never mind everything everyone in history ever said or did from the Aztecs up to Michael Collins.

"The only way to beat it is if you want to do my homework for me," I said. "And while I think it would be nice for you to have a hobby, I don't think this will expand your horizons."

"I can't fix the problem by doing it for you," she said, taking everything way too seriously again. "But I can try and give you the tools you need to fix it yourself. What about tutoring?"

Tutoring costs money. I mean, aside from the utter pointlessness. If I didn't understand it in class, then how was I going to understand it after class when my brain was already fried?

"I can't give up my cigarette and cider money for a tutor, miss," I said, trying to make a joke of it. I didn't want her to feel sorry for me but I wanted her not to push it.

"I don't want to get you in trouble," she said. "I don't see how that will help you in any way. But I won't be able to protect you from it if you keep carrying on like this, and if you did get in serious trouble, I'm afraid it will set you down a bad path."

"I think that path leads to my front door already, miss."

She looked sad.

"I did my French homework for today," I offered.

She closed her eyes. "I will help you in any way I can, Aideen. But you have to tell me what's going on."

"Everything is fine, miss. I promise."

She gave me a long look. "You remind me so much of myself at your age. Unfocused. Out of her depth. You're not a bad kid. You do need some discipline though."

"Sadly, caning is now illegal, miss."

"Sadly indeed. However, I meant a different kind of discipline. After school. Fifty laps of the track."

I nearly choked. "MISS!"

She leaned back in her chair and fixed her eyes on me. There was a glint of her usual sense of humour there.

"Unless you have a note?" she said, sounding completely innocent. "That you can show me right this minute?"

We both knew today was not a PE day.

There was no note.

There was no escape.

18

I thought my chest was going to explode. There was sweat dripping down my . . . my everything. And I don't mean a light sheen of sweat, I mean there was actual dripping. My legs burned for a bit and then they became numb and heavy. I stopped repeatedly and retched. Ms Devlin watched me from a deck chair she'd set in the middle of the field. She had a stack of papers to mark but it looked like she found my struggle more entertaining because she didn't seem to be doing a whole lot of work. She'd dressed me in long-lost gym gear. The T-shirt was too big and the shorts were too small and she'd slipped off her own trainers and thrown them to me.

"Aren't you lucky we both have small feet, Aideen," she'd said, amused.

I gagged.

These were working trainers.

After five laps I lay down in the grass and begged for death. It took Ms Devlin a minute to appear, blocking the weak January sun from my eye line. I felt tears rolling down my face but they could have been sweat. I wasn't sure.

"Aideen, that's ten per cent done."

"Miss, no," I croaked. "The Geneva convention prohibits this kind of torture."

I had no idea what the Geneva convention was but I thought I'd heard that line in a film before.

"The Geneva protocol prohibits biological warfare, Aideen. Nice try. Up you get."

"I can't. I literally cannot move. I live here now. The birds will take me eventually. Try to move on with your life. Don't blame yourself."

"If you're still spouting nonsense, then you have a few more laps in you. Take it at a walk."

I groaned but, sensing her resolve weaken, I thought I could give her another few laps at a snail's pace and then maybe she'd let me go because I'd tried so hard. What was there to go home to anyway? Would Dad be there again this evening? Drinking out of my mugs. Getting his gross molecules all over my sofa. Kissing my mother and pretending like he wasn't just taking a break from his real life.

Rage got me through another few laps. When it began to ebb out of me and I slowed down, Ms Devlin blew a whistle, entirely unnecessarily.

"All right," she said. "Hit the showers."

"Ew, gross. I am not getting in those showers. And I am definitely not drying myself off with an abandoned towel."

"Whatever, princess. Go home then. And if anything like this happens again—"

"What, a hundred laps?" I said.

Her face turned serious. "It won't be laps next time, Aideen. There's only so much I can do."

I nodded, understanding she'd gone to bat for me on this. She might not even have told Mr Walker what had happened.

I sloped off the field towards my schoolbag and pile of clothes. I threw everything into my schoolbag and slung it over my shoulder. Ms Devlin called my name again.

"Trainers," she said, pointing at my feet. They were basically welded to my swollen feet now, so I cursed as I kicked them off.

"That's not how you take off trainers, Aideen, you'll ruin the backs of them."

"You sound like my mam," I said. But as soon as the words were out I wanted to take them back. She didn't sound anything like my mam.

I exited through the main building, and as I passed the office I heard a familiar voice. Two familiar voices. Holly and Jill. I hesitated. She still hadn't replied to me about what had happened this morning with her and Meabh. But she was bound to be upset. I should put my petty feelings aside and go to her.

"Are you sure?" Jill asked.

"I'm sure. If it ends up being our last hard copy then at least we've gone out with a bang."

Holly's voice caught. There was a long silence and I imagined that Jill was giving her a hug. That should have been my hug to give. I looked down at my gross outfit.

Maybe it was my fault I wasn't the one Holly had gone to for comfort. If we were out of step with each other, perhaps it was because I was the one keeping secrets.

After a few moments I heard Jill whine, "I wish you weren't leaving. I don't want to be editor."

So Holly had picked Jill to replace her. That made sense. They were friends. And if Jill didn't want to be editor then that made it easier for Holly to take her place back when the election was over . . . whether she won or not.

I realised I was eavesdropping and I either had to go in and say hello or leave.

"You'll be amazing," Holly said. "You'll probably be even better than me."

I took a few quiet steps and pulled the door to the main entrance open. I was partway down the hill when I heard Holly call my name. Turning, I pasted on a smile. She was half jogging down the hill towards me.

"I thought it was you," she said when she reached me. "But you were wearing gym clothes so I was confused."

She took in my baggy T-shirt and tight shorts paired with my school shoes.

"What is going on?"

"Detention," I said, aware that my words were coming out in a tone I couldn't quite control. I sounded hollow and cold.

"Did Miss Sullivan realise it wasn't your work? You didn't tell her I did it, did you?"

"No. It wasn't that."

"So what, then?"

"Why didn't you answer my message earlier?" I asked. Holly looked surprised that I would bring that up. But in my annoyance I didn't feel embarrassed for a change.

"I'm sorry," she said, "I didn't get it till the end of the day and then I had to hand over the paper to Jill. Meabh told Ms Devlin that I couldn't stay on it because it wouldn't be fair and Ms Devlin agreed because she's a sour old bitch and Meabh is the principal's daughter."

"That's awful," I said, in my flat voice again. "I'm sorry you lost the paper."

"It's temporary," she replied. I wasn't sure if she sensed my tone or not. Maybe it was all in my head. "But why did you get detention?"

"I got caught rummaging around in Mr Walker's desk," I said. *Might as well spill it now, see if it changes anything*, I thought. But it sounded bitter even in my head.

"What? Aideen, what the hell? Why?"

"I was doing someone a favour," I said. I enjoyed her surprise.

I have things going on too.

I thought I saw a shift in her expression. But it was so tiny, over so quickly, I couldn't be sure.

"Who?" she asked. And this time it was her voice that sounded weird.

"I can't tell you that."

"Meabh?"

"No. Why would I be doing a favour for Meabh?"

If you could see guilt it would have surrounded me like a mist. But why? I hadn't been helping Meabh. This time. Fear of making Holly mad at me tugged against anger that I didn't really understand.

"Who, then?"

"I can't tell you that."

"Since when are there things you can't tell me?"

I almost laughed in her face.

Right, because we're so close now. There couldn't be anything I wouldn't tell you. It's fine for you to have this other life with your other friends, but not me.

Was I really being mad at Holly for having other friends? That wasn't OK.

"It's something I've been doing," I said, unsure if I was confessing or rubbing it in her face. "I've been fixing things for people. But I got caught this time."

She looked shocked. Didn't she?

"What do you mean? Fixing things?"

"People ask me for favours, things I can help them with, and in return they owe me one."

I could tell she was choosing her next words carefully. We were this close to a fight.

Or were we already having one?

"Like what? Helping people with presentations?" She

was talking about Kavi, but her tone was a slap in the face. I knew what she meant by that.

I didn't answer that. I thought if I opened my mouth I'd cry.

"Why won't you tell me who it is?" she asked. "I won't tell anyone."

"Well, that's what I told them."

"I'm supposed to be your best friend."

I'm sure you tell Jill things you don't tell me.

"I'm sorry. I'm not trying to keep things from you. I just don't feel right betraying someone else's secret."

We stood in awkward silence. I wondered if we were about to lay it all out. All the stuff that had been building up. I couldn't meet her eyes and I stared at a spot behind her shoulder instead.

"I should go," she said finally.

"Me too."

We went our separate ways.

The flat was empty when I got home. That wasn't surprising. Mam was supposed to be at work until six. But it had an abandoned feeling I couldn't put my finger on. I was turning over my conversation with Holly in my head. I'd felt both like a dog cowering from a raised hand and one snarling and snapping for no reason. Deep down, if I probed, I thought there was a tiny germ of disappointment that it hadn't descended into a screaming match. Where I could have said the things I really wanted to say, in the heat of the moment. But what were those things? They belonged to some ugly, growling creature and I didn't want them to belong to me. So I pretended they didn't.

I was also starving after my marathon around the pitch, and grimy and gross as well. I focused on those things. I hopped in the shower first and then, wrapped in a towel, I inspected the cupboards. Red lentils and beans. Gross. The fridge wasn't better. It had an almost empty carton of milk and a jar of mint sauce. We needed groceries. Badly. In that moment I wanted nothing more than a cheese toastie and I was willing to go to extraordinary lengths to get it. I resented the idea of having to get the rest of the shopping at the same time, so I planned to head to the corner shop and just get what I needed. I texted Mam to get groceries after work. I knew she'd have had a long day too but just this once I wanted to collapse on the sofa and let her pick up the slack.

My message didn't deliver. I got a sick feeling immediately. I told myself maybe there was nothing wrong. She turned her phone off at work. I'd just go get the groceries after all. My stomach churned. I told it, it would take me twenty minutes to get dressed and go to the Spar and come home again. In twenty minutes we'd have two toasties to make up for it.

I reached into my underwear drawer to look for the stash of cash I kept for rainy days and emergencies. I couldn't feel it. I kept stretching my fingers into the corner as though the roll of cash was playing hideaway with me.

But it wasn't.

It was like someone hollowed out my insides.

I pulled my arm out of the drawer and banged my elbow, swearing and rubbing it as I rushed into Mam's room and took in the sight.

There were clothes all over her bedroom floor. There was make-up in clumsy piles by the light-up mirror that didn't light up any more. I tried phoning her. Her phone was off. Of course.

Maybe the cash had fallen down the back of the drawers. I went back to my room and pulled all the drawers out of the frame.

I tried calling some of her friends, but two of them said they hadn't spoken to her in a year and the last one was a disconnected number. I debated whether to call Jacqui, her boss, wondering if I could maybe pull off casual over the phone.

"Hi, Jacqui. This is Aideen."

There was a long pause.

"Lisa's daughter?" I added.

"Yeah, I know."

"OK, um, is Mam working today, do you know?"

"I could ask you the same thing."

That wasn't good. I played innocent though.

"What do you mean?"

"She didn't show up today."

"Oh, well, I mean, I stayed at my friend's house last night. We have a big project for school. So I didn't know. She did say she was feeling sick yesterday morning. Maybe that's why she's not answering her phone."

Was that believable?

Jacqui *hmphed* in a way that let me know that it was not.

I hung up quickly before I could get my mam fired.

I logged on to Facebook. I only kept it to keep up with Mam. She loved posting embarrassing TMIs and playing Cafeland. She hadn't posted anything today though. With a sinking feeling I clicked on Dad's page. There was a close-up picture of him and Sarah smiling. They had checked into the airport this morning.

Off on a winter holibob with this one. She deserves a break!

For a second I was filled with a rage that felt bigger than what my body could contain. This would have crushed her.

Part of me wanted to scream. Part of me wanted to cry. Part of me wanted to lock the doors and never let her back in the house, because how could she fucking do this to me again. Why did she keep doing this? She knew how it always ended with Dad and she knew she couldn't cope with it. So why did she keep choosing him when I ended up suffering for it? Was I so worthless that nothing she did to me mattered? That she could keep hurting me over and over and over and still tell me she loved me and cared about me more than life itself?

I couldn't cry though and I couldn't scream and when I thought about locking her out I just worried about what might happen to her if she stumbled home and passed out in the hallway of the building. So I ignored the pounding behind my eyes and walked right out of the flat.

If she was going on a bender, she'd only be in one place. So I marched down to the bottom of the street and through the doors into the dark pub. I didn't see her. This wasn't the kind of pub where families went for food. It was a pub where drinkers went to drink. It was mostly empty save for a few obvious regulars. This made me feel worse. At least if I'd found Mam here, I could have maybe wrestled some money back from her. I would have known she was only a few hundred feet from our front door and would probably get home safe. Or if I waited a couple of hours she'd be drunk enough that I'd be able to come back down and drag her home myself.

I tried phoning her again but I knew before I even pressed the call button that there would be no answer. So I put my phone in my pocket and ran home, because if I didn't get home quickly I was going to cry in public.

I gave myself fifteen minutes. I bawled my eyes out. Face in my pillow. The kind of sobs that make your chest hurt. In a way I was relieved, really, that the tears had finally come.

Maybe it was more like twenty minutes. But then I stitched up the hole that ripped open when these things happened. That scar always healed in an ugly way but it was tough. I got up and splashed my face with cold water to try and look less like a puffy mess. It didn't do anything. I was just a puffy mess with a wet face. I dried my face with the towel that was hanging up and thought about how I needed to put on a load of washing. Did we have washing powder?

I remembered to take a few plastic bags with me before I left the house, playing my music as loud as it would go to try and drown out the thoughts in my head and the gnawing in my stomach.

The first time I went to the food bank I was nine and I was with my mam's friend Elaine. She started shouting about how I was being neglected and how there wasn't anything to eat in the house and wouldn't somebody do something. It was after that the social came the first time, and I never saw Elaine again, which was kind of annoying because she used to come round a lot and make me cheese on toast and paint my toenails pink. At the time I didn't even think of her as Mam's friend. I thought I had somehow acquired an adult friend myself.

The last time Dad left, I came here a few times. Mam was getting unemployment but sometimes the money disappeared before I could get the shopping in. She never noticed that somehow we still had food. She never asked where it came from. Getting other things was more of a problem. Soap, toilet paper, tampons, washing powder. You could get them at the food banks sometimes but not always when you needed them.

The second time the social got involved was when I was twelve and a teacher caught me stuffing my schoolbag full of loo rolls. Mam always pulled it together after they came round. She really, really tried, too. She went to the support groups and she stopped drinking and I'd never been taken away from her, though I had spent more than my fair share of weekends in respite. That's what they call it, to your face and everything. At the time I wasn't sure who was supposed to be getting a respite, me or Mam. But I was the one who had to share a room in a conference centre with a bunch of other kids whose parents were rubbish in some way while they made us do abseiling and canoeing even though it was freezing outside. There was always one kid who made it his mission to find out why you were there, probing and asking questions while you're orienteering in the drizzly April weather.

I never wanted to be back there. Not stealing toilet paper from school. Not talking to social workers. Not climbing a hill with a bunch of other kids who needed money, not a camping trip. I was older now. I could take more control. It wouldn't be like that again.

*

212

The nearest food bank was in a church hall about twenty minutes from our flat. When I pushed open the doors it was fairly empty. That was worse to me. If it was really busy at least you could disappear. You were just another person in the queue. When it was empty you got the personal shopper treatment, which was mortifying. I felt like they would memorise my face and remember me if I passed them on the street or sat near them on the bus.

"Is this your first time here?" A stocky woman in her forties approached me with a clipboard.

"Yeah," I lied.

"All right, come with me and we'll get you sorted."

I followed her and sat while she gave me a cup of tea and some biscuits and asked questions.

"How many people in your family?"

"Just me and Mam," I said.

"What age are you?"

"Sixteen," I said, feeling like I was lying because no one ever thought I looked sixteen. Sure enough, she gave me a once-over.

"Do you need any period products?"

My cheeks burned. "If you have them, I suppose." I wasn't on my period, but if Mam's bender lasted, then it was better to be prepared.

"Do you mind me asking what's happened?"

"My mam got sick and had to take some time off work and she doesn't get sick pay. The social worker drove me down here." That would fend off any well-meaning interference.

The lady shook her head. "This country's a disgrace," she said.

She asked me a few more questions and then got up.

"Can you put them in here?" I asked, handing her my Tesco bags.

"We have boxes and bags," she said.

"Just use mine, please," I said. My bags were new from last week's shop.

She took them and told me to wait where I was. I ate three more biscuits but left one on the plate so I didn't look like a greedy gorb or a starving orphan or something. When she came back, she handed me back two full bags.

"Is your social worker giving you a lift back? These are heavy."

"Yep," I said. When I lifted them I knew carrying them home was going to be a pain. But what was she going to do about it? And besides, I wanted to get in and out as quickly as possible. As soon as I was back on the street I could feel like a normal person carrying shopping. In this old musty church hall I felt poor and I felt neglected. I felt like a charity case. Don't get me wrong, it could be worse, but it could be a whole lot fucking better too.

The lady gave me a worried look I knew well and I gave her an "everything is fine, this is just a blip" smile even though I thought there was a good chance I'd be back in a few days

214

and I'd have to come up with a better excuse. I could just say Mam was *really* sick? Maybe I'd be able to boot Mam into gear and get her back to work before she got fired.

These were the things I was thinking when I heard my name.

You hear your name, you turn around, even if it's a bad idea. If my brain had a second to catch up I would have kept walking. Before I even saw her the voice registered. It was too late, I'd already turned.

Meabh.

She immediately cringed. She was carrying a huge box, but she scurried up to me as fast as she could given what appeared to be her very heavy load and booted foot.

"I'm so sorry, I shouldn't have called your name out like that. It was so insensitive. I didn't think."

Could the almighty not do me one single solid and strike me down right now? In ye olde testament it sounded like he did a lot of striking and smiting and yet when you needed a good smite into a pile of dust or a pillar of salt or whatever, he was nowhere to be found.

"It's fine," I said, wondering if that was enough and I could walk away now. "Well actually, it's not, but it's done now."

She winced.

"Sorry," she said again. "Can I help you with those?"

I shook my head. "I should probably offer to help you with that instead," I said.

"Right," she replied, picking up that I didn't.

We hung awkwardly for a second and then I nodded and left her standing there.

Outside it was getting dark and I hoped the January air would cool my cheeks. I hated being ashamed of being poor. I knew it wasn't my fault. I knew it wasn't even my mam's fault. I knew that it didn't make me a bad person or a lazy, stupid person. I knew all that. In theory. And yet somehow I never stopped feeling like it was some kind of moral failing.

When I was growing up on my street I hadn't felt so bad. I had friends whose parents also drank, friends who had social workers, friends who had nothing but toast for their dinner the night before the dole was due. They weren't around any more though. A couple had moved. Courtney's dad had a work accident and got a massive claim and they bought a house up the road where everyone from my estate buys a house if they make a bit of money. Mostly though we just grew apart. With me going to St Louise's on Dad's guilt money, I didn't see them at school.

There had been times too, after I'd just started at St Louise's, when they'd invited me out, to hang around, drink in the park and whatever, but back then Mam had been trying to stay sober and I needed to stay in and look after her. Stop her from cracking. My friends thought I was looking down on them. I wasn't. I was just afraid to leave the house. The gulf is too wide to bridge now. If I pass them on the street they don't even say hello.

"Aideen!"

I didn't turn this time. I kept walking.

Meabh hobbled up to me as fast as she could. I heard her boot clunking against the pavement and I slowed down in spite of myself. I noticed she did *everything* as fast as she could, and then I remembered her bananas schedule and realised it was probably the only way she could get everything done.

"Let me walk you home. I can carry one of those. They look heavy."

"Your foot."

"It's fine. And besides, I'm much stronger than you." She flexed her biceps and gave me a silly throwaway smile. My body flooded with a warm feeling that spread out from the centre of me. That was weird.

"Right, all those pull-ups," I said, mouth suddenly dry.

"Exactly. And I've been slacking since the 'accident' so I need the exercise."

I glanced doubtfully at her foot again.

"Honestly," she said, "I could probably take it off now, but I'm milking it for as long as I can."

I shrugged and gave her one of the bags. I didn't love the idea of her seeing where I lived but my arms were aching and besides, she'd found me at a food bank so she probably wasn't expecting to walk back to a six-bed mansion in the leafy part of town.

We didn't really talk on the way back. But when I kept

switching arms to carry the bag I had, Meabh took it off me without a word and carried them both with very little effort. That made me feel weird. Good weird. I decided it was hunger and that I'd make the Pasta 'n' Sauce I'd spied in the bag when I got in. Why was I mesmerised by the way the muscles in her arms tensed as she clutched the bags, though? There were only two explanations. One was that I was a cannibal. The other didn't bear thinking about.

When we reached my front door there was an awkward moment. I didn't want to ask her not to tell anyone that she'd seen me today. Somehow that would have felt worse. Admitting that I was ashamed. I didn't think I needed to ask though. She handed me the bags and I nearly collapsed under the weight.

"I can help you upstairs if you want?" she said.

A little part of me wanted to invite her in. I had a picture of us having a cup of tea, both of us with our feet curled underneath our bums on the couch. But it was cold upstairs and Mam might come home soon. I hoped she'd come home soon. Maybe she'd come home already and I'd somehow completely misconstrued the situation upstairs. Mam could have found the cash and become alarmed at having money in the house like that. She could have rushed out to the bank, but not before changing her outfit several times because she had a crush on the bank teller.

It could happen.

"No, I'll be OK. Thanks for helping."

"I'll see you tomorrow? Upstairs for PE?" she asked.

"Yes, I think I'll have syphilis tomorrow," I mused.

"Do you know what syphilis is?" she said, smothering a smile. Unsuccessfully.

"An old-timey disease?"

"It's an STD that causes sores on your genitals, rectum, and mouth."

"Wow. Are you implying I *couldn't* have syphilis because no one would want to sleep with me? That's rude."

"No. I'm sure you could get syphilis from anyone you want," she joked. Then she flushed. With her pink cheeks and dark hair she looked like Snow White. "Anyway . . . tomorrow."

"Tomorrow," I said.

She smiled, still flushed, and kind of rolled her eyes at herself as she waved me goodbye with both hands.

My stomach reminded me that I was starving.

19

I lay in the dark and waited to hear the turn of the key. My nose was very cold and I contemplated whether you only felt your nose when it was cold or if you felt it during other times. Was I even really feeling my nose in that moment, or the coldness? Was there a difference?

So basically anything to keep my mind off the reason I was lying awake.

At five thirty I heard a thump against the door and I jumped.

"Fuck."

That was Mam. Instantly I felt a wave of relief at the same time as a horrible dread. She was home.

But on the other hand, she was home.

I refused to get up and open the door. I wanted to avoid her, if I could, while she was awake. If she'd been out since this morning, she had probably crossed over into that weird place where nothing she said made any sense and she'd want to pick a fight. Somehow, after a lot of scraping, I heard the door unlock and she stumbled in. I'd removed anything from the hall that she might break but it didn't stop her making a terrible racket as she dragged herself to her bedroom. I felt my temper rise. She wasn't even trying to be quiet. I could be sleeping and she was just banging around out there.

It was a stupid thing to get angry about in the grand scheme of things, but in that moment I was absolutely livid. I wanted more than anything to go out into the hall and start screaming at her. I saw myself doing it. I thought of the mean, horrible things I could say and the look on her face if I said them. I'd tell her she was a shit mother and that I wished she'd die. That I wished that she'd drown in a pool of her own vomit because that's what she deserved. And when she started to cry I'd scratch my fingernails down her face.

When I heard her snoring in her bed I got up and locked the front door again. I picked her handbag up from the floor and put it on the table. I went into her bedroom, stepped over her shoes, and placed a glass of water on the bedside table. I shifted her onto her side and tried not to gag at the smell. She'd obviously thrown up already somewhere but that was a good thing. We didn't have a washing up bowl so I laid a towel underneath her head and hoped she wouldn't throw up again.

Then I tiptoed back to bed and tried to sleep. I think I dozed off but I stirred every time I heard her cough.

When I opened her door a crack the next morning, she wasn't snoring any more. The room smelled sour and musty at the same time but she hadn't thrown up again from what

I could see. My heart paused until I saw the rise and fall of her chest and then I closed the door again. I thought about staying home. Normally that's what I would do. But I felt something I'd never felt before. I wanted to be in school. I had to talk to Angela and get started on my next plan. Mam would be fine.

Guilt wrung my stomach like a dishcloth as I closed the front door behind me. Instantly I was plagued with thoughts about what might happen while I was gone. I stood outside the flat, stuck in place. If I left and something did happen, it would be my fault. I hadn't even checked to see if she was OK. Did I really see her breathing or did I imagine it? But I imagined her crawling out of bed around noon, croaking voice and creaking bones, and dragging herself to the bathroom to vomit. Maybe she'd tell me she had the flu. Maybe she wouldn't bother with the pretence and would tell me it wouldn't happen again. It was just a slip. And what would I say? The thought made me feel a gasping, grabbing tightness in my chest. Like someone was holding a pillow over my mouth, only the teeny-tiniest molecules of air getting through, more of a taunt than a lifeline. I squeezed my eyes tight shut and forced that part of my mind to turn black. It wasn't there. There was no problem.

Kavi found Angela and asked her to meet me in the PE hall. I'd realised how she could repay her favour, and I figured it was better to rip the plaster off quickly because she wasn't going to like it. When I arrived on the balcony for second-period PE (Ms Devlin largely unimpressed with my current diagnosis), Meabh was already there. I hung by the stairs for a second, watching her tap furiously on the keys of her laptop until she groaned and pressed down on the back button, deleting. Deleting a lot. She ran her hands through her hair and clutched at her scalp as she read over whatever was left. When she started tugging on the roots, I intervened.

"Is this for the debate?"

She started, nearly knocking her laptop to the ground. When she saw me her face broke into a genuine, warm smile. It was a nice smile. She had full lips and when they weren't pursed it made her face look completely different. Relaxed. Pretty. I didn't know what I'd done to deserve a smile like that.

"Debate speech going well, I see?"

"Yeah," she said slowly. "But we don't have to talk about that."

I bristled.

Oh, yes, sorry for asking, Queen Meabh. I'm obviously too stupid to understand your fancy words and—

"You're obviously going to vote for Holly and I don't want it to seem like I'm trying to get information from you about her speech or anything."

Oh.

That was . . . thoughtful?

Obviously I'd vote for Holly. She was my best friend.

Obviously. No question. Just because we'd had a fight didn't mean I didn't want her to win.

"We can talk about it if you want. I don't know anything about her speech."

She looked surprised. "But why would you want to help me now? Not that you *wanted* to help me before, but you *did*," she said, glancing at the stairs. "But now that Holly's running . . ."

"Trust me. I can't help you. I don't know the first thing about speeches and all that stuff. But you look like you're about to detonate. I could rescue the whole student body by letting you get it off your chest now."

She hesitated. I could see her wrestling with something but I didn't know what it was. I had no doubt I was going to find out though. I could see her building up steam.

"OK, so I have all these great ideas, right?"

That was a rhetorical question.

"But I don't know how to get people to care about them. I proposed the recycling cup scheme in the café last year but I just got the figures back and no one is really using it. No one is bringing reusable cups in, even though they get charged ten cents to buy a paper one. And no one is putting the paper ones in the recycling bins. And yes, the charge goes towards paying for other green stuff around the school, but do you know how much we've collected in the last ninety school days?"

I waited.

"One thousand, eight hundred euros."

"Christ."

"That's around two hundred paper cups a day. I mean, what the fuck? There's only four hundred students in our school. I want to write a speech that makes people care about what that means. I know it's one tiny little thing in the grand scheme of a world that is burning up and of course the onus of climate change is really on corporations and big business but I can't go, *Oh well, I guess there's no point in doing anything then!* I just don't know how to make anyone else care. About this or anything else. I can't get people to care about my community projects, I can't get them to care about bringing Polish classes into school, I can't get them to care about anything other than *can we get Friday afternoons off school?* and *can we have no homework on the weekends?* I mean, FUCKING OF COURSE NOT YOU ABSOLUTE GOBSHITES. THAT'S NOT HOW ANY OF THIS WORKS."

There was the Meabh I knew. Angry. Condescending. Terrifying. But I saw something else there too. Passion, frustration, and a whole lot of heart. It was a confusing moment, two versions of her collided at once. The old Meabh I couldn't stand and the new one I liked even though I shouldn't. I finally saw that I'd filtered everything about her through the wrong lens. She made sense to me now.

Before I could say anything, Angela appeared. She looked at me expectantly.

I glanced at Meabh. She shook her head as though she was shaking off the stress. "Go," she said, waving me on.

"We're going to figure this out," I said. We locked eyes for a moment and I felt this urge to wrap her up and take all her stress away. Not because she was annoying me with her tantrums but because I wanted her to only feel good things for a change.

Angela's arms were folded and she seemed nervous. When I got close she gave Meabh a once-over and then whispered to me.

"Does she know?"

I shook my head. "Come on downstairs and we'll talk."

We walked out into the hall and found a quiet spot.

"Are you going to rat me out?" Angela bit her lip.

I frowned. Didn't she trust me? Then again, why would she? We didn't really know each other.

"Of course not. Why would I?"

"I heard you got detention. I figured you got caught. I was going to text you last night but I didn't have your number and I don't know anyone who does."

"Where'd you hear I got detention?"

"Ellen saw you running laps in the field with Ms Devlin watching. She said Ms Devlin wasn't wearing any shoes because she threw them at you."

It did sound like something she'd do.

"You're half right. I did get caught; I did get detention. I did not rat you out and Ms Devlin gave me her shoes.

Granted, I can see why Ellen would jump to that conclusion given Ms D's generally threatening vibes."

"Oh. So what happened when you got caught?"

"I took the heat, what do you think?"

She raised her eyebrows. Her perfectly shaped eyebrows. "That's really sound. I wouldn't have expected you to do that."

"Why not?" I asked. "Do you think I'd just land you in it?"

"I don't expect you to prioritise me getting in trouble over yourself."

"Well, it's my risk to take," I said.

"I admire that. It's good business."

I felt my cheeks heat. Angela Berry thought I was good at business. "Anyway, that's not why I called you here. I need you to repay your favour."

"OK . . ." she said, wary now.

"You're having a party on Saturday night—"

"And you want an invite? Fine. Come if you must."

I wrinkled my nose. "Eh, no. First of all, you already invited me. I need to bring someone else there—"

"A plus-one, you're really pushing it." She winked. I nearly fainted.

"Wrong again." I cleared my throat. "This person is also already invited. I need to get them there. So I'm going to need your car."

She gulped. "Uh . . . I don't think so."

227

"Well, that's what I need from you."

"It's my *car*."

"So?"

"So it's a car. It's not a lip gloss. Do you know how much laxative tea I had to shill from shady sponsors to pay for that car?"

"Borrowing lip gloss is unhygienic. This is way better. Less chance of herpes."

"You have herpes?" she asked. This time she was the one wrinkling her nose.

"Oh, for God's sake. I did you a favour, you owe me one. That's the deal. You knew that. The thing I want is to borrow your car."

She met my gaze evenly and I could tell she was trying to come up with an alternative.

"What's going on?" Kavi appeared behind me. Which was literally impossible seeing as he would have had to walk past me on the stairs.

"Angela here doesn't want to pay her debts," I said, trying to lighten the mood.

I had visions of Kavi using his height and strength to be intimidating and menacing.

Those visions were not accurate. He was biting his lip.

"Um, I don't want to be rude and we, like, don't want to pressure you or anything because you know that's not really what we're about and I'm not really the blackmaily kind. But then I suppose who is the blackmaily kind? That's the question. Are we born blackmaily or do we become blackmaily through unfortunate circumstances? I mean, maybe everyone who's ever done something crappy to someone else started off doing it for the right reason and in a way that's kind of a nice idea because it means that humanity is basically good but then they end up in an ever more tangled mess and they stop seeing people as people and start seeing them as, you know, pawns in their wicked games and maybe that's even more scary than if they were born that way because that means it could happen to any one of us if we're not careful."

Silence.

Kavi was always there when I needed him but I never had any idea what he was going to say.

Angela looked unhappy, she bit her thumbnail as she thought about it. My heart pounded. I knew that I was full of hot air. If Angela wouldn't back down there was no way I'd do anything about it.

I almost gave up and walked away. It wasn't worth it. But I hadn't failed on one of my tasks yet and if I let clients set the terms of their repayment then I wouldn't get what I needed. It's not like Meabh had *wanted* to break into the school.

"We had a deal," I said, hoping to play on her sense of fair business practice – she was an entrepreneur too, after all – but I thought it came out too whiny.

"Fine," she said grudgingly. "You can use my car to transport your person, but I'm driving."

"You'll miss some of your own party."

"If something happens to that car I'll miss the rest of my life. My parents would kill me. They barely let me keep it after the sideswipe incident. Even though *I* paid for the damage . . ." She trailed off, grumbling at the end.

I thought about it. I didn't technically have a driving licence, after all. After a moment we shook on it and Angela left.

The air rushed out of me and my shoulders slumped.

"Hey," Kavi said softly, and he pulled me into a hug immediately, squishing my face against his chest. OK, more like his stomach. He was really tall. You know, compared to me.

I let myself breathe in the clean, cottony scent from his uniform and thought about how his mother must have washed it last night for it to smell so good. I don't know why I felt so rubbish. I hated the idea that Angela would be annoyed with me, even if I was just asking her to stick to the deal. Yes, she was a sixth year, and yes, she was intimidatingly hot, but it wasn't any of that. I didn't want to feel like a pest, like people didn't want me around. Which was stupid because I didn't need anyone to be my friend either. There was something safe about not needing anyone to like me. As long as they didn't have any reason to *dislike* me. I realise that's a low bar but I like to keep my expectations reasonable.

After a moment, Kavi held me at arm's length and although I hadn't cried, I could feel my eyes were red.

"Are you OK?" he said.

"I'm just tired. I didn't sleep." That was it. That confrontation was not a big deal. I was being emotional because I was exhausted. "I get it. I wouldn't want someone driving my car if I had one. I don't know why I'm taking it so personal."

Kavi looked like he was searching for something to say. Or was he waiting for me to say something else? Where was a distracting monologue when you wanted one?

"Do you want to talk about it?" he asked.

"It's fine," I said. "Seriously. Now we can tell Daniel Something that we'll take him to the party."

"I'll let him know, I saw him when I passed the Home Ec kitchen and I'm going that way."

"Thanks," I said. He saluted me and disappeared downstairs. He had seemingly become comfortable with skipping class. I hoped I wasn't a bad influence.

Back upstairs I sat down near Meabh. She was eyeing me with what I can only describe as a very Ms Devlin look.

"What was that about?" she demanded.

"Um. None of your business?"

"You're 'helping' other people. Aren't you?"

"No," I lied.

"You are."

"I'm not."

"You are. I know it. You're a terrible liar."

"I'm a great liar."

"You're not."

"I am."

"You definitely aren't."

"OK, fine. I am helping other people. So what?"

"That is a bad idea," she said firmly. "You should focus on your own problems. Have you got all your homework done for today?"

I rolled my eyes. She was becoming more like Ms Devlin every second.

"*That's* your problem," I replied. "You think you know what everyone should do and so you tell them and expect them to fall in line. You're a dictator."

Meabh shuffled uncomfortably and then shrugged. "I *do* know better. Am I supposed to pretend I don't so I don't hurt their fragile feelings? Maybe other people should just be smarter."

"You're upset about people not following the rules you set for them, right? You think it means they don't care about whatever cause you have on at the time."

"They don't care. People are terrible," she said hotly.

"Most people *want* to do the right thing," I said, "but if they *aren't*, then figure out a way to make it easy for them to be good people."

Meabh thought about this for a minute. She frowned.

"So you're saying I have to hold their hands like babies? They're incapable of making the slightest bit of effort themselves even if they know it's the right thing to do?"

232

I shrugged. "If you really want them to do what you want, you have to make it the best option."

"Leave them no other choice," she said, more to herself than to me.

"Well, I didn't quite put it like that, Kaiser, but sure."

"Well, what about this?" she said, suddenly excited. "Every year people doing Gaisce Awards have to go out and find volunteering opportunities, but we can create those opportunities in the school. We could set up a homework club for kids who are falling behind for whatever reason. You donate hours of tutoring."

I had the uncomfortable feeling that I was one of those kids and the *whatever reasons* were the kinds of things that Meabh would never have to experience. I also didn't think she had thought about what it might be like to be on the receiving end of one of her charitable notions.

"OK," I said steadily. "What if you're falling behind because, let's say, you have to work after school because your family is struggling, and you don't have time for your homework, let alone extra hours of tutoring? The people you're trying to help most are the people you might not be able to reach like that."

Meabh paused. She frowned. Her frown deepened, and I felt bad.

"What do I do about that?" she asked, sounding genuinely lost.

"I don't know. Those are problems you can't fix as a

233

student council president. You want to fix the whole world, but you can't."

"I could if I was in charge of the whole world," she pouted. "I could be so effective if people would just do what I want them to do. I'd fix everything."

I laughed. "I believe you."

"I'll work on it," she said immediately, beginning to type down some notes. Without looking up, she added, "But don't think I don't know that you're deflecting."

"Fine. Will you do my Maths homework with me again?" I asked with a grin. "I just used up all my brilliance."

I watched her wrestle with her desire to tell me what to do with my life and her desire to tell me what to do with my homework. Luckily for me, homework won.

20

I sent Mam three texts during the day to see if she was awake. She didn't answer and I kept checking my phone during class. Eventually I just turned the ringer on because I thought it was better than checking it every two minutes and getting in trouble that way. Of course last class of the day I got a reply and Mr Smith practically ate the face off the class trying to figure out whose text tone was an audio clip of Kristen Stewart saying, "I am, like, so gay, dude." Thankfully either no one knew it was me or they weren't going to tout.

Mam
All good love, don't worry.
Will make you dinner tonight.

There were three heart emojis in different colours and a GIF of a kitten rolling over. I guess that was meant to be an apology? Now that I knew she was OK, I felt a mixture of relief and dread. I was glad she hadn't expired in a pool of her own vomit but I didn't want to face whatever state she was in. Whatever she said about making dinner, she had to be seriously hungover – or worse, she had already knocked a few into her so she could face the day.

I was loitering by my locker, clearing out the discarded scraps of paper that lined the bottom like a hamster's nest, when Holly sidled up beside me. She'd ignored me all day and I had a pit in my stomach over it. Luckily I'd had my Maths homework, Angela and Meabh, and the ever-increasing worry that Mam was going to be fired and we'd be really fucked to distract me.

Holly leaned up against the locker next to mine and flashed me a grin. She tugged on a lock of my hair and then pouted. I sighed. She rummaged in her skirt pocket and pulled out a lip balm. The peppermint one that I like but will not (cannot) pay €4.99 for.

Really? You're not even going to say sorry? You're going to offer me some kind of scrap that I'm supposed to take as an apology? The lip balm is cheaper than the word, apparently.

I took it from her and unwrapped the cellophane, thinking that Meabh would be annoyed that there was unnecessary plastic. Could you recycle this kind? What was the rule? If you can scrunch it up you can't put in the recycling? I couldn't remember so I put the curl of plastic in my pocket to google later.

"Tingly," I said, smacking my lips after I'd applied the lip balm.

Holly smiled and then hugged me.

"Sorry," she said. "I was being a raging bitch."

Are you only saying sorry after I've already accepted your faux apology? Is that so I can't get mad at you because I've already forgiven you? She always did this. Made it impossible for me to stay mad without looking like I was the arsehole.

"You're stressed. You loved the paper."

"Yeah, it's that." Holly nodded. "Definitely that's been awful. But you've also never kept anything from me before."

You mean anything that mattered to you. I've kept plenty from you the last couple of years. But you don't want to hear about being poor and Mam drinking. It makes you feel sorry for me.

I had to tell myself to stop it. I could feel myself getting angry and if I let those thoughts take over we'd get into another argument.

"I'm not really keeping it from you. I told you the gist of things."

"It doesn't matter. I get why you need to be confidential. But it feels like you're cutting me out of this big part of your life."

She leaned in and rested her forehead against mine. It made my eyes blurry and my heart ache.

At the same time a flare of warmth lit me up from the inside and I followed that feeling instead. The one that erased all the bad feelings. Holly just wanted to be close to me. That was all it took to dissolve the crusty, calcifying stone of resentment that had been building in me. I pulled away.

"What's that?" I asked, pointing to a roll of paper she'd propped up next to the lockers.

"I thought you'd never ask." She grinned. "These are my campaign posters."

"Campaign posters?"

This was not a campaign poster kind of school. One year a girl who was running for secretary lost to a write-in vote for a meme, but that was the most invested students had ever been. Unfortunately, "egg that is bigger than before" was determined not to have legally won the election and Sorcha O'Brien ended up secretary after all.

Holly picked up the roll and unfurled one of the posters. It was like any campaign poster you'd see in real life. A big picture of Holly's face against a neutral background. VOTE HOLLY FOR CLASS PRESIDENT.

"Wanna help me put them up?" she said with puppy-dog eyes.

I thought about Mam at home waiting for me.

Then I thought about how I'd waited all night for her.

"Sure."

Holly handed me a chunk of Blu-Tack and we got two chairs from a nearby classroom to stand on as we worked on plastering the atrium with pictures of her face. It was more or less deserted.

"Well, are you going to tell me how it works, then, or not?" Holly said, sticking her first poster up by the door.

"The ... the social enterprise?" I said, remembering Kavi's words. Even though the atrium was empty it made me nervous talking about it out in the open.

Holly snorted. "The social enterprise? Where'd you learn that?"

That's right. I'm so stupid I couldn't possibly know something.

She didn't mean that to sound the way it did. After all, I *hadn't* heard of a social enterprise before yesterday, so I could hardly get on my high horse about it.

"Mr Smith. He was going on about it the other day. You know how transition years are supposed to do a business project? I mean, I don't think this would count to him, but I realised that it kind of fit."

For some reason I didn't want to bring up Kavi. He could get in trouble over these escapades. He already had. My confidentiality should cover his arse more than anyone's.

Holly jumped off her chair and dragged it a couple of feet along. "Fit how? What exactly do you do?"

"Well, I do people favours. And then they owe me a favour."

"Does that kid Kavi have something to do with it?"

So much for confidentiality.

I tried to make him sound like he was incidental. "Sometimes people have asked him to ask me."

"How did it start?"

Why did this feel like an interrogation?

"Uh . . . Kavi. He brought me someone. A friend."

I didn't love lying to Holly, but there was no way I was telling her the truth.

Holly looked dubious but she didn't press it.

"What are your plans this weekend?" I said, trying to change the subject. "We could do something?"

I had to break Daniel out on Saturday night but I was free the rest of the day. It was a simple fix; it should go off without a hitch.

"Visiting my nan Saturday. Might be free Sunday afternoon but I'm not sure yet. I'll text you on Sunday if I get home early and I'm not too tired."

Right, because I couldn't possibly make other plans. I'd just be waiting around for you to maybe be free.

"Sure, you can let me know," I said.

When we were done we backed into the middle of the atrium and surveyed our work. One thing stood out. Holly gave me a sidelong look.

All of my posters were stuck up about foot lower than hers. She slung her arm over my shoulder and we burst out laughing.

21

The flat did smell like dinner when I got home but nothing I'd brought back from the food bank would smell that good, which made me suspicious about where it came from.

"Is that you, love?" Mam called out from the kitchen.

I didn't answer. I went around the flat turning off the lights that she'd left on in her bedroom and the bathroom. They'd probably been on all day. I didn't take my coat off though because it was bloody freezing, but at least that meant Mam had enough sense not to put the heating on; our gas bill last month was astronomical.

When I walked into the kitchen she was flipping two chicken breasts in the frying pan.

"Where'd you get those?" I asked.

"I went shopping. I am able to do that, you know. I'm the mother." She said it in a joking tone and I didn't say anything.

"Child support," she said after a minute, cheeks reddening. "I know I fucked up the other night," she added.

How had I not remembered it was child support day? She didn't mention Dad by name though. She wasn't going to tell me about how he'd gone on holidays with his real wife or how he'd most likely not even told her that he was going. His name wouldn't come up again until the next time. I hoped there would never be a next time again. I hoped that every time. When was I going to learn to stop hoping?

"*Last* night," I said.

"It was a slip. You know they happen, Aideen, but I promise it doesn't mean I'm off the wagon. I went to group this afternoon. I called the doctor and I'm going to get him to put me back on the Antabuse."

Mam's support group. It was run by the place she did her detox in last year, when I had to stay with my auntie Jacinta for four never-ending weeks. You could go to the group anytime. It wasn't quite like AA. At least not the AA I'd seen on TV. There weren't any doughnuts or sponsors at Mam's group and there was no God bothering. People didn't get up and tell stories and no one said, "Hi, my name is Betty and I'm addicted to drinking Lambrini and scrolling Instagram," or whatever. There was an actual therapist there and they chatted as a whole group. Antabuse was a pill that was supposed to stop you drinking because the side effects of drinking on it were awful. But it didn't stop you wanting to drink.

She was looking at me like she was praying and I was God. I could wipe away her sins with the sign of the cross. Or I could smite her into damnation.

"What about your job?"

"I told Jacqui I had a bug but I was fine now and I'd be in, in the morning. And that I'd do extra shifts next week."

"She bought that?"

Mam flinched and I felt bad. Was I being too hard on her? She had been sober for a long time. Maybe this was a slip like she said? Slips happened. I remembered that from one of the social workers. There was one who took me bowling and tried to be my friend. She said stopping drinking was not a straight line. It was a cycle. People sometimes had to go back to the start again but it didn't mean that all the time they'd been sober was worthless.

"I'm normally a pretty good employee," Mam said, and I got the feeling she was trying to impress upon me that she was normally a pretty good mam.

I didn't say anything else and the tension grew thick.

"I paid the lecky bill," she said after a bit.

"Aye, and left the lights all on to celebrate," I grumbled.

"I got you a present," she said.

I wanted to say it was a waste of money but she was trying so hard. I didn't smile though.

She rolled her eyes and got up and went to the hall. She returned with a gift bag. She held it at arm's length away from me.

"Now, you only get this if you promise to stop being mad at me," she said. "I know I'm the worst mam in the world but I'm the only one you've got and I love the bones of you so you can't stay mad. I can't take it."

"So needy," I said, shaking my head.

She grinned and handed me the bag. Inside was an

advent calendar. Not a chocolate one but one of the ones that had things like nail polish and lip balms in it. She started getting me one of these a couple of years ago. The first year it had taken me two days to crack, and one day when she was out I opened all the little doors in one go. Mam walked in on me surrounded by tiny samples of bath oil and night cream. Since then she'd kept the calendar on lockdown and presented me with it on a daily basis.

"I found it in the sale bin," she said pointedly, "so it wasn't even that dear. You can stop panicking. And you can open all the doors at once!"

I looked at her. She was so excited. She looked really proud of herself. Truthfully I still felt really hurt and angry. But I could see what kind of gesture she'd made and if I reacted in any way other than pure joy she'd feel rejected. Though I didn't know how she could think that something like this would make me happy after everything she'd put me through. Still, I did my best smile and made excited noises as I opened all the doors. There were little face creams and lip glosses and nail polishes behind each door. Mam watched me closely, wanting to soak up my joy, so I did my best to give it to her.

When I'd opened them all I gave her a big hug and she squeezed me tight.

"That was brilliant," I said, and, though I did my best to hide it, I didn't know how she couldn't hear the hollow note in my voice. "I'm going to put these in my room. And you can't use any of them," I warned playfully.

She crossed her heart.

With my bedroom door closed I let my smile drop. I arranged all the little bottles and jars in a row on my dresser where she would see them and think I was really pleased about it. I knew she'd done it to make me happy but all it felt like was that she'd taken something that made me happy in the past and tried to use it as a bandage for my pain now. Pain that she caused. It tainted the good thing. I knew instantly that next December when I got another advent calendar I'd only be able to think of this moment.

First thing Saturday morning my phone dinged. And I mean *first thing*. I hadn't voluntarily got up this early on a non-school day in my whole life.

Kavi
You ready for tonight?

Aideen
You don't have to get involved.

Kavi
I'm so excited! I want to!

Aideen
You might get caught.

Kavi
So might you! It's better if I'm there.

Aideen
Why?

Kavi
At least you wouldn't be alone.

Almost like she could tell we were planning something stupid, Meabh's name popped up on my screen.

Aideen
I'll be fine. Seriously.
I don't need any help with this.

Meabh
Are you still going through
with this ridiculous plan?

I'd cracked and told Meabh about our plan for Daniel. I hadn't mentioned any names but told her the gist. She thought it was stupid.

Aideen
Yes I'm

Meabh
THAT'S NOT HOW CONTRACTIONS
WORK AND YOU KNOW IT.

Aideen
Mea b it shud b. No point wsting lttrs.

Meabh
1. LETTERS AREN'T RUNNING OUT.
2. IT'S ONE LESS CHARACTER.

Aideen
Stap shoutn babe.
Can here u frm hear.

Meabh
It could technically be seen
as kidnapping a minor.

Aideen
will u rite 2 me whn im in jail?

Meabh
Only if you promise not to write back.
I won't have time to decipher this
code for an entire letter.

Aideen

Mam got up early and brought me tea and toast in bed.

"I won't be here when you get back from work," I said.

"I'm going to hang out with Holly and then we're going to a party."

"You?" she asked.

"Yes," I replied, feeling a bit testy. "I go to parties. It's a normal thing to do."

I did not go to parties. And it wasn't that normal. I mean, most of the people in my class lived in the country and their parents weren't jetting out of town all the time. Half the time someone had a party it was the kind where the parents were putting a tray of sausage rolls on every twenty minutes. Unless there was an underground network of raging house parties that I didn't know about. Which could be true, I realised.

"Whose party?"

"A girl in school."

She looked even more surprised. I think she was expecting I meant someone from down the road, where a party meant clutching on to cans of cider at the end of the street. I mean, that's all this party would be, but everyone there would feel superior because they were doing it in a garden instead.

"Will there be drinking and drugs and sex at this party?" Mam asked, sitting on the end of my bed.

"No." Not for me anyway.

"Are you sure it's not Mass you're going to, then?" Mam cracked up.

"Have a good day at work, Mam."

"Wait, wait. Hold on. How are you getting there? Where is this party?"

I gave her a look. The look said, *Are you, the dirty stop-out of the century, really asking me these details?*

She gave me a look back. The look said, *I'm your mother, you insolent pup, answer my question.*

"It's out in Tydavnet. I'm getting a lift. I'll be home tonight. Late."

"But you'll be home? You can't stay out all night," she said, sounding the most Mam-like she had ever sounded.

I nodded.

She knew I was lying about something, but she wasn't quite sure what it was.

"OK, if you're going off to have sex, make sure you don't catch chlamydia please. GP appointments are fifty-five euros before you even get a script, and I'm not made of money."

"You really earn that World's Best Mum mug, you know that?"

I shook my head at my mother's version of the sex talk, but I felt a lot lighter than I had yesterday. How did she do that? How did she make it seem like her stumbling in, totally hammered, was years ago and everything was OK now? I knew I couldn't trust her. I wondered if she would drink when I was out of the house. Maybe that was why she didn't mind me going out. But I wanted to believe her. I wanted to believe this was just her regular brand of lackadaisical parenting and that she wasn't cracking open a hidden bottle of wine as I stomped downstairs. I had done a sweep of the house when she'd been in the shower and hadn't found anything. But she had all day to buy drink.

If I stayed in I could stop her.

But I'd promised Daniel.

Mam popped her head back into my room just as she was about to leave. I don't know if she saw through right into my brain or if she just took a good guess at what I was thinking.

"I'm going to be fine, you know," she said. "I'm going to group after work. I want you to go and have a good time."

I shrugged like I hadn't been worried. "I will."

This pleased her. She gave me a big smile and an exuberant wave.

"Off to glitz and glamour," she said.

She did *seem* like she was in one of her good spells – the days following a bender where she tried so hard to be good and make things better. Maybe Dad hadn't been around long enough to get to her this time. Like a disease she hadn't had enough exposure to, to get really sick. It would be fine. Time to concentrate on the next problem. The one I could actually fix.

22

I met Angela in a car park in town. I told her it was more convenient for me instead of her picking me up at my house. It wasn't, but we arrived at Daniel's unscathed. Except for the new fear of dying in a fiery car crash I'd developed. Angela parked at the bottom of their drive. It was a large, detached house with a neat lawn, a flower bed, and a shed. It was a dream home.

The plan was that Daniel was going to put in some face time with his grandparents and then pretend to feel sick and go to bed. Then he'd throw his pillows out the window and jump. The aim was, hopefully, to land on the pillows. We'd wait for him in the car and drive him over to the party. Seeing as I wasn't even allowed to drive the car, it was the easiest favour I'd done yet. I was more of a facilitator for this one.

Angela and I sat in the car with the radio on. After a minute of me trying to think of something to say, she began grilling me on the mechanics of the social enterprise. She asked me how many favours I'd done and whether I always used repayments to "fund" other favours. I explained as much as I could without giving too much away.

"So you've never used one to, like, get someone to do your homework or something?"

"That sounds like a great idea, but frankly if I start handing in good homework at this point in my education, I think it would only be a red flag."

"You know, you have a really good thing here. You could tweak it a bit. Formalise it. Have applications or something, but it's a pretty solid model. But what would you do if you needed something from someone, but they didn't owe you anything?"

I had no idea.

I was saved from answering by a text.

Daniel
Change of plan. I just said I was going
to bed and my mam has told me to go
and stay in the attic room and granny
and granda are staying in my room
because they can't climb all those stairs.

Aideen
so go out the attic window

Daniel
I could. But you know, I'd die.

I glanced up at the house. The front of the house only had a small round window where I guessed the attic would be, but it definitely was too high up to escape from.

Aideen
Well what do you want
me to do about it?

Daniel
There's a ladder in the shed that Dad
uses when he's cleaning the gutters.
The attic window is at the back.

I sighed.

Aideen
Fine!

Daniel
There's a spare set of keys under the
frog at the back door, the biggest one
is the shed.

"There's been a hiccup," I said to Angela. She raised
an eyebrow.

"I won't be long," I promised.

"I'm missing my own party," she grumbled, but she
didn't do anything except turn up the radio and lean back
in her seat.

The lights were on in the house but the curtains were drawn
so I wasn't too worried jogging up the driveway, but I didn't
want to take all day about it either. At the back of the house

there was a patio and a back door. On the step was a ceramic frog wearing a tutu. The keys were nestled underneath and I had to shake a woodlouse off them. I shook my head at someone leaving their keys outside their house like that and imagined leaving mine underneath the perpetual beer can that sat on the front step of my building. Middle-class people are not wise.

The shed was a bit trickier; when I opened it, it was full to the brim with junk. At least six bikes, even though I knew there was just Daniel, his parents, and one brother. There was also a lawn mower, buckets of paint, an old bath, and right at the back . . . the ladder. I had to clamber into the old bath and wrestle with the ladder to get it off the hook. It was one of those extendable ones and it was surprisingly heavy, but I finally made it out of the shed with only a few bruises and one scrape down my leg that burned. Around to the side of the building I saw Daniel Something peering out of the window forlornly. His expression changed when he saw me and he grinned and gave me a thumbs up. It was freezing outside but all the effort had me sweating at the back of my neck, and yeah, if I'm honest, the underboob. He opened his window and shout-whispered to me.

"HI!"

I rolled my eyes, feeling irritable from all the effort this "easy" favour had cost me so far. I tried to extend the ladder fully and nipped my finger in the process.

I groaned and clenched my jaw so I didn't shout the

bad words I wanted to shout. Pissed off, sweaty, and hurt, I slammed the ladder against the wall with a louder bang than I meant. I froze for a second. Daniel froze. We both listened for any disturbance. A second passed and nothing happened.

"All right, come on to fuck," I shout-whispered.

I held the ladder and Daniel shimmied out of his window. He was wearing a shiny green shirt and painted on jeans. As a breeze wafted towards me, so too did the overwhelming scent of Brylcreem and Paco Rabanne. Daniel paused on the top rung of the ladder and took his phone out.

"For God's sake, what are you doing?" I hissed.

"Photo op," he whispered back. He angled himself in the frame and I watched in slow motion as he slipped. I watched him reach and grab the ladder with both hands, my heart in my throat. I watched his phone fall out of his hand as he did, and that's when everything went black.

When light returned, I had a throbbing pain between my eyes and as my vision adjusted and I pushed myself up to sitting, I saw Daniel was clinging on to the windowsill, his tiptoes barely reaching the lip of the gutter and the ladder had fallen to the ground beside me. I was lucky it hadn't landed on top of me.

"Are you OK?" He looked worried. I wondered how much time had passed. Not more than a few seconds surely.

Then there was a screech and my head turned towards

the noise. I'd been out just long enough for Daniel's mother to make it from her living room to the back of the house and find me lying on the ground with her ladder and her son scrambling back through the window, his tight jeans highlighting his bum as he toppled into the room.

Daniel's mam lifted me by the elbow and dragged me in through the back door and pointed at the kitchen table.

"Sit," she said through gritted teeth.

A rumbling racket of feet on the stairs boomed overhead and in a few seconds Daniel had burst into the kitchen.

"Mam, don't be mad," he said breathlessly.

"Oh right, son, I won't now that you've said so. Would you like a cup of tea and a biscuit," she said with mock politeness. Then her tone shifted. "Get you upstairs before I lose the head. I'm not having you two sitting down here coming up with a story."

"Mam—"

"Up," she said. Her voice was quiet and authoritative. Daniel gave me a pained look before he turned around and slunk out of the room. I heard plodding on the stairs this time.

His mam turned on me with her hands on her hips. She was a thin white woman with long hair pulled into a sleek updo and she was maybe only an inch taller than me. She wore a silk blouse and a fine gold chain. She looked like she might be a doctor or a receptionist or something.

"Explain yourself," she said sharply.

"Uhhhhhhh ..." I dragged out the noise, hoping

something would come to me, a very good reason for trying to aid her son's escape.

"We're in love?" I said, trying to take a leaf out of Kavi's playbook. But I was unconvincing and she gave me a pursed-lip look that plainly said she both did not believe it and even if she did it wasn't an excuse that would hold any water with her.

"What's your name?" she demanded.

"Glenda," I said, saying the first name that came into my head. Why Glenda, I don't know.

"Glenda," she said flatly.

I nodded, not meeting her eyes.

"Well, Glenda, you're not leaving here until you give me your mother's phone number and she comes out here to pick you up. I would like a word with her."

"Oh, she's dead," I said quickly.

"And your father?" she asked skeptically.

"Dead." I shrugged. "Super duper dead."

"I'm so sorry for your loss," she replied dryly. "Who do you live with?"

"Oh, no one, ma'am." I looked at my hands sadly. "I'm eighteen."

She looked me up and down and snorted. "Little lady, you're thirteen if you're a day."

I was deeply offended. Why do people always think you're young when you're short? There are short adults, for God's sake.

"I'm sixteen," I snapped. Whoops.

She rolled her eyes at me like she couldn't believe I was that stupid. Damn it. She was a fellow short. She knew I'd be annoyed by that. One-nil to Mrs Something.

"Well, I suppose if you're a minor and you just tried to break into my house—"

"I was not breaking in. Daniel was breaking out." That wasn't a crime.

"And how did you get into my shed?"

"Uh . . ."

"Right, well, you have two options, Glenda. Give me your mother's phone number or I will have to call the Gardaí to come and take you home instead."

I ran through the options. I wasn't going to be arrested, I was pretty sure of that. But if I didn't tell them who I was, they'd take me down to the station, surely. They'd call social services for sure. Damn it.

"Fine," I said. "I need to look it up. I don't know it off by heart or anything."

"Don't even think of giving me a fake number," she said. "I'm going to insist she come and get you herself."

As I scrolled through my phone, I cursed myself for not getting Angela's number. She could have come up with some kind of plan. Was she was even still outside? She might have decided she'd waited long enough and took off. My guts twisted.

258

Meabh.

I'd give her Meabh's number.

Worst-case scenario, Meabh didn't have a clue what was happening and gave me away. I wouldn't be any worse off than I was now and I could call my mam if I really needed to. That was definitely a last resort though. And what about Daniel Something? I was failing him. This was my first proper failure. Reluctantly I called out Meabh's number and internally I blessed myself and prayed she'd tell Mrs Something that she had to let me go.

The low brrrrrng-brrrrrng of the dial tone kept going. Mrs Something looked at me the whole time. Then I heard it switch onto voicemail.

"You have reached the voicemail of Meabh, please leave a message after the tone."

Mrs Something *hmphed*.

"I have your daughter here in my home. She has been trespassing. Please call me back as soon as you get this message."

She gave the phone a dirty look like my "mam" had refused her call on purpose.

What now? The kitchen clock told me I'd been on the premises for at least twenty minutes. Wasn't Angela wondering where I was? Oh, who was I kidding. She'd definitely left. She wasn't going to miss her own party to wait around for me all night.

Mrs Something took a seat at the kitchen table and folded her arms. She had the unmistakeable look of someone gearing up to a lecture.

"I'll have you know that Daniel's grandparents are visiting this weekend and you are spoiling their trip."

I tried to think of something to say that wasn't just . . . OK? But I was saved from my impossible feat of imagination by the doorbell.

Bing bong.

Mrs Something huffed and stood, pointing at me. "Don't you go anywhere," she said. She almost made it to the kitchen and then she paused and turned around. She walked to the back door, took a set of keys out of her pocket, and locked it. She locked me in the house. Like a prisoner! Surreptitiously I patted my pockets, remembering I had another set of keys. They weren't there. They must have fallen out of my pocket when I collapsed outside.

"Are you messing with me?" I said, unable to stop myself. "This is false imprisonment."

"Take it up with a lawyer," she scoffed.

"My mother is a lawyer," I replied.

For a second she looked worried. Then she gave me a long look from head to toe, taking in my clothes, my shoes.

"I don't think so."

She flounced out of the kitchen closing the door behind her.

I'd never met someone I hated more. Would it have

been wrong to burn her house down to get out? I'd kill Daniel and the Elder Somethings in the process, of course, but you know, collateral damage . . .

"I've broken down outside and my phone has no reception. I'm sorry but could I trouble you for your phone?" a woman with a thick Scottish accent said, loud enough to hear through the kitchen door. I should have shouted at her to run. Apparently if you turned up at Mrs Something's house unannounced, she might tie you up in the basement and keep you as her trophy.

"Pssst."

I jumped. My mind went to Kavi immediately. Then I heard a quiet rap on the window and when I squinted into the dark, the light from the kitchen causing a glare, I just made out the top of a head. A head with braids.

"Angela?!"

Only her eyes were visible. She was crouched outside looking in. I hurried to the window.

"Och, I'm just on hold. Oh no, wait with me a moment. They might need your Eircode," the Scottish woman said.

"It's H-eighteen—"

"Oh, I won't remember that. Head like a sieve. It'll just be a second."

Angela mouthed something at me and pointed at the door. I glanced over my shoulder, afraid Mrs Something would hear me. I made a locking motion and then pointed to the outside.

"Lovely home you have here," went on the Scottish woman. "That's a beautiful vase. Waterford crystal?"

"Yes, thank you. Any luck?"

"Still the hold music, sorry!"

Angela looked confused, so I went to the back door and she followed. I pulled on the handle. It didn't budge of course. She grimaced. Then I pointed outside again. She got it. I stood on my tiptoes, trying to see, as though I could help from here. And I kept glancing over my shoulder waiting for Mrs Something to burst back in.

"Well, you take one cup of sugar, three cups of flour, six eggs . . ."

A dawning realisation came over me when I heard the Scottish woman giving out a very strange recipe and I burst out laughing. I clapped my hand over my mouth and then I quickly gave one hard rap of warning on the window and practically jumped back into my seat at the table. Mrs Something burst in the room.

"What are you laughing at?"

I held up my phone. "Stand-up. Des Bishop video. You know him?"

"Give me that," she said, holding out her hand.

As if I'd hand over my phone to her! "G'way and shi—"

CRASH. The sound came from the hall and whatever had broken sounded expensive.

Mrs Something skidded into the hall.

"I'm SO SORRY," the Scottish voice squealed.

262

A click, whoosh, and a waft of cold air let me know Angela had found the keys on the grass and opened the door. I ran towards it and practically mowed her down.

"Come on," she said, pulling my hand, but I pulled back and stopped her.

"Daniel," I said. I couldn't leave him here. We had to do something. I wasn't going to fail.

"We're already on it," Angela said. "Now come on to fuck."

I didn't have time to question who the "we" was. Although I knew Meabh was the one in the hall distracting Mrs Something. Just then Daniel caught up to us, running much faster than me. I trailed at the back of our group as we skidded round the corner to the front of the building. Angela's car was at the bottom of the drive, headlamps on, like a lighthouse beckoning us to safety. I turned to look back at the front door. Meabh was standing on the front step wringing her hands and saying sorry over and over in a Scottish accent.

"DANIEL!" Mrs Something screamed as she spotted him running. We were crunching along the gravel drive now and a set of motion-sensor lights lit us up. I ground to a halt, realising Meabh was trapped with Mrs Something. She couldn't run. But then in a blur, like a sprinting knight in shining armor, Kavi appeared, racing around the other corner of the house towards Meabh. He didn't even slow down as he barrelled towards her and threw her over his shoulder.

"Keep going," he shouted at me. Mrs Something began chasing after us, shouting.

"GET BACK HERE, DANIEL."

Into the dark night air Daniel shouted back.

"BYE, MAM, I LOVE YOU. I'LL SEE YOU AROUND THREE."

23

"Oh my God, that was so much fun," Daniel said, getting into the car. Angela took off as quickly as possible. Daniel's mam was waving a broken piece of glass and yelling in the rearview mirror.

"What are you guys doing here?" I said to Meabh and Kavi. "How did you know?"

"When you didn't come back for ages I panicked. I called Kavi," Angela explained.

"I called Meabh," he said.

"I was already outside when she phoned," Meabh said. "I heard her telling you to give her your mum's number. I didn't answer because we didn't know what your plan was and we'd already decided on ours."

"You're going to be in so much trouble, Daniel," I said.

He shrugged. "Yeah, I mean, it could have gone smoother, but you know, she's way too strict. If I'm going to have to stand up to her, I want to do it when there's a getaway car."

I laughed, glad that he didn't seem to be annoyed, even though I still felt like I'd failed the task.

As we drove towards Angela's house, the rain began

beating down. Her windshield wipers were no match for it.

"Shit, guys, I can barely see," she said, swerving to miss what looked like nothing from where I was.

I turned around and whispered, not very subtly, "She mounted the pavement twice on the way here and it wasn't raining then."

"It was dark, Aideen," Angela said testily.

"That's what headlights are for," I replied. "Why the accent?" I asked Meabh then, changing the subject.

Meabh blushed. "I don't know," she said, covering her face with her hands. "It just came out."

"I didn't hear the accent," Angela pouted. "Do it now."

"No way."

"Go on," Kavi said. And the rest of us pleaded with her. A chorus of, "Go on, go on, go on."

Finally, cheeks a deep pink, Meabh blurted out the first thing that came to mind.

"Keep yer eyes on the road, lassie."

We all howled.

"That's so offensive to the Scottish," Angela said.

"Seriously though, keep your eyes—"

"Ahhhhhhhhh," we all screamed in unison as the car hit an unmistakeable something and Angela screeched to a stop.

A few seconds of silence followed. I dislodged my heart from my throat.

"Is everyone OK?" Angela asked.

A chorus of yeses answered.

"What do you think we hit?" I asked.

"I can't look," Angela said. "If it's a cat I'm going to kill myself. Go look, Kavi."

"Why me?" he protested. I could see him looking out the window at the lashing rain.

"You're the boy," Angela answered.

"I'm a boy," Daniel piped up. "But this is my good shirt. I'll ruin it for you ladies though."

"Sexist," Meabh replied. "Chivalry is simply another form of misogyny that places women on a pedestal, thus denying them full humanity and agency."

"So you go look, then," Angela retorted.

"No, I don't want to. It's raining."

I rolled my eyes, opened the door, and stepped out in the downfall. I was instantly drenched right down to my underwear.

"It was a glass bottle in the road," I said, getting in the car again, shivering already. "But we have a bigger problem. The tyre is busted. Do you have roadside assistance?"

Angela grimaced.

"You have accidents all the time. How are you not more prepared?"

She didn't even look apologetic. "I keep meaning to . . . But I never get around to it. There's a spare tyre though."

I stared at her. She stared back. I was not going to win this one.

"I have no idea how to change a tyre," I said.

Meabh buried her face in her hands and then spoke through the gap between her palms.

"I do. But I'll need help. I can't kneel on the ground with my boot on. But I can talk someone through it."

Kavi sighed and looked at Daniel's party clothes. "I guess that's me."

We pulled up to the house, three fifths of us soaked to the skin and turning blue. The rain had stopped as soon as we'd got back on the road, which had only taken about twenty minutes thanks to Meabh and Kavi's teamwork. When we got there, there were several boys playing a very muddy game of Gaelic in the garden.

"That can only end well," Meabh mused as we got out of the car.

"I'm sure it wouldn't pass your strict health and safety regulations," I said.

"I know you're making a joke about how I am overly invested in rules and regulations, and there are some criticisms to be made of bureaucracy, but most health and safety regulations are important for preventing injury. The weird ones are usually because there's some arsehole who did something really stupid and then sued because nobody had told him not to."

I yawned pointedly.

Daniel Something was halfway up the drive and looking like Dorothy landing in Munchkinland. Angela was several steps ahead of us, ready to rejoin her party and leave us behind.

"OK," I said, in a changing-the-subject tone of voice, "let's see if we can't get out of these wet clothes."

I looked at Meabh when I said that and then immediately regretted it, feeling a hot flush warm me up. Neither Kavi nor Meabh seemed to notice and we traipsed up to the house, squelching as we did.

Angela showed us in the front door and gave us a tour. By which I mean she pointed ahead and said, "Kitchen," and pointed to her left and said, "Living room."

She started to leave us but Meabh grabbed her by the sleeve.

"Maybe we could use your tumble dryer?" Meabh said pointedly.

"Do you have one?" I asked.

Meabh frowned. "Of course she does, who doesn't have a tumble dryer?" Then she realised what she'd said and met my eyes.

"Sorry. That was a stupid thing to say."

I shrugged it off. It was weird when things like that happened. Like when I was really little I didn't know we were poor. And then I figured it out and I avoided saying certain things that I knew marked me as "the poor kid".

But sometimes there were little things that I hadn't thought about and they popped up and embarrassed me. Like not assuming that someone has a tumble dryer, when other people would assume that of course they do.

I could see Meabh felt terrible and I didn't want to have to say it was OK. But I didn't want her to feel bad either because she hadn't meant anything by it. The others didn't seem to notice anything weird about our exchange.

"One time," Kavi started, and I pinched the bridge of my nose before the story even got going, "when I was little I told my brother that he should get in the tumble dryer and we'd turn it on and see what happened and then my mam found me trying to help him in, you know like stuffing his limbs in there, and she almost had a heart attack and started screaming that appliances are not for people and then she told my brother to get out of the tumble dryer and never go in there again, but when he tried to get out again he was stuck and we had to call the fire brigade to cut him out of it. Then we didn't have a tumble dryer for ages but now we have one that's a washing machine and tumble dryer in one."

Kavi to the rescue.

"Of course," Angela said, pointing towards the kitchen letting the story wash over her. "Laundry room is beside the kitchen, there's towels and stuff upstairs in the hot press." She hesitated and then whispered conspiratorially to me, "There's some extra beers in the fridge in the garage if you want them. Just pace yourselves." Then she swept past suddenly. "Hey, you. Spill on my rug again and I will end you."

I watched Angela confiscate a can and then we went to look for the towels. There were a fair few kids from school milling around but it wasn't quite what I expected. I think I'd seen too many movies and thought there'd be people doing keg stands and dancing on the tables. In reality there were a few people in the living room sprawled around a sofa playing what appeared to be a *Murder, She Wrote* drinking game while Angela Lansbury solved crime on the TV, and in the kitchen there were several pockets of people doing an awkward half-chat, half-dance shuffle with bottles of Corona in their hands. Just when I thought I hadn't been missing much by being a hermit, a girl shrieked "I SAW YOU KISS HER, RONAN!" and everyone turned around and started watching them fight.

"That's the party content I came for," I said.

I peered through a gap in the assembled audience and realised it was Jill. She was a bit drunk but mostly she was absolutely fuming.

"IT WASN'T A REAL KISS, IT'S A PARTY," Ronan shouted back.

"OH RIGHT, RONAN, BECAUSE AT A PARTY YOUR TONGUE IS NO LONGER REAL AND HER MOUTH IS NO LONGER REAL AND I SUPPOSE IF YOU HAD SEX YOUR DICK WOULDN'T BE REAL EITHER."

Ouch. Well, I could have told her that would happen; Ronan was a scumbag. But she wouldn't have listened to me.

Kavi, Meabh, and I squelched upstairs and looked for somewhere to change.

I tried the door nearest to me. Locked. I tried the next one. Towels. Jackpot. I threw one each to Kavi and Meabh. The next one was the bathroom.

Kavi sighed. "I'll take the press. Youse can use the bathroom."

The bathroom had a large bath and was themed of the seaside. Something I've never quite understood. I'm not sure what it is about peeing that makes people think of lighthouse ornaments and soaps shaped like seashells in a seashell.

"I'm too cold and wet to be awkward about this," Meabh announced as soon as we were alone in the bathroom clutching our towels.

"You made it more awkward by saying it."

"I didn't. If you say it then it dispels the tension. You're acknowledging it and moving on."

"I don't think so. I think it makes it far more uncomfortable than just pretending it's not happening."

"Should we stop arguing about this and take our clothes off?" Meabh suggested.

"Yeah, OK."

I unzipped my coat and shrugged it off onto the floor, where it landed in a squelchy heap. Meabh did the same, and shed a zip-up camogie team hoodie at the same time. Most of the bathroom was taken up by the tub and there wasn't a lot of space so twice Meabh elbowed me in the process.

"Sorry."

She was wearing a damp white tank top and I could tell that she was wearing one of those sports bras with the fancy crisscrossy straps. Then I realised that I shouldn't be noticing that. Meabh pulled off the top and threw it on the ground and I realised she was used to changing in front of other girls from playing camogie. And she *was* wearing one of those crisscrossy bras. She was unbuttoning her jeans when she paused, noticing that I was frozen in place.

"Do you want me to turn around?" she asked.

"No," I replied. "You can if you want. Or not. It's no big deal. I don't care. I don't have anything special under here that you haven't seen before."

"I haven't seen anything you have under there before," she said. "You always skip PE. When do you think I've seen you undress?"

"That's not what I meant." I blushed. "I mean, I just have. You know. Like regular boobs. You've seen boobs. I mean, probably."

"You think I go around the changing rooms looking at girls getting undressed?" she said, affronted. "How can you think I'd do that? I'm not a pervert just because I'm a lesbian. You should know that better than anyone."

"That. I didn't. I don't." I covered my face with my

hands. "I don't think that. I meant I don't need you to turn around because I don't think you're going to be looking at me like that because why would you because you get changed around girls all the time and it's not weird for you."

"I really feel like I should turn around now."

"No," I said, and I yanked my jumper off. I wasn't wearing a T-shirt so I was now standing in my black bra from Penneys and felt glad it wasn't the white one that came in the two-pack, which has since turned a depressing grey. "I'm fine, really. See." Hurriedly, and with zero grace, I scrambled out of my jeans and I stood there in my underwear and spread my arms wide. "Totally fine with it."

Meabh stared at me for a second. A long second. I felt warmth rise in my cheeks. Was she thinking I should work out? I'm kind of chubby and she obviously exercised a lot and was quite thin so maybe she thought I should be too. I had no idea why but my heart began pounding and I began to notice the smallest details. There was a small appendix scar peeking out from her waistband where she'd unbuttoned her jeans. Her skin was pinching in goose bumps all over her stomach. I couldn't help but notice where her nipples pressed against the fabric of her sports bra and when my eyes reached her neck, this thought, this picture flashed in my mind. I looked at her and she was looking back at me. It felt like she could see what I'd imagined. I'd thought of kissing her there, of pulling her close and feeling her skin against mine. I thought about trailing my fingers down her waist and sliding them down past the open buttons of her jeans to—

"Are you guys changed?" Kavi sounded confused.

I jumped. Meabh jumped.

"Just a second," I said, and I cursed my voice for wavering.

Meabh threw the towel I'd dropped on the ground and I wrapped it around myself. With surprising deftness she removed her boot and shimmied out of her jeans and I did not look. Nor did I find that her choice of underwear (a pair of green polka-dotted boy shorts) made me think about what it would be like to take them off with my teeth. Oh, for fuck's sake. What was wrong with me? In the space of a few seconds I'd turned into some kind of sex pest. Bless me, Father, for I have sinned.

Meabh was annoying.

I did not fancy her.

Yeah, because bickering never leads to sexual tension. Dumbass.

No. There was no sexual tension. OK, so maybe I'd had a weird inappropriate moment, but tension involves both people having the inappropriate thoughts and Meabh would never think about me like that. And I would never think about her like that again.

My inner voice snorted.

Meabh wrapped herself in a towel as well and we both awkwardly shuffled out of our underwear. She was naked under there now.

What a stupid thought. She was naked underneath her clothes all the time. Oh, holy mother. Was that what I was going to think every time I looked at her now?

"Let's go. Poor Kavi is standing in the hall on his own in nothing but a towel," I said.

I scooped my clothes into a bundle with one hand, using the other to keep my towel firmly in place. When we emerged I noticed something I'd never noticed much before.

"Kavi!" I exclaimed. "You're hot!"

Without his shirt on I could see that Kavi had broad shoulders, and although he wasn't Marvel-superhero ripped or anything, he could hold his own on a teen soap opera.

"There isn't one way to be hot," Meabh said, chastising me. "Kavi has the kind of traditionally glorified body we're used to seeing on a pedestal—"

"Yeah, yeah," I said. "That's a bit rich coming from Miss Pull-Ups over here."

"What now?" he said before Meabh could retort. I could see she had something to say.

"Dryer, obviously," I said before she could.

"None of us are wearing any clothes," Meabh said, pointing out what I'd overlooked. The dryer was downstairs, through the kitchen.

I looked at Meabh. She looked at me. I looked at Kavi. He was looking back at me.

"This is your fault," Meabh said reasonably, and pushed a bundle of clothes into my arms. Kavi copied her.

276

"Fine," I grumbled. "You two tagalongs are useless."

I turned and began to stomp down the stairs. Then I froze. My stomach dropped. At the bottom of the stairs was Jill, sobbing into her friend's shoulder. Her friend Holly. Holly, who very clearly was not visiting her grandmother.

"I'm so humiliated," she was saying. "Amy said she did sleep with him. She didn't know we were together. He told her we'd broken up. I hate him so much. I hope something awful happens to him."

"Karma's a bitch," Holly said. "Something bad will happen."

"His mother would absolutely kill him if she knew. She's so religious. I could just tell her, she'd murder him for me. But then she'd tell Amy's parents and it's not Amy's fault."

I watched Holly stroke Jill's hair and murmur comforting words and I felt my eyes water against my will. I thought I knew what Jill might feel like right now. *I* felt betrayed and stupid and like Holly must be laughing about me behind my back. She'd told me she was at her grandmother's. She didn't want to tell me she was going to a party because then she'd have to ask me to go and she didn't want me there. But 1 was good enough to hang around with on Sunday afternoon if she'd recovered from her hangover. Maybe she was waiting to see if Jill would want to do something instead. She liked Jill in a way that she didn't like me any more. Maybe some part of her still loved me, but it was a memory, an old version of us that no longer existed.

I had been caught between two conflicting messages that made me feel like I was losing my mind. I'd felt like I was being paranoid or clingy or seeing slights when they weren't there. But really all it was, was that Holly didn't have the balls to tell me she didn't want to be my friend any more. If she had, it would have hurt. But it would have hurt less than the slow pick, pick, picking of the last couple of years.

I felt someone jostle me and I looked up. Kavi was taking the bundle from my arms.

"I'll go," he said. Meabh was watching too. I wondered what they saw on my face.

I pulled Meabh by the hand back into the bathroom. I wasn't going to sit around on the landing in a towel listening in to Holly and Jill and worrying that they might come upstairs.

I let go of Meabh's hand and got into the bath. I sat width-ways, my knees pulled up to my chest. Meabh got in too but she sat at the other end of the tub. We didn't say anything for a few moments but I could tell she was working up to something.

"Spit it out," I said, hoping she wasn't going to talk about me staring at her before in an attempt to "dispel the tension."

"Why did you say it was a bit rich coming from me?" she said, and I could hear the pout in her voice. I turned my head and saw the pout on her face. She was staring at the wall opposite like it had personally offended her.

"What?"

"You said 'a bit rich coming from me'. You called me 'Miss Pull-Ups' when I said that there was more than one way to be hot."

I gave her my most incredulous look. Then I laughed. She was probably trying to distract me. But maybe she was also genuinely annoyed.

"Because you have one of those 'traditionally glorified bodies' or whatever. You look like some kind of advert for Nike in your sports bra. It's easy to spout body positivity when you could model for *Sports Illustrated*."

Meabh wrinkled her nose at the idea of *Sports Illustrated* but she also blushed.

"I think you have a great body," she said, almost in a whisper.

I didn't know what to say to that but I didn't hate hearing it.

"I have no boobs," she said, in the most genuinely plaintive tone I'd ever heard. It made me laugh. "Who's gonna want to see me naked? There's nothing to see!"

"Well, first off, all of the media lesbians are elfin and flat chested and they get to wear clothes that are sexy in an androgynous kind of way. You don't see TV lesbians with big tits. We don't exist cos we don't look good in button-ups." I thought about it. "Besides, more than a handful's a waste," I said.

She snorted. "Not to me," she said. "I feel bad about it

because it makes me feel like I'm being objectifying or something, but I want a girl with boobs."

I felt my cheeks heat up. "You can have one. There isn't some kind of soul mate matching-up service based on bra size." I put on a gruff voice: "Nah, you two can't date, one of you is an A cup and the other has double Ds. What was that? True love? This is the Titty Equity Commission, take that shit somewhere else."

Meabh laughed.

"I never thought we'd one day be having a conversation about breast preferences," I mused, grateful that at least she hadn't tried to talk to me about Holly. I don't think I could have had that conversation with Meabh. There was too much history. Maybe she realised that too.

"I guess I never thought that either," Meabh said.

Kavi pulled the door open, breathless and somewhat flushed. I patted the space in the tub between me and Meabh.

"Hey, Kav, c'mere and tell us what kind of boobs you're into."

He blinked. "This feels like a trap."

Meabh nodded. "Yeah, I don't think I'd be OK with any answer you give."

Kavi nodded seriously and clambered into the bath to sit between us. I closed my eyes until he was sitting in case the flapping of his towel revealed too much. He stretched his arms overhead and then rested one on each of our shoulders. If it was any other man on God's green earth, I'd find that move creepy. But it was Kavi, and I knew he was being sweet.

"How'd it go down there?"

"Uh. A girl asked if she could do a belly shot off my stomach. That was weird."

"It was weird that she asked or it was weird when she did it?" I joked.

"No, it was OK when she did it. It was more that she wanted to that was strange."

Meabh and I spluttered in unison.

"Oh my God. You let her?"

"She was cute." He shrugged. "She had really long blonde hair though and it tickled a lot."

"Fair enough. So tell us. How come you keep those abs a secret? If I had abs I'd walk around naked all the time like, *hey, look at this, everyone*. If I did all that work I'd make sure people knew about it."

Kavi looked pleased. "I got my uncle, my living uncle not my dead uncle, to start taking me to the gym this summer. Mainly it was because I was tall and thin and people kept making fun of me for being weedy and also maybe I think there might be something to do with me being brown too but I don't really wanna talk about that with you guys, no offence, and then I thought maybe if I got muscles girls would like me and then maybe other lads would also stop picking on me and it would be nice, but really it hasn't done anything because you can't walk around with your shirt off that much and so no girls noticed and the lads don't care anyway. But it was OK really because I got to spend a lot more time with my uncle and that was nice and it turned out we have a lot in common, and it made my mam really happy and then my little brother started coming too so now it's like a family-bonding thing."

I felt a rushing in my ears.

"Who picks on you?" I demanded, ready to scramble out of the bath and kick some ass.

Kavi shrugged. "Just people. It's not terrible. Little things. Comments."

"I'll kill them," I said. "I will pull their eyes out of their sockets and hold them in my hand so they can watch me dismember their own body."

Kavi frowned. "I don't think eyes work like that. You could use a mirror or something."

"You're too small and weak to dismember someone," Meabh said.

"Alone," I replied, raising my eyebrows. "Miss Pull-Ups, you can be the muscle. I'll be the artist."

"The artist?"

"If I'm going to murder people I'm going to do it in style. I'm not going to half-arse it. It's not Maths homework. It's a passion project."

"I really don't want you to murder anyone," Kavi said.

"I get you." I winked. "You can't be involved. You have motive."

"Seriously, Kavi, there must be something we can do?" Meabh said. "It's not right, people giving you hassle."

"I don't think you can make people stop being dicks," he said thoughtfully. "They either will or they won't in their own time. I don't need them to be on my side. I just need someone who is, so I'm not alone. I need people I can talk to. And I have that now."

I felt a hard knot in my chest and burning in my eyes. Meabh looked like she might cry. I think she knew what it was like to want people to be on her side. To *like* her. I decided I wouldn't call her annoying any more. I didn't know what it was like to be Meabh, and I certainly would never get what it was like to be Kavi, but I knew what it was like to feel alone.

Around two thirty, we had to leave. I found Angela and, slightly drunk, she threw me the keys.

"I thought I wasn't allowed to drive your precious car?"

"I trust you," she slurred, throwing her arms around me. Then she held me at arm's length and squinted. "You *can* drive, right?"

"Of course," I shrugged. I had driven my cousin's car round the back roads when I'd stayed in the country with my auntie Jacinta, so I had experience if not what you might call a "licence".

I made a hasty exit, afraid she'd change her mind or I'd run into Holly and Jill, but it meant waiting in the car while Kavi and Meabh peeled Daniel off the living room floor. I turned on the engine to warm the car up and noticed Dylan Cheung talking to one of the boys on the Gaelic team. He looked miserable. I rolled down the car window to eavesdrop.

The other boy gave Dylan a limp pat on the arm.

"Look, I'm not supposed to tell you this, but he's told all of us on the team not to talk to you."

"And you're just going along with it?" Dylan said, not hiding his pain at hearing this.

"You know what Ronan's like." The other boy looked at his shoes instead of at Dylan.

"He's my cousin, for fuck's sake. What is his problem? He made my life miserable on the team. So I quit. Now he's still not happy? What did I ever do to him?"

"You know what you did, mate. You were better than him."

The boy gave Dylan a manly slap on the arm instead of having the balls to be a human being. Dylan shrugged his hand away. When the boy was out of sight Dylan wiped his nose with his sleeve and kicked the wall a few times. I wanted to go and comfort him but I didn't think he'd appreciate me popping up in his vulnerable moment.

Kavi appeared a few minutes later, fireman-lifting Daniel. He looked like a hero from a romance novel. He flopped Daniel into a seat and wrestled a seat belt on him before sliding in beside him. Meabh took the passenger seat and shrugged at me.

"I guess I wasn't needed after all."

I ditched Daniel at his house.

The light was on in his living room. We all stared at the brightness like it was a terrible vision we couldn't look away from.

"I'll pay for your mam's vase," Meabh said.

Daniel nodded. He braced himself for his fate and got out of the car, letting a chill in.

I dropped Kavi home next and noticed the lights were still on at his house.

"Were you allowed out tonight?" I said, raising an eyebrow.

"Yes," he said defensively. "Mam's just a worrier. She'll have stayed up to make sure I'm OK. It's embarrassing, I know."

"It's not," I said. "It's nice."

He waved goodbye to us and then it was just me and Meabh.

We drove in silence, other than a few directions, to her house, and I could feel the tension from earlier creeping into the car. Pictures of her in her underwear kept flashing back to me. The long stare she gave me. Her comment about my body. It was a good thing the roads were clear because when I pulled up to her house I wasn't quite sure how I'd got there. I'd been in my own world.

"Tonight was really fun," Meabh said. She put her hand on my arm. It felt strange. It was just my arm and yet it felt weirdly intimate. Her touch was gentle but deliberate. I looked into her eyes. She bit her lip. My gaze fell on her lips then. It was so quiet I could hear her breathing like she was trying to keep it steady. My heart pounded. Her lips parted. I wanted to lean in.

Then a light blinded me and the silhouette of Mr Kowalski took up most of the door frame.

"Meabh, were you allowed out tonight?" I asked with a groan.

"Not exactly."

24

Of course Meabh hadn't been allowed out. I don't know how I forgot about her bananas schedule, but it definitely didn't include midnight gallivanting and parties. On Sunday morning I texted her.

Aideen
How mch trble u in?

Meabh
He said he was really disappointed in me and he didn't think that I would lie to him. He said he thought that I was above silly behaviour like going to parties and sneaking out.

Aideen
Above bein norml ... Cud b worse?

Meabh
It's the way he looks at me when he says it.

I didn't know what to say about that.

*

In the evening I told Mam I was going to go for a walk and get some fresh air and she gave me a funny look because that's not something I would ever do or say, but she let it go. I met Angela in town to give her her car back. She had somehow survived the party and looked fresh as a daisy in spite of everything.

"Thanks," I said, handing over the key and getting out of the car.

She got into the driver's seat and was about to close the door when she looked at me and frowned.

"What's wrong?"

"Nothing," I replied. "Tired."

She put her key in the ignition, her hand on the door handle, about to shut it.

"Oh, come on. Get in, I'll drop you home."

"That's all right. I don't mind walking back."

I wanted to keep my life. I had a feeling Angela's bad driving wasn't solely down to the dark night and lashing rain.

"That wind would slice ye. Get in the car."

I got in. At least if she dropped me home it'd be quicker. Mam wouldn't be alone for so long then.

"How's your dad?" I asked, once we were on a clear stretch of road.

"He's not good," she said bluntly.

I wondered if I could ask the question I was thinking.

"He'll be OK, though," she added without me having

to ask. It sounded like a warning. Like if he wasn't OK then God was going to have to answer to Angela. "But I hate talking about my crappy problems. Tell me about your crappy problems instead."

"Who said I have any?"

"Everyone has crappy problems," she said.

"Ah, you don't want to hear about them. They're stupid compared to what you've got going on." My mam might break my heart sometimes but she wasn't dying. Not yet anyway.

"Nah," she said, "I love hearing other people's problems. Makes me feel better about my own life. Like mine isn't the only one going to shit."

"That's beautiful."

"Are you going to tell me or not? Come on. My dad's practically dying. It's the least you could do."

I laughed in spite of myself. How could I talk about Mam without being obvious? Should I? It wasn't like me, but all of a sudden all I wanted to do was talk about it. Like I'd been keeping so much shoved down and I couldn't hold it in, didn't want to hold it all in.

"I have a . . . friend—"

"Just the one? Loser," Angela said, but there was no bite in her voice.

"Yeah. Well. Kinda," I said, thinking of Holly, even though I wasn't talking about her. God help me, which was worse, Holly being my only friend or my mam? "Anyway, she's done something really crappy and it hurt me and I don't know how to tell her that because she doesn't take criticism well."

"You write them a letter," Angela said seriously.

"A letter?" I said, skepticism leaking out of me.

"Yeah. Dearest Friend, Stop being a pure gobshite, you're making my life miserable. Kind regards, Aideen Cleary."

I laughed, but even the idea of saying something like that out loud to Mam made me feel sick. I could imagine the crushed look on her face if I told her truthfully how much she'd hurt me. I didn't want to be the one to make her feel bad.

"She wouldn't like that."

"She's not meant to like it? People don't have to like everything you do or say. You know, I didn't take you for being spineless. You have a whole social enterprise doing mad stuff just to help people. That's pretty impressive."

I smiled but it made me sad. "It's complicated. She doesn't mean to hurt me," I said. I didn't want to talk about it any more. People kept telling me I needed to stick up for myself and all I could hear was that I was a doormat. Was I supposed to choose hurting other people just so I could get my feelings heard?

"Doesn't matter what she means." Angela rolled her eyes. "It matters how she makes you feel. Why should she get to make you feel like shit and not hear about it?"

"I guess I'm just used to protecting her."

If I told Mam she was hurting me, she'd feel bad. If she felt bad, she might drink, and I'd feel bad. If I didn't tell her, then it would just be me who felt bad.

"Well, who the hell are you? Wonder Woman? Jeez. Stop being such a martyr and tell your friend she's an arsehole."

"You have a way of cutting through the crap, Angela."

"I know. I think I should be a therapist or something."

I wouldn't go that far.

Angela pulled up to my building and I wondered what she thought of it. If she'd think bad things about me because I lived here. I decided she didn't look like she was thinking anything bad.

"You got this," she said.

I got out of the car. "That wasn't so bad. You only clipped one wing mirror and it's still on." I pushed it back into place.

She pulled away from the kerb, her gears grinding noisily, and she stuck her hand out the window to give me the finger.

Holly
Hey! Do you want to hang out this evening?

I thought about ignoring it, but the idea of not replying again felt like I'd be screaming in her face: I'M MAD AT YOU. I couldn't do that.

Aideen
Sorry. So many favours today.
Can't hang out this evening.

It might have been manipulative. To tell her that I was doing favours and bring up the part of my life I'd shut her out of. It didn't feel good. It felt like I was picking at her the way she'd picked at me. Was I as bad as she was?

When I got in the door, all the lights were on again.

"Mam?"

"I didn't think you'd be home so soon," Mam said. The phrase instantly made me queasy. Why did it matter that I was home earlier than she thought?

She was sitting curled up in front of the TV with a blanket around her legs. She had a mug in her hands and she was watching *Fair City* on catch-up. I did a quick scan of the room but couldn't see anything to indicate she'd been drinking. No bottles or cans, but that's too obvious. Other things like cigarettes that she smoked upstairs instead of using her vape because who cares about tobacco smell in the flat when you're hammered. Or a ring on the arm of a sofa from sloshing bottles. But there wasn't any of that. Still, I couldn't shake the uneasy feeling. Instead of going to my room and tackling at least one piece of the mountain of homework that was due for tomorrow, I plopped down on the sofa and pasted a smile on my face.

"Got a lift home. What have you been up to?"

She shrugged and pointed at the TV.

Are you avoiding speaking because you're tired, or because you don't want me to hear you slur? Or am I being paranoid?

"Would you make me a coffee?"

Coffee? Are you trying to sober up? Did you ask me to make it because you don't want to get up and stumble?

"Sure."

I stood at the kettle and watched the back of Mam's head as though she'd slip and give me a clue. Nothing.

"Here." I set the coffee down on the arm of the sofa. Mam smiled at me and I tried to see if her·eyes were unfocused without staring. "I'll take that one," I said, pointing to the mug she already had in her hands. It was empty.

"Sit down and relax. I'll get it later."

She didn't put the old mug down until I'd taken a seat. Then she picked up the new one from the arm of the sofa. She sipped her coffee and watched the end of *Fair City*.

She washed both mugs before she went to bed. When she kissed me on the head, all I could smell was coffee. I turned the TV off and stared at the black screen for a while. I wanted to trust her. Or maybe it wasn't so much that I wanted to trust her as I didn't want to deal with what came next if she was drinking. Quietly, I checked around the kitchen, in the cupboards, under the sink, in the bin. Obviously she could have hidden any cans or bottles in her room. Maybe that was why she'd gone to bed. Or maybe

I was paranoid because it was so hard to believe that a slip could just be a slip.

I was about to give up and go to bed when I had another thought. I crept out of the flat and down the hall. The exit sign on the far end of the corridor was the only light. The bulbs in the light fixtures had blown ages ago and no one had replaced them. The back stairwell smelled terrible, as usual, and I cursed myself for not putting on shoes when I opened the bin room and the ground was sticky and covered in stray rubbish. The bag on the very top of the pile of rubbish in the skip was a Tesco carrier bag tied by the handles. Feeling like some kind of gross bin pervert, I took it and untied the handles. Inside were six empty cans of lager and a receipt. The receipt was from the Tesco in the shopping centre where Mam worked.

I couldn't be certain it was hers. It wouldn't hold up in a court of law. But I knew it was. The sinking feeling in my gut knew it. I could practically hear the click of the pieces falling into place. I just knew. Like I always knew. I wasn't paranoid; I'd developed a gut instinct. So it wasn't just a slip. She was drinking again.

What the hell was I supposed to do about it?

The next morning Mam dragged herself out of bed before I even got up. Once upon a time that might have made me think she hadn't been drinking after all.

This was not my first rodeo.

She had obviously stashed a can somewhere and wanted to drink it before I got up. She was sipping on coffee again when I came into the kitchen.

"Good thing I'm off today. Didn't sleep a wink last night," she said, blowing on her drink. "Must have been the coffee last thing."

"Maybe you shouldn't be drinking it now, then," I said, wanting my voice to come out cold and stern so she'd know I was annoyed, but instead it came out like I was making a casual suggestion. Why did that always happen? I didn't like the idea of Mam being off all day in the house on her own. Doing God knows what. Well, I knew exactly what.

"Oh, I wouldn't get through the day without it," she said. The toast popped then and she turned to take it out of the toaster, preventing me from making a very cutting comment about how it wasn't coffee that she couldn't live without. Damn it. Obviously I wouldn't say something like that to her.

"Are you all right, love? You look funny." Mam buttered a slice and handed it to me.

I held the toast in my hand and looked at it.

"Love?"

"I feel really sick," I said suddenly. "I can't go to school today."

A small part of me thought of Meabh and our almost kiss. I wanted to see her. Feel out her reaction. But that could wait.

"Don't give me that," Mam said. "You're fine, you're grand."

"No, really. I feel terrible. I can't go," I said, and I applied a very convincing I'm-going-to-throw-up-or-maybe-faint tone to my voice.

Mam pursed her lips. We both knew she couldn't make me go. We didn't have that kind of relationship. I wondered if she knew why I was doing this. Was she panicking and trying to decide if I was onto her, or was she simply annoyed that I was in her way?

"All right," she said, as though she was giving in, as though I needed her permission. "Get back to bed, then."

I whined. "I don't want to go to bed. I want to watch the morning shows. Can you make me a cup of tea?" I made a pouting face, like I knew I was being a pain in the arse but I expected her to indulge me because I was sick.

"If you're really sick, you should go to bed," Mam said.

I ignored her and curled up on the sofa, looking as helpless as possible. I pulled a blanket around my shoulders, rested my head on the arm of the sofa, and made puppy-dog eyes.

"So thirsty . . ." I said weakly, and gave a pathetic cough.

If she hadn't planned on using her alone time to knock back a few cans, Mam would have found my annoying child act irritating and amusing in equal measure. She would have made a joke and felt my forehead and made me cups of tea. As it was, she rolled her eyes impatiently, but put the kettle on anyway. Even though I knew what I was doing, it still somehow hurt, knowing I was a nuisance.

I zipped that hurt away into a tight secret space and reminded myself that I was doing this on purpose. I was being annoying on purpose. Mam might not realise that I was doing her a favour by sticking around all day, but I was. Maybe if she went the rest of the day without drinking she'd get it out of her system and she'd know she didn't need it. I could be her annoying detox fairy. She'd thank me later.

All day I followed her around, pretending to be needy and sick. I made her lie with me on the couch. Whenever she'd get up to do something I'd find a reason to follow her. If she was getting up to make tea, I'd give her a couple of seconds and then get up and wander into the kitchen.

"Are there any biscuits?" I asked mournfully.

"No," she snapped, clearly sick of having a shadow. "Go sit down, if you're so unwell."

I started to cry. It came surprisingly easily.

"What are you crying for?" she said, throwing her hands up in exasperation. I could tell she was getting more irritated as the day went on.

"Don't shout at me," I said, sniffing pathetically. "I'm sick."

I did my best impression of being a big baby who couldn't handle having a stomach bug. I'd committed, too; whenever I went to the loo I stuck my finger in my throat until I retched loudly. I didn't throw up but I made a good impression of it. Meabh and Kavi had texted me to find out why I hadn't been in school. I didn't answer. I don't know why. I didn't want to tell them the truth. But weirdly I didn't want to lie either.

"Oh, come here, you pain in the arse," Mam said wearily, and pulled me in for a hug. "What if I go to the shop and get you some biscuits? What kind do you want?"

Shit. Backfired.

"Oh, no. Don't. I couldn't eat them anyway. It'd make me worse."

"Well, what would you like?" She held me at arm's length and put on her best attentive-mother act. "I'll get you anything you want."

I bet you would. And what would you get yourself in the process?

"No. Really. Can we just watch a movie or something? I don't want to be on my own." I was laying it on a bit thick, but Mam just rubbed her eyes.

"Yeah," she sighed, "whatever you want."

By bedtime I could tell that she wanted to claw her own skin off. I don't know if it was because of me being a pain in the hole or because I hadn't given her a chance to down a drink. She was shaking her foot restlessly and picking at her nails all evening, but when I told her I wanted to sleep in her room, she didn't seem surprised.

She tossed and turned all night. I couldn't sleep because

I was afraid the moment I drifted off she'd get up. I wasn't even certain there was any drink left in the house, but I wouldn't put it past her. Whenever she rolled over, I'd roll over. All night I sighed or coughed or got up to use the loo so she knew I was awake.

The next morning we were mirrors. Grumpy and bleary eyed and greasy from no sleep.

"You still sick?" Mam said, though the words seemed like a lot of effort.

I inspected her. I'd only made her want a drink that much more. One day of sobriety wasn't enough. She had probably been drinking fairly steadily since her bender and I hadn't noticed because I'd been caught up in all my favours and problems with Holly and Meabh.

I nodded and rubbed my stomach for good measure.

"Well, I have to go to work," she said, with very little sympathy. I'd drained every last drop.

I sprang up. "I'll walk in with you. I need to get some medicine."

"I'll bring you stuff home," she said. "What do you want?"

"No, I can't wait till you get home. I think I'm getting a head cold and I need Lemsip or something."

"Let me see if we have any in the drawer."

I wasn't worried about that. We never had anything like that just lying around the house. It involved a level of organisation neither of us was up to. I bet that Meabh had a whole drawer of emergency things. Maybe she had one of those first aid suitcases. She almost certainly never got cramps in the middle of the night and realised she'd forgotten to buy ibuprofen or tampons.

I was right. We didn't have any Lemsip. I walked Mam to her work and then took her purse, saying I needed money for the chemist and that I'd bring it back. I walked home with her purse in my pocket instead. She texted me twenty minutes later asking where I was and I pretended I'd been delirious with my new cold. I picked her up from work, claiming that I really wanted some chicken soup and she couldn't get some for me because she had no purse so I thought I'd walk in and meet her. When she pointed out that there was a Spar near our flat I pretended I didn't hear her.

We did this for four more days.

I made up excuses to escort her to and from work. She didn't ask me what the hell I was playing at because some part of her must have suspected and she was afraid that if she asked, I might tell her. I let my phone die and didn't charge it. I couldn't face Meabh and Kavi asking me why I still wasn't at school. They'd be mad, but my sober companion act with Mam was working, and that made it worth it. As far as I could tell she hadn't had a drink since Sunday evening, or maybe Monday morning.

The problem was, the week had felt like for ever. It was exhausting, staying on her all the time, and by Sunday I was getting a knot in my stomach, wondering how long this could go on for. It may have felt like for ever, but it had only been a week. Was a week enough for her to start keeping it up by herself? For her to want to keep it up?

The decision was taken out of my hands. We were watching *Fair City* when someone rapped on the door. Mam and I looked at each other, confused. We didn't know people who dropped by. Mam shrugged and was about to get up and answer it when a thought occurred to me. Had Meabh or Kavi found out where I lived and come round to check on me? Or Holly.

"No," I said suddenly, "you sit. I'll get it."

It wasn't Holly. It wasn't Meabh or Kavi either.

It was weird to see Ms Devlin outside of school. Obviously I knew she didn't sleep in the gym cupboards and probably had some kind of real life with a partner and children and that sort of thing. But as much as you can know these things, it is never not weird to see your teacher outside of school. It is doubly weird when it's not a supermarket or McDonald's but your actual doorstep. Even weirder, she wasn't wearing gym gear. She had on jeans and a stripy top and she was wearing glasses. I'd never seen her glasses before and yet now that I had it was very clear that she was meant to wear them. They suited her face.

"Uh, miss . . ." I said, gathering myself. "I know I'm your favourite student and all, but it's a Sunday. The Lord's day and all that."

"Can I come in?" she asked, ignoring that she was interrupting my good praying time.

In response, I slid through the smallest gap I could manage and closed the door behind me.

"*May* I come in," I corrected her, flashing her a beaming smile. "Sorry. It's not really a good time, miss. My mam . . ." I sort of trailed off, not sure what would be a good enough excuse.

"I'd really like to speak with your mother, Aideen. I've been calling her mobile but it's off."

I was confused for a second; then I remembered it was my mobile she'd been ringing.

"She's really sick, miss. She's in bed now actually." I dropped my voice to a stage whisper as though I was trying not to disturb her.

Ms Devlin raised her eyebrows. "Lurgy, is it? Gangrene? Quinsy?"

I made a mental note to google quinsy.

Forcing a laugh, I shook my head. "No, miss, regular old flu."

"Have you been off caring for her?"

That was a trick question. The social would have something to say about me missing school to care for my mother.

"No, not at all. She's come down with it today, just as I was feeling better."

"So you're feeling better," she said. It wasn't a question. It was another trap. Although I'd kind of walked into that one myself.

"Well. I mean. I feel a bit better but I'm still not feeling great. Probably contagious. You're probably getting all my germs right now. Good thing you didn't come in the house or you'd be caught in a swamp of germs. It's so thick with the bastards in there that the air is legit green. I swear."

Ms Devlin sighed. She pushed her glasses up her nose and peered at me pointedly.

"You don't look like someone who has had flu, Aideen."

"Miss, unless those glasses have some kind of James Bond body-scanning powers, I'm not sure how you can prove that."

Ms Devlin looked at me evenly, waiting. Then I realised what I'd said.

"I mean *tell* that. I don't mean. I mean you can't tell by—"

"Save it," she said in her PE teacher voice. "I'm not here to prove anything. I'm here because you didn't come to school all week and no one could get through to your mother."

"I'm fine, miss. It was just the flu."

"So I'll see you in registration tomorrow?"

I hesitated.

"Aideen," she said, and her voice became quiet and more serious than usual. "This is a matter that I should only be discussing with your mother for the moment, because you are a minor. But your attendance since September has been dreadful, and with this week's absences you are dangerously close to the limit. The school has some discretion but I know that they are this close to contacting the education welfare board and that means there will be an investigation. There could be a fine, which I know you don't need."

I couldn't help but flush at the implication. I thought about what Ms Devlin must have seen coming here. Things that I forget to see. Rubbish strewn all over the streets and burned-out bins, cars blaring dance music that paused to let one of the boys out and then squealed off, broken beer bottles in the building's entrance and the smell of the bin room seeping through the walls. Maybe I should have let her in the flat. It was nothing special but it was clean and tidy. I didn't want her to think that it was like the outside. But really the thing she said about education welfare was a bigger problem. That's just a fancy term for the social worker who gives you hassle about going to school. I couldn't have them coming to the flat. I was barely keeping it together for me and Mam. I couldn't put on a show for the social too. I had a terrible feeling that I would burst. Or that it would burst out of me. The worries. That I might break down and actually tell them that I couldn't sleep at night because I was afraid that Mam would get up and leave and that she would come back drunk hours later. Or that she wouldn't come back. I couldn't do that to her. I couldn't betray her like that. I wouldn't give myself the chance to either.

"I'll be in tomorrow," I said. "I'll be there early! I promise. Let me walk you out."

Ms Devlin was not stupid. She knew I was getting rid of her, but I wasn't stupid either (at least not about this), so there wasn't much she could do about it right now. There was the worry that she'd pull a Goody Two-shoes busybody move and call the social about her concerns, but maybe if I acted really good for a few weeks she'd forget about it. She could move on to the next charity case she wanted to rescue.

When I closed the front door, my first thought was that I'd left enough time for Mam to find the drink I was convinced was still hidden in the flat, and then I wondered what I was going to do tomorrow when I couldn't mind her all day. Monday. The salon was closed on Mondays. She'd have the whole day to fuck it up. But when I entered the living room it didn't look like she'd budged an inch. She was curled up with a cup of tea and beginning to doze off. I crossed my fingers – you know, like, my metaphorical fingers – that this week had been enough to give her a head start. Mam *wanted* to stay sober, I reminded myself. She needed me to help her this week because the first week was the worst. Probably.

"Who was that, love?"

"Bloody number eight saying we had his Amazon package. I told him we didn't and sure I went downstairs and there it was sitting in the window beside the postboxes."

"Next time he comes round, you tell me," she said sternly. "I don't want you talking to the likes of him."

She cared about me. I knew Mam knew why I'd been following her around all week. Hopefully she'd feel too guilty to start drinking the second my back was turned. All the same . . .

"Maybe you should go to one of your groups after work tomorrow?" I tried to sound casual as I flopped back in the seat beside her. "You've not been because you were taking care of me all week but you said you were going to, and I'm all right enough to go back to school now."

"Sure thing, love," she said, and she took my socked feet in her hands and rubbed the toes. "I'm glad you're going back. Wee Holly must be lost without you."

Yeah right.

25

Holly leaned into Jill and whispered something, and Jill laughed and I felt so lonely. I'd arrived into registration slightly out of breath, as I'd had to run past Ms Devlin to get there before her. Meabh was at the front of the room but there was no free space beside her. I took a spot near the door, realising too late that it was next to Ronan. He was making obscene gestures to the boy next to him and I did my best not to hear a thing they said. I wondered if Holly had texted me while I'd been off. I hadn't charged my phone yet. I think I was afraid to see that she hadn't.

Ms Devlin entered the room several seconds after me. She raised her eyebrow when she saw me panting on my bouncy ball.

"Nice form this morning, Aideen," she said.

I laughed. "Don't know what you're talking about."

"All right, lads, I want to remind you that the student council election is on Friday this week. There's a debate on Thursday after final period that I'd like you all to attend—"

"You might not have a life, miss, but I'm not going to any debate after school. I'd rather be kicked in the balls," Ronan scoffed.

"That makes two of us. You're dismissed," she said, with a wave of her hand.

It took Ronan a second to catch on. The snickers around the room were the only thing that alerted him.

"Miss, you cannot just say you wish I'd get kicked in the balls!"

"Certainly I couldn't say those words, in that order, where anyone could hear me. But as long as my meaning is ambiguous, then I think it's fine. Yes, Holly?"

I swivelled to see Holly with her hand in the air.

"Miss, I think this is a problem. No one is going to come if it's after school. Can we not make it an in-school event? Like last period or something?"

"Ronan can still go get kicked in the balls, though, if that's OK with you," Jill added.

My stomach flipped as I watched Ms Devlin consider this. I knew what this debate was. A chance for Holly to shine and for Meabh to come off as stuffy and boring and aggressive. Holly had said she wanted to beat Meabh publicly, and she wanted the whole school to see it.

"I think that's a good idea, actually," Meabh said. "As many people as possible should hear our ideas."

Meabh still thought if she brought the best ideas people would vote for her.

For someone who had "reading the news" in her daily schedule, I don't know how she maintained such naive optimism. I wanted it to be true for her though.

"I think we could work something out," Ms Devlin said thoughtfully. "I don't see why seniors couldn't take one class to engage in the democratic process. Mandatorily. And I have a first-year English class at that time. They could come too and watch persuasive writing in action."

Meabh and Holly wore equally smug expressions.

One period later I was back in the PE hall. I hadn't a clue what had happened in Geography class. In the week I was away, I'd missed something vital. It had been worth it, though, I told myself. I was worried about Mam. I carried it around with me like a heavy stone in my chest but I was hopeful she wouldn't mess up the good start I'd given her. A little part of me was happy too, knowing I'd get a chance to see Meabh soon and talk to her properly. Underneath all the worry there was a giddy flutter in my stomach and it became stronger the closer to the PE hall I got.

"I'm glad to see you back today, Aideen," Ms Devlin said when I approached her with my note. "I spoke with your teachers while you were gone. Miss Hennessy told me there had been some improvement before you got 'sick'. I want to see that continue now that you're back."

She didn't use air quotes around the word *sick*, but I heard them all the same.

"Miss Hennessy . . ." I said, rubbing my chin. "Remind me?"

"Your Maths teacher," Ms Devlin said dryly. "The one who uses numbers instead of words."

"Riiiight. I'm practically a model student," I said, and I found myself feeling cheerful, like the weight in my chest had lightened a little. "Am I getting one of those awards they give out at the end of the year? Did you call me back because you want to ask about my trophy preferences? Gold is fine."

"The committee will be in touch about engraving later. We want to make sure we spell your name right, of course," she replied. "Actually, I wanted to ask you what you've been doing differently."

"What do you mean?"

"I mean you've been struggling in Maths for as long as you've been at this school. I've been pestering you since September about handing in homework and you ignore everything I say. All of a sudden I'm hearing you're actually doing it. At least in one class."

"I had some help." I couldn't keep the smile from my face when Meabh came up, even if no one had actually said her name.

"From?"

"From a friend."

"Is your friend a secret?"

"I guess not." Why was I so reluctant to tell Ms Devlin anything? I felt like it was like being arrested. Where anything you say can and will be used against you. "Meabh Kowalska." There was the smile again. Betraying me.

"Ahhh. She's helping you when the two of you are up there slacking off." She jerked her head towards the balcony.

"Miss. Honestly. Meabh is not slacking." I felt very defensive of her. "She has a sprained ankle. And I have the vapours." I handed her my note.

"The vapours?"

"Yes. Vapours. From my womb."

"That sounds serious."

"You're right. Maybe I should go home and lie down."

"How are things at home?"

I wanted to kick myself. I'd set my own trap.

"Fantastic," I said. "Could not be better."

A slip is a slip is a slip. It didn't mean going back to square one. She'd had a whole week of being sober. A week was a good start. I bet in AA there was a chip for that. In Mam's group there were no chips. Maybe I should make her a chip.

"I could get you help in your other subjects. We talked about this."

"Miss, honestly, I don't know how much more you want from me. I've done my Maths homework. I'm getting that trophy. Your expectations are so high."

She rolled her eyes. "I'm glad things seem to be going well. I have my eye on you, though."

Weirdly that didn't make me feel nervous. It was kind of nice to think someone had their eye on me.

*

311

Meabh was hunched over her laptop up in the balcony. I felt the giddiness ramp up yet again and I felt very aware of my body being awkward. It was full of nervous energy. Meabh had already spread pages of notes around and she had tied her hair back and she had one pen behind her ear, one in her mouth, and a long pen mark on her neck. She'd thrown her jumper off and so she was just in her school shirt. I could just see the shadow of a lime-green sports bra underneath.

What should I say?

Her skirt was hitched up again and her long legs caught my eye. She'd kicked off her boot but still had one shoe on. I remembered our almost kiss the night of the party.

How should I say it?

I remembered seeing her in her wet T-shirt, watching her peel it off, and I felt a hot rush through my body. I wondered what she would do if I kissed her now and I thought about how much more fun that would be than doing Maths homework every PE class.

How do you have a normal facial expression? Mine was being weird.

A montage of images flooded my head. Even though I knew that Meabh would never consider letting me kiss her neck, loosen her school tie, unbutton her shirt, and slide my hands up her thighs on school property. It would be sacrilegious to her.

But I could picture it.

"Hi," I said, hoping I sounded casual but sexy but mysterious and exciting. It was a lot to ask of one word.

She grunted in reply and didn't look up.

OK. Well, she was working. I knew it would take a lot to distract her from work. But Ms Devlin had often called me "a lot" so I was more than capable. I mean, granted, she meant in a different kind of way, but that was fine.

I sat on the bench nearest to the zone Meabh had designated her work area. That zone encompassed an approximately three-mile radius of nerd debris, but I got as close as I could and stretched out on it, trying to appear as though I was just naturally lounging while scrunched-up papers scratched my leg and a pen lodged under my hip. I propped my head up on my hands and fluttered my eyelashes. Was I doing sexy right? Should I be doing this pose on a piano instead?

"So . . . I'm sorry I haven't been in touch since the party. Or, well, after the party," I said, hoping to nudge her memory. "It was really fun though. Thanks for helping."

"*Hmph*," Meabh said.

I did not like that tone.

"Uh . . . are you OK?" I said, reaching out and putting my hand on her arm. I felt like I was in trouble, so now was not the time to think about Meabh's arms or to notice that I could feel her biceps through the fabric. But they were tensed. Not a good sign, but I just wondered what it would it be like if she used them to pin me down.

Jesus, stop it. Somehow now that the *Meabh is hot* switch had been flicked, no pun intended, it was all I could think about when I looked at her.

But she shook my hand off her arm.

"I don't have time for you right now." Her voice was cold enough to douse my sudden hornball energy. I sat up, feeling stupid and humiliated.

"What's your problem, what did I do?"

"Nothing," she snapped. "You didn't do anything."

"I don't know what you're talking about." She was mad. It made my heart pound, and not in the *Meabh is so hot* kind of way.

"I know you don't," she said. She was being infuriatingly smug too. She had that stupid smug face that she always got when she was right and everyone else was wrong. "That's kind of the problem."

"I hate that face," I said, feeling a surge of anger. Where did she get off being mad at me? "All I've ever done is try and help you."

"Oh really?" she said loftily. "See, I think I've been helping *you* all this time. I've helped you with Maths. I've helped you carry your groceries home. I've helped you with your stupid favours. You couldn't even be there for me on the worst week of my life."

Each sentence was like another sucker punch. She

314

thought I was a burden. She thought I was stupid and I needed her help. She thought I was some kind of charity case. She didn't even *like* me. I stood up and curtsied to her.

"Well, thank you, Queen Meabh. All the poor, stupid people are supposed to be grateful for your kind assistance, right?"

She looked shocked. She hadn't expected me to stick up for myself. No one ever did. *I* didn't expect it. The words just sort of burst out of me and they didn't stop.

"You think that you help me with my Maths homework a few times and that means you're saving me, right? And you can put it on a transcript or you can talk about your good deeds in an interview someday. Fuck. You. Your dad is disappointed with you and that's your biggest problem? You have no fucking idea what the worst week of my life would look like."

She looked stupid, sitting on the floor with her ridiculous manifesto, and I walked away from her, down the stairs, and out into the brisk breeze. As I watched the class doing suicide sprints on the field, I replayed the look on her face and took a moment of pleasure from the vicious feeling I'd had. Now, in the cold morning air, I felt empty, but in a good way, like I'd finally released something toxic that had been building up inside me.

I didn't think about whether it had been aimed at the right person.

*

When the bell rang at eleven for our morning break, I went to find Kavi, hoping he'd know what specific stick was up Meabh's ass. I thought I remembered him having Geography at this time so I headed in that direction. Usually when I wanted Kavi he simply appeared. Often when I didn't want him, too, so looking for him was a new experience. I stopped a few people who had the same Geography class but they couldn't remember if he'd been in or not. I found him, though, walking towards the café with a reusable cup in hand. When he caught sight of me, a weird expression took over his face. I jostled against the crowd until I reached him, then pulled him into an empty classroom.

Of course, when I look back on the conversation that happened next I want to burn it from my memory. But the technology does not yet exist. It's one of those conversations you replay for a long time after and you still feel as terrible as you did when it happened.

"What's going on? Meabh's mad at me. And I can tell there's something wrong with you, too, and you haven't even said anything."

"I'm angry too," he said evenly.

I waited a beat for the long story about another time when he was angry. It didn't come. Apparently angry Kavi didn't ramble.

I racked my brain. OK, I knew he'd sent me a message and I hadn't read it or replied. But I had a good excuse. "Why though?"

His eyes bugged. "You have been MIA for six days! You haven't answered a single text. They haven't even delivered since Wednesday."

"OK," I said. So maybe I'd missed an opportunity for a favour but as far as he knew, I was sick all week so he could hardly be mad about that. "I'm sorry. My phone died. I was sick."

"I thought something really bad had happened to you."

He seemed really upset and I started to feel the familiar tug of guilt. I didn't like it.

"I was sick. That's all. It's not a big deal." I heard the words come out irritably and I knew Kavi didn't deserve that, but he shouldn't push me on this. I was entitled to privacy. And all I'd done was ignore my phone for a few days.

"I don't believe you. Sick people can text. And yeah, Meabh's mad too. Something really bad *did* happen to her and you weren't here."

"What, so you two were just sitting around all week talking about me behind my back?" I was getting angry now. It was a good thing I hadn't told them what was actually going on; that would really give them something to gossip about.

"Yes! Obviously we were talking about you! You come up from time to time. Especially when you disappear. That's what happens when you have friends who actually like you."

It took a second for that to hit me because I wasn't expecting it from him, but when it did, it stung.

317

"What happened to Meabh?" I asked.

"*Someone* uploaded a video of Meabh chasing after a first year with a reusable cup that he'd thrown in the bin. She threw it at his head and gave him a lecture. You know how she is . . ."

I tried to withhold a smile. I could fully envision that scenario.

"But they sent it round to half the school and the comments got nasty. There were so many of them."

Ouch. I thought about Meabh on her phone reading through pages and pages of people hating her.

Kavi wasn't done though.

"It's all anyone was talking about last week. Meabh was devastated," Kavi continued. "I know people call her annoying all the time. They make fun of her for being the way she is, but it *is* who she is and seeing everyone hate her for it like that, it was too much. She missed school over it."

Meabh's never taken a day off school. Nothing could have told me how bad it was more than this. A hot flush of shame burned inside me.

"I had to go around to her house and talk her into coming back. And she's so amazing she just decided to try harder. She said she still wants to make things better for everyone. Even if they hate her for it."

Kavi was silent for a few minutes. I felt like there was something else he was trying to say. He didn't quite look at me when he asked.

"Who do you think posted it?" he asked, clearly attempting an even tone.

No. I couldn't even think that. It was too cruel, even for her.

Was it?

Besides if she was going to try and take down Meabh, wouldn't she use the paper to do it?

That would be too obvious. She'd need more than a stupid video for an article. She'd need a real story.

"You don't know it was her," I said.

He looked disgusted. "I don't know why you can't break away from her. Especially now. After this."

"Jesus, Kavi, give me a fucking break. I have stuff going on too."

He had no idea how I'd spent my week.

"So tell me what's going on," he said, frustrated. "I've been here. I've reached out to you. You'd see that if you turned on your damn phone. I would have gone to see you, too, but I don't know where you live."

"It's none of your business. Where I live or what's going on."

He eyed me steadily and gave me a minute to change my mind. I stared back. Finally he gave up.

"I don't know what's going on with you. I wish you would tell me, but I respect that maybe you have a good reason not to. But I am not disposable. I'm not a toy you can play with when it suits you and then ignore when you have other stuff to do. If you want to be my friend, you have to stop treating me like I don't exist if you're not looking directly at me."

I was stunned. I didn't do that. What the fuck? Just because I didn't text him back for a few days? Just because I didn't tell him all the details of my shitty life? Who the hell was he to demand I tell him everything?

"I never said I wanted to be your friend," I said snidely, feeling the hot flush turn to anger. "You didn't really give me any choice."

Kavi didn't react. His face was blank.

I left him there like that.

Too far, dickhead.

Shut up. Shut up. Shut up. You're the stupid voice in my head that thinks all these mean things and now that I actually say them it's wrong?

It's not Kavi you're mad at. It's not Meabh.

Yes it was. He was being intrusive and demanding and he had no idea what was going on in my life and if he was going to have a hissy fit every time I didn't answer a message, then he was too high-maintenance for me. And Meabh. Well, if the comments on Meabh's video didn't include the words *high-maintenance*, I'd eat my face.

You sound just like Holly.

I muddled through Maths, completely lost. We'd moved on to a new topic and my brain hurt. I should give up. I'd just got my head around trigonometry and now we were on something totally different. How was I supposed to keep up?

By going to school maybe?

It felt like it was too late. My brain flooded with all the things I didn't understand. Eight subjects, and I was drowning in all of them. How was I ever going to get back on track when I couldn't even remember the last time I was *on* track? How could I keep social services off my back, the teachers off my back? What was I going to do about my best friend, who was horrible to the girl I maybe kind of liked? Meabh didn't deserve any of this. Even if she didn't like me back any more. And Kavi. I'd hurt Kavi because I was too afraid to tell anyone about Mam and because I'd let myself take out my shame and frustration and anger on the sweetest person I knew. How would I stop Mam from drinking? She could be drinking right now. She could be hurtling us both towards disaster in spite of everything I'd done to stop her.

My heart was beating so fast I thought I was going to throw up. My chest was too tight to let air in. I was suffocating in this room. The windows were closed. They were painted shut. How the hell was anyone supposed to breathe like that? We were all stuck breathing each other's air. It was making me sick. I could practically feel that the air I was taking in was used and grimy and secondhand. I scrambled back from my desk and ran out of the room, not stopping to hear if Miss Hennessy called my name. I ran the length of the hall and down the stairs so no one could follow me.

For some reason I found myself at the sick bay door, and for some reason I knocked.

Sister D answered.

"I don't feel right," I said, breathless.

She ushered me in with a comforting hand on my back. Something about the softness of her touch made me want to hug her.

"Lie down, dear."

I got into the sick bay bed, with its flat pillows and thin mattress you could feel the springs through.

Sister D shoved a thermometer into my mouth.

"Your eyes are hanging out of your head. Were you up all night playing computer games?" she asked, mild chastisement in her voice.

I shook my head.

"Is it your period, dear?" She nodded knowingly.

I shook my head.

She took the thermometer from my mouth and inspected it. I highly doubted her eyesight was good enough to read it.

"Stomach bug?"

I shook my head. Then I remembered I could talk.

"I feel—My chest feels tight, like I can't breathe."

She drew a stethoscope from her pocket and put it to my chest. She motioned for me to sit up and I did.

"Turn around and lift up your jumper."

I did as she said and she pressed the stethoscope to my back as well. When she was done she gestured to me to lie back down.

"I have just the thing for you," she said, and she opened the cupboard, popped a pill from a foil pack, and poured me a glass of water.

"Diazepam?" I asked hopefully.

"Benadryl," she replied.

"I don't have allergies. I don't need an antihistamine."

"You need to sleep. Look at the bags under your eyes. Goodness gracious."

Skeptically, I swallowed.

I remembered thinking an antihistamine wasn't going to do much for me.

I remembered that when I woke up and saw from the clock on the wall that it was after one.

Holly was sitting in the seat beside my bed. She had a coffee from the café and a pain au chocolat, which she handed to me. She felt my forehead with the back of her hand like she was a human thermometer.

"You are having the worst luck," she said, sipping from her own coffee cup.

"You know you get ten cents off if you bring a reusable cup in."

"Yeah, I know, but I always forget."

"I'm fine, anyway," I said. "Just tired."

I didn't know what else to say. I also knew I wasn't

looking her in the eye but I couldn't bring myself to. I didn't want to look at her. I wasn't sure what I'd see. Would I see my life long best friend? Would I melt? Would I see someone who was cruel and horrible and mean and I'd explode in anger?

"I've been worried about you," she said, and she patted me on the thigh.

"Have you?"

I wasn't sure if I wanted that to be sarcastic or not. It came out with a softness I didn't like the sound of. It reminded me of Dad telling Mam he loved her. She would always say *Do you?* In a way that made me feel sorry for her. Like she wanted it to be true more than anything, but she couldn't quite believe it.

"Of course I have, silly."

You could have come around to check on me. You *know where I live.*

She had come to see me now, in the sick bay, though.

"How's business?" she said then, changing the subject. "You must have loads of things backed up since you've been off."

"It's not a business."

"You know what I mean."

"I really need to get up," I said. "Lunch is nearly done and I can't miss the whole day. Ms Devlin will go apeshit."

"I'll walk with you," Holly offered. "I can read you bits from my debate speech. See what you think?"

324

"I have to go to my locker first." I grimaced. "Besides, I wouldn't understand your speech."

Holly laughed. "I know, but it'll help me get it into my head."

I caught her eye for the first time since she had walked into the room. She didn't blink. She didn't think there was anything wrong.

I know. I know. I know.

26

When I got home, Mam wasn't there. Monday was her day off so immediately I was stressed. I charged my phone to call her and sat beside it for the longest few minutes, waiting for it to have enough charge to turn on again. My stomach twisted and my head pounded. She could not do this to me again.

When the phone finally came to life, I went straight to my call list. But a flurry of messages came through. Missed calls and texts from Kavi and Meabh. I hesitated. Then I opened them. It would only take a second. Mam would still be doing whatever she was doing in a second. Even though I'd already fought with Kavi and Meabh, I felt growing dread as I began to read. They started off jokey and telling me to come back to school, and then got increasingly worried. I cringed thinking of how I'd let these messages pile up like they meant nothing. Meabh even messaged me about what happened with the video. She'd sent me a link to it. I pictured her upset and vulnerable and hoping I'd respond. I clicked through to the page but it had been taken down already. I wondered if that was because the person who put it up felt guilty or if it was because they didn't want to get in trouble. I didn't like that I didn't know the answer to that.

A hard knot formed in my chest. It hurt and I wanted to cry. I knew Meabh was right and I hadn't been there for her. It didn't matter why. It only mattered that when things were bad I had been too wrapped up in my own problems. And Kavi was right too. If I didn't ever tell them what my problems were, then how could I expect them to understand? But the thought of telling them everything was too awful. Right now everything was in my control. What happened with Mam, who knew, where I lived, how we managed it. I was managing it. I had so far. I couldn't be friends with people who would take that away from me. And they would. They would want to "help". The road to social workers was paved with good intentions.

"Are you home?" I heard Mam's voice as she came in the door. Relief and fear mingled. She was home. But had she been drinking? I almost tripped in my haste to get to the hall before she could hide anything she'd bought.

She was taking her coat off when I reached her and was hanging it up on the hook.

"See, I remembered," she said, expecting praise for not leaving it at her arse. I followed her into the kitchen, where she flipped the switch on the kettle and sighed. She flinched when she turned and saw I was standing right behind her.

"What the fuck, love?" She laughed. "You scared the bejesus out of me."

"Where were you?" I asked, aware that I sounded angry even though I hadn't planned to. I felt like a bottle of Coke all shook up, ready to explode, and I couldn't pretend to be calm.

"I've been at work," she replied slowly, either not getting why I was annoyed or pretending not to. She loved to do that.

"It's Monday. The salon is closed on Monday. That's not even a good lie."

"Excuse me?" she said, affronted. "We were doing a stock take."

Mam poured boiling water into her mug and added milk.

Suddenly adrenaline flooded through me, making me shaky and reckless.

"Have you been drinking?" I asked. I hadn't in my whole life ever asked her that question directly. We tiptoed round it. But I couldn't do that any more. If she was going to lie I wanted her to do it right to my face.

Mam was surprised. For a long moment she searched for a way to answer me. That's how I knew she was searching for a lie. You don't need to come up with a good truth.

I opened the cupboard nearest to me. Then the one below. The fridge. The one under the sink. When I didn't find anything I moved to the living room.

"What are you doing?" Mam followed me, hands on hips.

I looked behind the TV. Got down on my hands and

knees and looked under the sofa. I upturned a vase, letting a bunch of dusty plastic flowers fall to the ground.

"Aideen!" Mam said, annoyed. "Stop it."

In the hall I looked inside Mam's boots and in her coat pocket. She didn't follow me this time. I lifted the lid off the cistern and shook out the rolled-up towels. I looked under her bed and in her pillowcase. I felt in her chest of drawers and pulled the bottom one off its rail so I could see inside. I looked in the bottom of her wardrobe and in an old sports bag she uses to "hide" Christmas presents every year. I even looked in my own room.

When I went back into the living room she was sitting on the sofa with her arms crossed, her tea half drunk.

"Are you quite done?" she asked. She didn't sound mad exactly but she wasn't happy.

I threw myself into the armchair and glared at her, but my adrenaline and my confidence that I was right were already ebbing away.

"I don't know if I can trust you," I said. I couldn't look at her as I said it. I looked at the TV instead. It was off and reflected my mam back at me in its black glossy screen. One degree removed from watching the hurt on her face.

"I know," she said. "But it was one slip. I was sad. I'm sorry."

I'd never heard her say before that she was sad. Of course I knew Dad made her sad. That's why I hated it so much when he came back. She'd be doing well, on her feet, and he'd come around and ruin everything, and it would take no more than a few days.

"Mam, the thing is, there are always going to be things that make you sad. So what then? Do I have to worry every time . . . something bad happens?" I avoided his name.

She appeared to think about that.

"I don't know about what's going to happen in the future. I'm sorry. I wish I could give you a guarantee. All I can say is that right now, I am doing OK. I'm not drinking. I promise. I know you don't have any reasons to trust me after all these years. But I'm asking you to please try."

I looked at her, properly this time, not through the TV, trying to figure out if I could believe her. It was possible. She promised.

She'd promised before.

But that didn't mean that this time, her promise wasn't real. Trust is funny like that. It's like faith. If you have proof then you don't need trust. You need trust when you have doubts. I said a silent Hail Mary and hoped that faith would come.

Orla
I need to talk to you. Meet me before
registration in the toilets on the first floor.

"How's things with your secret boy?" I asked, yawning and leaning against a sink while chugging a Coke for breakfast. I was already PMSing and the early morning hadn't helped.

Orla looked in the two stalls, checked behind the doors, and didn't answer me until she was sure there was no one there.

"We broke up," she said, though she didn't look devastated.

"Did you get caught?" I asked, remembering her strict dads.

She shook her head. "No, just turned out he was a gobshite. Fellas. You know how it is."

I did not.

But I nodded anyway.

"I think I fancy Ali, you know, in my year? But I don't know if she likes girls."

"Only one way to find out," I said.

She looked at me as if to say, *And that is?*

"Ask her if she liked Fiona Apple's latest album."

"Of course." She hit her forehead with the heel of her hand. "But look, that's not why I asked you here." She took a folded piece of paper out of her skirt pocket and handed it to me.

I unfolded it. It was a printed-out article from the school paper.

TALUS WHAT REALLY HAPPENED!
Presidential hopeful Meabh Kowalska's recent ankle injury took her off the camogie team where she has served as captain for three years, but a

source informed us that this impairment may have been self-inflicted.

I turned cold all over. I scanned the story for my name. It wasn't there. Reading closer, I realised it sounded as though Meabh had simply launched herself down the stairs. Who knew about that? How did they find out? It wasn't the full truth, but as far as I knew only Kavi, Meabh, and I knew what had happened that day. Meabh wouldn't tell anyone, for obvious reasons. It didn't even occur to me to doubt Kavi; there was no way.

"What is this?" Although I knew what it was, of course. What I meant was, how do you have this, who wrote it, and what the fuck am I going to do about it?

"I was sent a draft of the new paper late last night. It's not being printed until tomorrow night but they always send it to me early so I can check it over."

"Who sent it to you?" I said, cutting her off.

"Jill, of course. She's the editor."

"There's no byline on it. Do you know who wrote it?"

Orla squirmed. "No . . . but I may have overheard something. Just after the last issue came out, when Holly had just stepped down. There was an article Jill wasn't sure about writing, and Holly told her to."

The same conversation I'd overheard that day after my laps with Ms D.

I skimmed over the article again. This would destroy

332

Meabh. It was due to come out the day before the election. She would look ridiculous. She would definitely lose. Her dad would know and if I knew anything about Meabh, it was that disappointing him or embarrassing him was not an option for her. And she'd already been through this with the video. I didn't think she could handle another scandal. And this one was much worse. I could not let this get out.

"Can you stop this from being published? I mean take it out before it's printed. I will owe you anything you want."

Orla looked pained. "I would do it, of course I would. Meabh helped me when I needed it, and she's been through enough the last week. I know what that feels like."

I remembered Orla saying she'd been bullied over text and I thought she probably knew how Meabh felt better than most of us.

"But Holly always checks the first copy that prints. Jill's probably going to do the same thing now she's editor."

I nodded, already on to the next possibility. I opened the door to the toilets to leave, so focused on how I could possibly get around this that I forgot to even say thank you.

"If there's anything I *can* do . . ." Orla said, her voice trailing off as I ran down the stairs. I couldn't waste any more time. I needed to go to the source.

For the rest of the day I stalked Jill. We didn't have many classes together but she had most of her classes with Holly so I knew where she would normally be. Unfortunately it also meant she was always with Holly. Finally, though, I passed them both in the hall and heard Holly say she was going to the toilet. I hid among a throng of taller students headed in the opposite direction so she didn't see me. Then I doubled back and caught up with Jill.

"Hey," I said casually.

"Uh . . . hi—oof!"

I grabbed her by the hand and pulled her into a cleaning cupboard.

"What the hell?!" She pulled her hand away. "What's wrong with you?"

"We need to talk," I said.

"In a cupboard? Are you serious? I have class."

"Yeah, yeah, Jill, we all have class. You're not special. Look, I know about the article about Meabh."

"What article?" Jill asked. She was bad at playing it cool. Her voice sounded strained.

"The one about Meabh breaking her own ankle."

"How do you know about that?" she asked.

"I heard it around," I said. I couldn't show her the screenshot or she might suspect Orla, but there were plenty of people on the paper who could have blabbed.

"No one knows about that article but me."

And Holly. And Orla. But that wasn't enough people. She'd realise eventually if I didn't cover for Orla.

"I hacked into the system," I lied. "OK?"

She pursed her lips, skeptical of my abilities. "You can do that?"

"Yeah, I invented an . . . algorithm. I call it Flubberygiblets."

Jill rolled her eyes. "I'm going to German. I'll see you later."

"No! Please. I'll tell you the truth."

I really needed her. I couldn't see how anyone else could take the article down, other than the person who wrote it, the editor of the paper. This was my only chance.

She paused and I made one clarification.

"Off the record." Thank God I'd watched enough TV to know to do that.

Jill nodded reluctantly. Her journalistic curiosity was getting the better of her. Even if she wasn't going to be able to publish it, I'd just let her know I had a story of some kind.

"I've been doing favours for people. I fix something for them, and then they owe me one. One of my favours involved breaking into the computer system. Someone else did it for me because they owed me. That's how I saw the article."

"Bit convenient," she said doubtfully.

"I don't know what to tell you. It's the truth."

"Well, I still don't get why you needed to kidnap me."

"I need you not to print that article. It isn't true and it isn't fair. "

She folded her arms. "I have it on pretty good authority that it is true. I have a source."

"Who—"

Jill held up a hand. "Don't even bother. I would never tell you."

"Your source is wrong," I said. Technically that was true. "And come on, Jill, don't you think this is too far? Hasn't Meabh been through enough? Or do you hate her that much?"

Jill shifted her weight. "I don't hate Meabh. I mean, she's—"

"Annoying, yeah, I know." The word irritated me now.

"But I don't have a problem with her."

"If you print this, don't you think it's going to look like you've done it to help Holly win? Isn't that kind of unethical?"

She bit her lip and I smelled weakness. Time to swap my stick for a carrot.

"And I'll do you a favour," I said.

"I don't need anything," Jill replied.

"You don't *need* anything. But what about something I think you'd like?"

"And what would I like?"

I smiled. "Revenge?"

I texted Laura, the girl I'd got the pill for, and called in my chit. She was surprised to find that all I wanted was a piece of the letterhead and some literature from her dad's pharmacy, and promised to get it for me at lunch. That just left one person to get on board.

I found him leaning against the wall after school, waiting for the bus. He was alone, and a few feet away half the Gaelic team were surrounding Ronan as he ran his fingers through his blond curls and told a stupid story.

"Your cousin is a knob," I said.

He looked at me, smiled, and then dreamily stared off into the distance. "Sometimes I dream about smashing his face against a wall and watching the blood drip down the bricks."

I laughed, then I straightened my face. Dylan and I weren't friends exactly but we'd had a few classes together over the years.

"You have to spend a lot of time with him, though, don't you?"

"Every day after school. I go to his house and wait for my dad to pick me up after work."

"Your parents don't let you stay home by yourself?"

"Ronan and I used to be friends. I used to like going. I love my aunt. She's a bit of a Holy Joe but she's really good to me. I don't want to tell her what he's been doing."

"But your aunt is really strict, isn't she?"

It was one question too many. Dylan gave me a sidelong glance.

"Why do you care?"

I had nothing to lose. Except the last thing I needed to make sure that article went away. I took out an envelope and handed it to Dylan.

He took it, bewildered, and opened it up.

Crossan's Pharmacy
101 Castle Street
Ballyeden

Dear Ronan Walsh,

Due to your recent prescription for azithromycin, it is our pharmacy's policy to follow up with information regarding sexual health and well-being. Please find enclosed some literature on sexually transmitted infections and prevention.

If you require any further information or would like to speak to your pharmacist regarding sexual health you can drop in to our branch on Castle Street or you can visit the website.

A copy of this letter has been forwarded to your GP.

Kind regards,
Crossan's Pharmacy

Dylan looked up after reading it with the biggest grin on his face.

"Is this real?!" he hissed, keeping his voice low. Ronan and his friends weren't far away, though they were not paying any attention to us two losers. "Oh my God, his mam is going to kill him. She'll absolutely murder him. How did you get this?"

He was giddy with joy. Perfect. That was the petty energy I needed right now.

"It's not exactly real . . . but it could be."

He was less giddy now. He turned the envelope over.

"It's got a used stamp on it."

I'd nabbed a letter from the school office, steamed it open with a kettle from Home Economics, and then ironed it nice and straight. I'd put a blank label on top of the school's address and filled it in with Ronan's address.

"It's got *Mrs* Walsh on the front," Dylan said.

"Oops. Typo." I smiled serenely.

We exchanged meaningful looks. I nodded. Dylan nodded. A silence of understanding settled.

"Sorry, I don't get it," Dylan said.

I guess not.

"OK, you bring this letter with you to your aunt's house. You set it where she will see it. It has her name on the front so she'll open it and then . . ."

"Then Ronan will be in deep shit."

I was particularly pleased with finding a way to get back at Ronan for cheating on Jill *and* for the way he'd treated Ms Devlin. I wondered if he'd remember when he saw this, the way he'd tried to shame her for the exact same thing.

Dylan grinned. I realised I'd picked someone so fed up of Ronan's shit that I didn't need to offer him anything in return. He'd earned it, though.

"As payment for this favour, I will do something for you."

"What?"

"I'll make it so that everyone wants to be your friend."

Dylan raised his eyebrows. "I've heard about you, you know. Doing favours for people. Why are you doing this though? I didn't ask you for anything." He frowned then, "Did someone else ask you to set up Ronan?"

"Maybe," I said.

The humiliated ex-girlfriend would probably come to Dylan's mind sooner or later but I figured he'd be on her side anyway.

Dylan looked thoughtful. "Why do you do it?"

"I don't know." I shrugged. "I like helping people."

"There's lots of ways to help people. There's lots of people to help. Why this? Why do you want to fix their problems?"

I didn't know what to say to that, so I said the only thing that came to mind.

"Because I *can* fix *their* problems."

27

We had registration in an actual classroom on Wednesday morning because the drama club were setting up the hall for the debate the next day. I'd walked in on them first thing not realising we'd been moved and the stage had been built already. A large black grid had been lowered over it, and from what I could tell they were unscrewing some lights, moving them, and screwing in other ones. I heard a lot of talk about gels and parcans and a debate about whether a gobo would be tacky, whatever that meant. They obviously felt very important and were acting like they were professionals, wearing all black. One of them with a folder kept saying how they really needed to do a tech run with the candidates. The election had got totally out of hand as far as I was concerned. A debate, honestly. Who did we think we were?

Still, I was giddy to start the day because I had something fun planned for Dylan. He'd texted me a thumbs-up to let me know he'd planted the letter. Neither of us knew if there'd been any consequences yet. He said his aunt Donna hadn't noticed the letter by the time his dad came to pick him up.

I didn't have to wonder if she'd found it though. As soon as I entered the classroom Ronan and Ms Devlin were having it out. I took a seat near the front to watch. Everyone was watching it unfold.

Ms Devlin had her feet up on her desk and was leaning back in her chair. Her trainers were mucky and she was trying hard to look serious.

"Miss, this is totally unfair. She can't decide to stop me playing. You're the coach!" Ronan's face was ruddy with rage and he was barely keeping himself from shouting.

"Ah yes, Ronan, see, the funny thing is, as your mother, she is definitely allowed to stop you playing. I have no say in it."

"I'm sixteen," he protested. "Surely there's some kind of rule about me being old enough to decide for myself. Can't you please talk to her? Tell her I'm the best player. You need me."

A couple of the other boys from the team piped up then.

"Yeah, come on, miss, we need him."

"He's our midfielder, miss."

"Yeah, you lose midfield, you lose the match."

Ms Devlin shrugged, a jovial expression on her face, like she was enjoying this immensely.

"I'm afraid you overestimate my competitive spirit," she said. "Take it up with your mother, Ronan."

Ronan threw himself into his seat with mutinous glares at Ms Devlin, who appeared not to notice. I heard him say to the boy next to him, "If I ever find out how the fuck I got a letter from a pharmacy I've never been to . . ."

"Why didn't you tell your mam it was fake?"

"Of course I did. But she searched my room and found condoms. Didn't matter that if I was using condoms, then I wouldn't have the fucking clap, would I? She's just pissed I was getting the ride at all. Now I've to go to fucking Mass every morning and I'm going to be off the team for the final. We definitely would have made it this year."

A few of the boys clapped him on the shoulder in comfort.

I looked across the room to catch Jill's eye. Her lips were so tight I knew she was holding in a huge grin. She met my eye for a brief second and I knew that article would not be printed. At least this week. Holly was sitting beside her, and I wondered what she'd think when she realised it wasn't printed. Jill would lie and say she didn't know what happened. Would Holly still want to print it if she won on Friday? If it couldn't help her? If she lost she almost definitely would, out of spite. But that was something I'd have to deal with later. For now, Meabh was safe, and hopefully she was still in with a chance.

I glanced then at Meabh, who was highlighting parts of her manifesto and making notes, her nose all scrunched up. I didn't know if I was helping her win, but I wasn't going to let anyone make her lose.

*

Seeing as the PE hall was out of use for PE, Ms Devlin had agreed to let me use it during my free period to work on my project with Dylan. She was impressed that I was involved in "such a commendable endeavour," or whatever she called it.

"What is all this?" Dylan tapped a box with his foot.

"These are your supplies. These are going to make people forget about stupid Ronan's stupid prank."

"You think?" he said, not quite sure but optimistic. "It looks like a box of crap."

"Only if you have no imagination!" I said cheerfully. "These are what we need to set a world record."

He looked at me. I beamed.

"I'm going to need more information."

"Right. OK, so, I had a look at some of the easiest-to-beat world records. I thought we do a whole bunch of them and make you the guy who set like ten world records."

I watched his face for a reaction. He grinned, then it faded into a frown.

"Don't you need a Guinness person to come and watch?"

"Yes. *Technically.* Don't worry about that. It's a two-part plan. Part one: we set the records here, in school. Everyone hears about it. You become a huge sensation."

He raised his eyebrow at *sensation.*

"All right, well, it becomes a talking point. And then we rally support to make it like an event. Which leads to part two: we invite Guinness, and it becomes a whole school thing with everyone supporting you, because they've already seen you do it!"

Dylan chewed on the inside of his cheek. He inspected the boxes. I held my breath, afraid he'd say no. I really didn't have a better idea and I didn't want Ronan's foul mood to backfire onto Dylan, even if he never realised Dylan had been the one to plant the letter.

"It does appeal to the showman in me," he said finally, with a wink. "But how are we going to make sure everyone knows about it?"

"Don't you worry about that. It's sorted. You worry about *this*." I pointed at the box of items, most of which I'd pilfered from around the school. "I stole these eggs from the Home Ec room and I want to get rid of the incriminating evidence."

I helped Dylan unpack the first task onto a table tennis table I'd pulled from the storeroom: most eggs cracked with one hand in a minute.

Twenty minutes later we were dying with laughter. The video footage I took on my phone was so shaky from laughing, one of the tech guys who'd got interested in what we were doing agreed to hold it instead. But he started laughing so much that eventually we took a break so he could find a way to keep it steady. We ended up taping the phone to a mic stand with gaffer tape.

By the time the bell rang, Dylan had successfully:

Peeled an orange blindfolded in 15 seconds
Cracked 38 eggs with one hand in one minute
Blown a pea across 24 feet and 8.1 inches (something
    we all spontaneously cheered for)
Clipped 52 wooden pegs to his face.

Dylan failed to:

Type the alphabet on an iPad in fewer than 3.14 seconds
Peel more than 8 bananas in a minute
Hold more than 26 tennis balls in one hand
Assemble a Mr Potato Head in less than 16.17 seconds.

Afterwards he lay back on the floor, catching his breath. It was surprisingly sweaty work and he had pink marks all over his face from the pegs.

"Do you think this will really work?" he asked, sitting up.

"I do." I grinned. I wasn't even lying. "It's so funny. Everyone is going to love it."

"And it goes up tomorrow?" he asked, wiping his forehead.

"First thing," I said. "You're gonna be huge, *dahling*."

"Is everything sorted?" I asked Daniel. We met behind the prefab building and I was shivering and rubbing my hands together to try and prevent frostbite setting in. It was the kind of morning where you felt the cold get into your bones.

He nodded. "You got the text, didn't you?"

Daniel had accessed the school's records and sent a mass text to the student body with a link to the school paper's website and a countdown to just after 9 a.m. this morning.

"Yeah. It's definitely going to work though, isn't it?"

"Do you mean the link or the plan?"

"Both."

"The link is fine. It wasn't hard. The plan . . . well, the video is funny. I promise. Do you want to see it now?"

I shook my head. I didn't think that would help. It would just give me more specific things to worry about.

Stomach acid leaped around my stomach and I wasn't sure if it was nerves or missed breakfast.

"And the other thing?" I asked. I couldn't quite meet his eye. I watched a spider crawling out of a knot in the door frame behind him instead. Daniel took a folded sheet of paper out of his pocket and held it out to me. I hesitated before taking it.

"Thanks," I said, nodding.

He patted me on the shoulder and left.

I turned the piece of paper over and over. I'd asked Daniel to find out who had posted the video of Meabh. I'd confided in him that I thought it might be someone I knew but I had to find out for certain.

"Do you really think that's necessary?" he'd asked me.

"I need proof."

He said he'd trace the IP address to a location and get me the answer.

I knew it was just a video of Meabh being Meabh and honestly it made me laugh. I loved that she was that passionate. But it had hurt her and it had given people an excuse to make fun of her and talk about how annoying she was. I wanted so badly for it not to be Holly. Holly would never make up a fake story or spread false rumours. But she would use the truth against you. She could make you feel like it wasn't her fault that you were hurt because she hadn't lied.

Finally, nausea threatening to overcome me, I unfolded the sheet so hurriedly it ripped. I could still read what it said though.

I'm not the fucking CIA. You already know who did this.

I choked out a laugh and blinked back tears at the same time. He was right. I didn't need proof.

There was a buzz around the room. Everyone was waiting and curious. Holly and Jill were sitting at the back, heads bent together over Holly's beloved hard copy of the paper. It had come out that morning, without the offending article.

Holly was confused, but there was something else too that I struggled to identify.

Jill spread her hands. "I have no idea what happened! It was in the final draft!"

Holly saw me looking at them and I watched her consider

if this was my doing. I looked away quickly and took a seat near the front. Meabh was oblivious and examining what appeared to be notes for her speech.

Ms Devlin marched into class about five to nine and before even calling the register she folded her arms and stared us all down.

"As you know, today is the electoral debate between your candidates for student council president. Holly and Meabh. As both girls are in our own registration class I will expect you all to vote on Friday. However, I don't trust a single one of you, so just as the debate is now mandatory – and I will be taking attendance – in an equal show of mistrust, the voting tomorrow will happen during registration."

Holly winked at me and I knew she must have suggested this to Ms Devlin, like she said she would. She wanted Meabh's defeat to be as brutal as possible. I couldn't even muster a fake smile back. She'd been so busy the last few days I hadn't even needed to avoid her, but things would come to a head soon. It was like a rumble of thunder in the distance.

"Miss, you can't force people to vote. That's, like, fascist," Ronan said.

"Ah, much like with your mother deciding what sports you can and cannot participate in, school has its own peculiar rules."

"Miss, you can't—"

"Una Bannon?" Ms Devlin started calling the register over the sound of Ronan's complaints.

At 9:05 I heard the chiming of several alarms going off at once. Ms Devlin looked up, frowning.

"Ronan. Put your phone away. You too, Alison." She seemed more surprised than annoyed.

"But, misssss," Ronan whined, "the countdown."

She opened her mouth to cut him off but whatever she expected him to say, it wasn't that.

"What are you talking about?"

"The countdown clock."

Someone else piped up and filled her in on the text the whole school had received this morning. Alison held out her phone and Ms Devlin inspected it curiously. Seeing her resolve weaken, the class began a cajoling chorus of, "Please, miss, can we look. Come on, miss."

"Fine. But—" She held her hand up to silence the cheer. "I'm putting it up on the projector and we can all look together. You better hope this is suitable for school viewing or you're all in major shit. Phones away."

She got one of the boys to retrieve her rarely utilised laptop and connect it to the projector on the wall. I really hoped this wouldn't backfire. I was seized by a fear that people wouldn't think it was funny or they'd think Dylan was stupid. My heart only settled when the page came up on the projector and all I could see was a video of Dylan, the preview shot of which was him in a silent scream with fifty-two wooden pegs stuck to his face. Immediately a roar of laughter went up and even Ms Devlin looked amused.

Daniel had done a great job editing it. The background music was overly dramatic and orchestral and it made the whole thing even funnier. He had clipped out all the boring bits and included slow-motion replays of the best parts. By the end almost the whole class was cracking up. Ms Devlin had honest-to-God tears of laughter down her face. I didn't think I'd ever seen her laugh. I didn't think I'd seen any PE teacher in the world laugh. No one has.

Only Ronan didn't think it was funny. He was seething in the corner and when his friend leaned in, laughing, Ronan pushed him away so hard he fell off his chair. I snuck a peek at Holly and even she was giggling and pink in the cheeks. For a second it reminded me of her, but from a few years ago. There were times when we'd laughed so hard it had hurt our stomachs, over the kinds of things you tried to tell other people about but they never made them laugh because you had to be there. I felt a powerful ache, a longing to erase everything that had happened the last couple of years, the dirty, ugly mess our friendship had become. If I offered her a clean slate, would she take it? Or would she roll her eyes and pretend she didn't know what I was talking about?

Meabh looked around from her seat and mouthed at me, *This was you*. It wasn't a question. I winked and put a finger to my lips. She smiled and I forgot about Holly.

28

At the end of the day I stood at the back of the PE hall, my stomach twisting. I really wanted this to go well for Meabh.

We weren't the only class who were being forced to attend the debate. All fourth years and up were here, and Ms Devlin's first-year class. They were tiny and excitable and I felt very mature next to them until a teacher tried to usher me into sitting down because she mistook me for one of them.

As people piled into the room I heard snippets of conversations. Everyone was still talking about Dylan's video. By nine thirty in the morning there had been several GIFs and memes floating around, the most popular one including a shot of Dylan trying desperately to hold on to dozens of tennis balls in one hand, a look of extreme concentration on his face before they jumped out of his hand in every direction. It was the look on his face that made it. I'd been the one piling them on, but per my request, Daniel had cut me out of the shot. Someone had posted the whole video on social media and that had racked up over two thousand likes so far from people who weren't even at our school. I'd overheard one of the boys off the team asking him if he'd come back now that Ronan was benched. I'd smiled as I heard him shrug it off with disinterest. I was happy for him, but as soon as I knew that plan was working, my mind turned to the debate.

The blackout blinds, the ones the drama club used when they were putting on a show, had been drawn down, so the PE hall was quite atmospheric for three in the afternoon. The stage, which I had learned yesterday was made of rostra, was lit dramatically, with both footlights and parcans, and there were two fixed profile spots. I waved to my new drama tech friend from yesterday, who was sitting up in my balcony with a lighting desk and a grin on his face. His moment to shine had come. Or rather, his moment to make others shine.

Laura sidled up to me and hip-bumped me.

"That was you this morning, wasn't it?" she asked.

"I'm sure I don't know what you're talking about," I replied loftily.

"I'm glad. Someone needed to do something. Dylan was getting terrible shit for nothing. Now he's a hero. It's brilliant."

"How are things with the ex?" I asked.

She shrugged. "I'm so over it. I like someone else."

"Yeah?"

"Yeah, I don't really know him that well but he seems super sweet and he is such a ride. We did shots at Angela Berry's party. Well, I did, he just—"

353

"Can we please stop gabbing and take a seat, ladies?" Ms Devlin marched past.

"Coming?" Laura asked.

I was confused for a moment. Why would I come with her? Then I realised she meant for me to sit beside her for the debate.

"Sure," I said, trying not to sound surprised. You don't want other people to know your first thought is, *Why do you want to sit with me?*

We took two seats at the back beside her choir friends, who said hello in eerie harmony. In front of me Dylan was surrounded by people jostling to sit beside him. Laura pulled out a bag of popcorn and offered me some. In spite of all the fear I had about this stupid debate and what might happen, I laughed.

When the lights went down, I wasn't laughing any more. The twisting in my stomach was threatening to bring up that morning's toast. The vice principal came out onstage, squinting into the full-blast spotlight, and talked a bit about how wonderful it was to have a proper election and how that was what the democratic process was all about and some stuff about how the youth are more politically engaged than ever blah blah blah. He explained how the "event" would go and I thought the term *debate* had been applied rather loosely. When I thought about the debate I fully imagined Holly and Meabh at each other's throats, both of them shouting increasingly louder and ending in a fist fight or a knife battle, perhaps. As it turned out, they would each give a speech and some students would ask questions after. That was it. There wouldn't even be a winner.

"Bit tame for these two," Laura whispered to me.

Holly opened the "debate" with her speech. She talked a bit about her time at the school and on the paper and why she wanted to be student council president. She didn't go the anarchist route of promising people three-day weekends and free-pizza Mondays, which she obviously couldn't deliver, but she made some modest suggestions about little things she'd like to change. A student lounge in the old art building for sixth years, no uniforms for Junior and Leaving Cert students during exam weeks, bringing back the ski trip for transition years, that sort of thing.

I realised, watching her, that she didn't have to have amazing ideas that would make a significant impact. She had something better. She was funny. She made jokes that the whole room laughed at. She was charming and engaging. And she'd begun to realise she had this glow and it was something she could use.

The room cheered for Holly as she finished her speech. I wanted to close my eyes as Meabh walked up the steps and took her place. Her jaw was tight and her expression said *I can't believe you all think that was good. Idiots.*

I sent silent psychic messages to her, to loosen up, relax her shoulders, her jaw. I listened to the ideas she had and I could see that she'd put so much thought into everything.

For every idea she had, she gave reasons why it would work, how it would be easy for people to get on board with, how it would save the school money. But I knew that the rest of the room couldn't see what I saw. Someone so passionate she didn't know how to rein it in and tone it down. People around me were shifting in their seats or whispering to their friends. They were bored. Meabh didn't even seem to notice. She ploughed ahead and raced through a million different points. I knew it was because she thought they were all as important as each other and she had to let everyone know every detail even if it meant speaking at double speed.

I glanced at Laura. Her face was stuck in a kind of shell-shocked grimace. When she noticed me looking at her, she gave me a sympathetic look.

"She sounds really smart," Laura whispered to me. "She knows what she's talking about."

She did not have to say, *But no one cares, they're bored stiff.*

When Meabh finished, there was a beat before people began to clap. They were so tuned out I don't think they realised it was over.

When the applause had died, Ms Devlin stood up at her table and clapped for both Holly and Meabh and congratulated them.

"Now we'll have questions from our audience. Anyone, any questions for the candidates? Don't be shy."

One of the first years put her hand up and Ms Devlin pointed at her to speak.

"What would you most like to change about the school?"

Immediately, I could tell that this was a prepped question. It didn't even make sense, seeing as they'd both already talked about things they'd change.

Holly beamed and Meabh rolled her eyes. I winced. I didn't think she realised she did that as often as she did. It was like every feeling she had was written all over her. She couldn't help it. And unfortunately most of her feelings were being infuriated with other people's stupidity.

She must find me so annoying

And yet, never once had Meabh made me feel like that. At least not since diorama-gate. I could probably let that go after all these years. Holly, on the other hand, a perfect performer, made me feel like that all the time.

"I mean, apart from a hot tub in the gym, which I think might be a long shot" – Holly paused for the laugh – "I would love to see our school embrace a more inclusive spirit. There are too many groups and gangs and cliques that make people feel like they don't belong. Our school should be a family. You might not get along with every single person all the time, but when you're family, you're always welcome."

Meabh rolled her eyes again and I could see her mutter to herself. So could everyone else, of course, if they were looking at her. I knew what she was thinking. What the hell did that even mean?

Meabh didn't let people clap for that. Before they could get going she leaned into her microphone.

"As I said before, I have multiple areas I would like to address, but if we are going to talk about inclusion then I think we need to look at our admittance criteria, which unfairly disadvantages people from lower-income communities. We need to address at a systemic level what we are doing to encourage a more diverse student body, especially those who have not had the advantage of attending one of the feeder schools in higher-income neighbourhoods."

No one was sure whether to clap now or not. After a silent moment Ms Devlin called on another first year with her hand up. I had the impression that the first years had all been tasked with thinking of a question to ask.

"What have been the good parts and the bad parts about running for president?"

"It's been a lot of work," Holly said with a laugh that felt like she was confiding in the whole audience. "I had to write proposals to hand in, I had to write a speech, I had to quit the paper, which was really hard."

I was impressed that Holly didn't show one ounce of bitterness. There was no side-eye, no hint of a snide tone.

"But it's also been fun. I got to challenge myself to really think about what would make the school better, I got to learn a lot from the student council advisor and, my favourite part, I got to have posters of my face everywhere. Lads, do you know how fun that is, to have everyone talking about you? I feel famous!" She finished with a chuckle that let everyone know she was only joking and that of course all the hard work was the reward and posters are silly.

Meabh looked mutinous. Her brush with fame in this election cycle had not been fun and I had to wonder if Holly had brought it up to rub it in.

"It's been really difficult and stressful," she said, "but it's something I care so much about that it's worth it."

I thought about Meabh having to endure teasing, knowing that people were making fun of her for her admittedly sometimes excessive enthusiasm. For her "annoying" personality. For the kind of thing people had always hated about her when it was just who she was. I thought about how I wasn't there for her when it happened and how I hadn't faced her since. I thought about how I'd done the same thing to Kavi, telling him I had never wanted him around when all he wanted was a friend.

"One more question?" Ms Devlin asked the room.

And then the bell rang.

The debate. The election. Our school. There were only a handful of people in the room left who cared, and everyone else was already halfway out the door.

29

I left school deflated and pissed off. Meabh hadn't done herself any favours in that debate, and she didn't even realise it. She was going to lose. I barely remembered getting home, I was so lost in mulling over the debate. I tried in my mind to soften Meabh, manipulate the memories to convince myself it wasn't so bad. I knew I was lying to myself though. I thought about how much work she'd put in. I'd watched her writing and rewriting policies, sweating over them on the PE balcony, and I knew that was only a fraction of what she'd really done. And she'd never played dirty with Holly. She wanted to beat her on the issues.

I knew Holly had done horrible things, but when had she become a person who could justify those actions just because she didn't like someone? Then again, I'd listened to her say terrible things about Meabh for years. Their stupid rivalry was this thing that had always been there in the background. The two of them endlessly competing or sniping at each other. And I'd been there too. I'd been just as bad. I'd been the kind of person who thought it was OK to let my best friend say whatever she wanted about Meabh, even when it was mean or unfair, because you hate the people your best friend hates. That's the rule.

But if I hadn't noticed my part in this problem, maybe Holly hadn't realised how bad she'd gotten either.

I caught myself. I was doing it again.

Somehow my mind always jumped to making excuses for her. I still wanted to find a way that it wasn't her fault. As I walked home I tried to figure out why I did that. Why did I always want to see the best in her and ignore the worst?

Then the voice came, like it always did, when I least wanted to hear it.

If you accept that there's a problem, then you have to do something about it.

I was almost home but I turned instead and headed in the opposite direction, sending a text and not waiting for a reply.

Holly came downstairs already changed into sweatpants and a T-shirt. She looked soft and happy and she beamed when she saw me.

"Come upstairs," she said. Wordlessly I followed her up to her room. It was so familiar and yet strange at the same time. I'd spent so many nights here and this was the first time I felt out of place.

She curled up on her bed with her feet underneath her.

"Are you OK?" she asked, seeing my face. She sounded worried. She wriggled over and patted the space beside her.

It made me want to cry. There was a part of me that wanted to cuddle up with her. Put on a movie and play footsie and pretend like nothing had happened. I sat on the end of the bed instead.

"What's going on?" she said, and I saw her realise that something was off with me.

"I'm going to vote for Meabh."

She wasn't expecting that.

"Why?" She looked genuinely hurt. I felt tears well up and my throat burn. This was so sad and it was so horrible and I didn't want to do it.

"I think she deserves it," I said. "And it's awful of me to only tell you that now. And it's a horrible way for me to tell you that I can't be your friend any more."

I hoped she'd shout at me. I'd betrayed her, after all. I'd slept with the enemy, so to speak.

"Why?" was all she said again, in a small voice like a little girl.

"You know why." I blinked back tears. "You don't like me. You talk to me like I'm stupid. I know I'm stupid but you talk to me like I am and it hurts. You don't want to be around me any more and I am sick of feeling like I'm a burden to you. I feel like you're only friends with me because you think you have to be."

"That's not true," Holly protested. She scrambled towards me and took my hands. "I know I can be a dick sometimes, but that's not true. You're my best friend."

I took my hands out of hers and folded my arms, leaving her hands lying limply in her lap.

"You don't treat me like I am. You talk down to me. You leave me out of things. You don't even notice when I'm not around." Tears were streaming down my face and I was acutely aware of how everything I was saying was so embarrassingly needy and childish.

Holly reached out and wiped some of my tears away with the back of her hand. I wanted to grab it and press it against my heart but I didn't.

"I'm sorry I haven't been a good friend," she said, a pleading note in her voice. "I swear I'll be better. I don't want to hurt you."

"It's too late for that."

"I can be nice to Meabh. I know you like her. I can learn to like her too." She offered the words up like a last hope.

I shook my head. "I know you put that video up. And I know about the article you told Jill to write."

She blinked. "How do you know?"

She didn't deny it. I appreciated that. Maybe she knew there was no point. Maybe she saw that I had no time left for pretence.

"As soon as I heard about it, I knew it was you." I hadn't wanted to admit it then but when I got that note from Dylan, I stopped lying to myself.

She at least looked ashamed, her cheeks turning pink. She couldn't quite look at me.

"I didn't know it would be so popular. I took it down when I saw the comments were getting bad."

"I know." I sometimes thought Holly did things without really thinking about the consequences. I hoped that seeing the consequences had made her think. That wasn't enough though. "How did you know about Meabh? About her ankle?"

"I heard her ask you," she admitted. "I came back inside to fill my water bottle and I heard you two talking. The hall was empty. I didn't mean to listen but it wasn't hard to overhear. When I saw that boy Kavi coming I hid in the store downstairs."

"Why didn't you say anything?"

"I don't know," she said, and it felt like she really didn't know. She struggled to figure it out. "I guess I wanted you to tell me. And then you didn't and I was annoyed that you didn't. I don't know. It was stupid." She looked at her hands and then she started crying too.

"I was the one who took it down. Jill didn't know." I didn't want to drop Jill in it. Her friendship with Holly was her own thing to work out.

"I figured you called in a favour somehow. I realised then that you liked her. I don't know how I didn't see it before."

"Please don't publish it after . . ." I said. After the election. After she was president.

Holly nodded. "I told her to keep you out of it, you

364

know. Jill, I mean. In the article." She twisted her hands and paused. "Doesn't that count for something?"

"I don't know."

She wiped her eyes and took a deep breath. "Is there anything I can do to fix things between us?"

I wanted to say yes. I thought the answer was no.

"I don't know," I said. But I let her hold my hand for a while.

I left Holly, heartbroken and confused. I thought I would feel better after I spoke to her. That it would be a release. I didn't. It wasn't. Things felt more messy than ever. Could someone treat you badly and still love you? Someone could treat you badly and *you* could still love *them*, so maybe the reverse was true too. But just because you loved someone, it didn't mean you had to give them another chance. Or maybe that's exactly what it meant. I thought about it the whole way home. I didn't come up with an answer. Exhausted, even though it wasn't even five p.m., I trudged up the stairs, weighed down by my heavy heart.

Mam was asleep on the sofa.

She hadn't hidden the bottle of wine this time.

Maybe she'd hidden the first one, the second one even.

I put a blanket over her and kissed her forehead.

30

For the second time that day I turned around and left my house. I choked back more tears, feeling like I had enough to drown myself with. I couldn't fix things with Holly. I couldn't help my mother, not tonight. But there was something left. Something I could fix, someone I could help. Or I could at least try.

"Thank you for meeting me," I said.

Kavi was stony-faced and he sat back on the bench on the balcony. I listened to the sounds of the school basketball team practising below. Then I realised I had to say the actual words.

"I'm sorry," I said.

He looked at me.

"OK, you want more."

His face very clearly said *duh*.

"You were right. I was not treating you like my friend even though you've been the best, most attentive friend I've had in years. I think I resisted it because I feel like I don't deserve a good friend like you."

He opened his mouth to interrupt but I didn't let him.

"And I'm not saying that so you feel sorry for me or forgive me because I'm pathetic or whatever, I'm only saying it because I want to let you in. You aren't going to do all the talking any more."

Kavi stood and then wrapped his arms around me and pulled me into one of his hugs. I squeezed him back and he kissed me on the top of my head.

"Is that it?" I asked when we broke apart. "I really thought you were going to make me work harder for it."

"Why would I punish you?" he said, bemused. "I know you mean it."

I loved him for being like that and I promised myself I would never, ever take advantage of it again.

"OK," I said, clapping my hands together. "We need to do something about Meabh."

"Agreed." Kavi nodded quickly. "That debate was terrible. Do you think she knows it was terrible?"

"I think she knows people weren't responding to her the same way they responded to Holly, but I'd hazard a guess she thinks that's their fault."

"Is she right?"

"In an ideal world, people would pick her because she's the best. This is not that world and she needs to start realising it now."

"Are we going to tell her that now?" he said uncertainly.

"Dear God, man, are you wise? She's at a breaking point. She might stab us both and eat our bones and bathe in our blood. That's an awkward conversation for another day. I have a different, probably doomed plan for right now, but I don't know how we'll get it all done ourselves."

"Tell me what it is and we'll figure it out."

It wasn't revolutionary and it wasn't a trick or a scheme with any kind of guaranteed success. It was good old-fashioned door-to-door canvassing.

In January.

In the rain.

On foot.

With no materials.

Or addresses.

Instead of walking downstairs and running out of the hall without looking back, Kavi looked thoughtful.

"I think we can do it," he said. "But I don't think we can do it alone."

"You're right, we can't do it alone," I said. "But I know some people we can call."

"I didn't know you helped that girl," Kavi whispered to me, pointing at Laura behind the palm of his hand.

"Yeah, so?"

"She's belly shot girl."

I snorted. Some choir girl!

The group were watching us expectantly.

"I hope there's a good reason I'm hanging out with a bunch of fourth years." Angela tossed her hair over her shoulder. The assembled party gazed back at her with a tinge of awe. "Oh, I know you. You did that video. It was funny actually. Fair play."

Dylan blushed.

I stood up and twisted my fingers. Why was I so nervous about this? The worst that could happen was they said no.

"I want you all to know that you're not obligated," I said. "You can all leave if that's what you want. I'm not blackmailing you or anything. There's no consequences for saying no. I won't use it against you. You are all entirely paid up. You don't owe—"

"Oh, for God's sake, spit it out!" Angela groaned.

"We need your help," Kavi said. Like the words weren't buried deep down, weighted with anchors, too heavy to float out into the air.

Laura, Orla, Dylan, Daniel Something, and even Angela waited for more. They didn't protest or run out of the room.

"OK," I said slowly, feeling like I was walking into a trap for some reason. "The election is tomorrow. You all saw what happened this afternoon. I want to help Meabh Kowalska win the election and I want to go out tonight and knock on doors and tell people about the good things she'll do and why they should vote for her."

I held my breath for the rejection.

"And you want us to go too?" Laura asked. I tried to find the indignation in her tone, but she sounded like she wasn't sure what I was asking.

"Well, yes. If you want to."

"Yeah, definitely. She did the worst Scottish accent in history for me." Daniel grinned.

"She changed my tyre," Angela said thoughtfully, "and I find her hilarious. Did you see that video of her with the coffee cup? She's an icon."

"I changed your—" Kavi started, but I elbowed him. Meabh helped. That counted.

"She helped me—" Orla started.

"Uh, let's maybe not say what she helped you with," I interrupted quickly. Orla grinned.

My heart swelled seeing all these people talk about Meabh so positively. Even after the cup incident. I wished she could have heard it.

"I'm on board," Dylan said. "I was going to vote for her anyway. Holly is full of shit." Then he glanced at me. "Aren't you her BFF or whatever though? Why are you doing this? Did she ask you to throw the election for her or something? I *knew* she didn't really want to be president."

"No," I replied. "Nothing like that. I think Meabh deserves to win. That's all."

"Definitely makes a stronger point than a letter," Angela said, raising one eyebrow. Then she held up her hands. "No judgement."

"Anyway," I said loudly. "We need you guys to come out and canvass with us. But to do that we need the home addresses of all the senior students. Fourth years and up."

Daniel's head popped up from his phone and he saluted. "On it."

"Hitting all those houses is going to take a lot more than just us. Laura, do you think you can rope your choir into it?"

She thought about it. "Most of them maybe. My dad's pharmacy sponsored our robes this year, so I could guilt them into it."

"Whatever it takes."

"We need to print of a tonne of flyers with the main points on them." I looked at Orla, who nodded. "On recycled paper," I added apologetically.

"We have some in the office," she said.

"What about me?" Dylan asked.

"You're my star recruit. You're the most likeable fella in school right now. You're the celebrity endorsement."

Angela snorted. I figured her eighteen thousand Instagram followers would have an issue with that.

"Let. Me. Guess," Angela drawled. "You want me to be your chauffeur?"

"Not at all," I said, hand to heart. "I'm shocked you would think that."

She raised an eyebrow.

"I want *you* to let *me* drive so we all make it through the evening alive," I continued.

Angela gave me a death stare.

"I'm kidding. Sort of. I was hoping you could do some live stories for us on your social media?"

She narrowed her eyes at me, fully aware that although I might genuinely want her support on social media, I also really didn't want her to drive but I still needed her car. I held my breath.

"Yeah, go on, then."

Meabh's house made me nervous. Standing on her doorstep and ringing the bell put me right back at being seven years old with my not-good-enough diorama, and I prayed that her dad wouldn't answer. Did he stay at school late?

Meabh's face was furious when she saw me on her doorstep. It was the face I was afraid of.

"Can I come in, please?" I asked, meek as I could manage.

She said nothing but stepped back and led me upstairs. It was weirdly reminiscent of earlier, with Holly. Though that felt like a million years ago. I followed her and she opened the door to her room.

There was a framed photo of Hillary Clinton on the wall and papers all over the desk and floor. I counted seven mugs of half-drunk tea or coffee dotted around the room. One wall was completely dedicated to what appeared to be a straight-up murder board. It was covered in different-coloured index cards. I peered at them and realised they were her plans. The blue ones were headed by the title

"Polish Language reform". I skipped that. The green ones were predictably "The Green Initiative". A lilac one read "A community school or a school for the community; introducing social and educational outreach". When I looked at the papers spread around I realised they were largely made up of research papers and were highlighted within an inch of their life.

Meabh sat in her desk chair and waited.

"Not very environmentally friendly," I joked.

She didn't laugh.

OK, now was not the time.

"I'm sorry," I said. "I ignored all your messages and that was so rude and I'm sorry and I was a terrible friend and it's even worse because you know . . . well, you know." I realised I'd accidentally acknowledged the possibility of something more between us and neither of us had really said that out loud. I suppose saying "you know" wasn't exactly bursting into song and saying I love you, but it was the closest I'd gotten to saying *I think I might like you in a more-than-friend way and I think you might feel that way too on account of some moments we've had.*

Meabh didn't shout. She did something much worse. She burst into tears.

Not again.

"Why does no one ever like me?" she wailed. It was very dramatic and almost made me laugh.

"I do. I do like you," I insisted. "I like you a lot."

"No you don't."

"I do."

"You don't."

"I do."

"You think I'm annoying," she said. "Everyone thinks I'm annoying."

"Yeah. So? I still like you."

"People were so mean. I think it was mostly joking . . . But they seemed to forget I am a human being, you know? They were making jokes about everything. Even my haircut, for God's sake."

"I like your hair," I said, and I privately congratulated myself on being smooth with the ladies. *I like your hair.* That was going to go down in history as one of the great lines.

She looked at me again and smiled. It was a shy sort of smile. I wanted to feel that smile under my lips.

"Your ideas were really good today," I said. "You'd be a good dictator."

"You made them better," she said. "I'd need you as an advisor."

"What? Are you telling me that you aren't perfect?!"

"Maaaybe."

"Dictators are traditionally not open to a lot of input," I said, feigning confusion.

"I'm sure they have private advisors."

"No, they don't."

"Yeah, they do."

"Doubt it."

"Probably though."

We both laughed. Meabh's smile faded quickly.

"I'm still kind of mad at you."

"I get that," I said. "But I have a surprise for you. Come downstairs."

She followed me out of her house. The car was parked just outside her front door.

Angela was already filming a live video. Orla had a box of flyers on her lap, Daniel Something was in the boot and Laura was sitting on Kavi's knee and he was spitting out stray wisps of blonde hair. He didn't look upset about it. There was space for Meabh to squeeze in beside them. We probably wouldn't die.

"What is going on?" she asked. I barely heard her because I was concentrating on how she'd taken my hand and was pulling me back into the hallway, out of sight of the car.

"We're canvassing. We have over a hundred houses to hit so you'd best get your arse in the car." I looked at her bare legs; she didn't shave and I could see fuzzy hairs sticking up in the cold. "Well, maybe put some clothes on and then get your arse in the car."

She blushed and looked down at her feet.

"Why are you doing this?" she asked.

"You know why," I said.

"Because you like to help people?"

"Nah."

"Because you believe in my platform?"

"God no," I joked.

She smirked. "Why, then?"

"Cos I fancy you. I'm hoping that if I go to all this effort you'll look at me and think, *Well, she might be a dumbass, but she tries*. And then, I dunno, maybe you'll flash me or something."

She laughed out loud at that. "That is not why."

"It is," I said earnestly. "I think you'll flash me."

"You do not."

"I do."

"You don't."

"I really do."

"You—"

I cut her off with a kiss. I didn't think about it, I just leaned in and held the back of her head gently. Her lips parted and she kissed me back. My other hand wrapped around her waist and I pulled her close so I could feel the length of her body press against mine. The kiss deepened and I felt a sense of urgency. Like I'd been wanting to kiss her for so long that it had burst out of me and now I could barely control it.

A honk of the horn brought us back to reality, just as I was feeling the urge to throw her down on her own stairs and kick this thing up a notch. We were both breathless and caught by surprise. I'd expected something soft, quick, gentle. But I got heat. Of course I got heat. Meabh didn't do anything without passion.

She looked at me, dumbfounded for a second and slightly glazed over. Then she shook herself and frowned.

"Did you kiss me to shut me up?"

"Yes, and if I'm going to do it again, I'm going to need to get a stepladder," I said, rubbing the back of my neck.

"Or we could just do it lying down next time," she said archly, and my heart sped up. In a single second I pictured one thousand different scenarios of me and Meabh kissing. Most of them involved the memory I had of her in her underwear.

"Come on," Angela called out. "Are we doing this thing or what? People are waiting for my next update, you know."

I squeezed Meabh's hand, then let go and walked out of the house towards the car.

"Jeez, Angela. Don't be such a clam jam," I muttered, as I climbed into the driver's seat again.

"I'm going to get some trousers," Meabh said, waving sheepishly to everyone and pointing upstairs. At that moment, however, Mr Kowalski appeared from the kitchen. For a second he looked alarmed at the assembled party in his driveway. Then as he looked closer and saw that we were all students from school, his alarm grew.

"What's going on here?"

"Uh, we're doing our civic duty, sir," Kavi said. "We're canvassing for Meabh tonight."

He turned to the staircase where Meabh looked back at him meekly.

Mr Kowalski frowned. "Meabh, you don't need to do this. The best person will win."

It was clear from the adoration in his voice that he thought that was Meabh. And of course, she was his daughter, so why wouldn't he think that? But it dawned on me from the way Meabh cringed that Mr Kowalski was not a secret tyrant. He was something more complicated than that. He thought Meabh was perfect. And that was far too much for her to live up to. When I thought of her weird schedule I wondered suddenly if it wasn't that Mr Kowalski had forbidden Meabh from quitting anything, it was that Meabh had simply never been able to tell her dad that every new thing she picked up to impress him was another burden she had to carry. Giving something up had to be beyond her control. She couldn't quit because that would make her a failure. And perfect girls don't fail.

"I just want to know I did everything I could," she said.

"Go on then, pumpkin." He smiled indulgently. Then he peered in through the car window. "Aideen Cleary, do you even have a driving licence?"

I pretended not to hear that and shouted to Meabh that we'd turn the car around and meet her at the end of the drive. I rolled up the window and reversed out of the drive as cautiously as I possibly could, Mr Kowalski's eyes burning holes in the back of my head the entire time.

*

Six hours later we'd hit 78 houses out of 119. Orla had arranged the addresses by Eircode so we would hit the most amount of people with the least amount of wasted time. The choir had taken half the list and their own van to hit one side of town, though Laura stayed with us, announcing airily that she and Kavi would work together.

So for five hours we tumbled out of the car, walked up to doors in pairs and said our bit, then moved on to the next house until everyone in that area had been spoken to. Then we all piled back in the car and drove to the next most densely populated area. Some students were very confused about what we were doing. Some students promised to vote for Meabh without question, though I couldn't tell if it was to get rid of us or not. Some said they were going to vote for Holly anyway. A few hadn't even realised there was an election on. But others actually changed their mind. One house in particular stuck out to me.

"My name is Meabh Kowalska and I'm here to ask you to vote for me in tomorrow's election."

The boy shook his head. "Sorry. No offence but I'm voting for Holly."

He tried to close the door but Meabh stuck her boot in the way. I bit my lip.

"Can I ask why that is?"

He shrugged.

"You must have a reason," Meabh said impatiently.

He threw his hands up. "You're mean."

Meabh scoffed.

"Mean how exactly?"

"You shout at people all the time. It's scary. You threw a cup at someone because they put it in the wrong bin."

"Hey—" I started to tell him to shove his vote up his arse but Meabh put her hand on my arm.

"What do you care about, Justin?"

"Huh?"

"What do you care about more than anything else in the whole world?"

Slightly bewildered, he said, "My Switch."

Meabh closed her eyes, gathering patience and then opened them. "OK. Justin. Imagine I walk into your house right now, up to your bedroom, and I find your Switch and I throw it out the window where it breaks and it can't be repaired."

He nodded. "OK?"

"Now, how would you react? Would you be angry? Would you shout?"

He mumbled something affirmative.

Meabh was getting more annoyed. I thought about stepping in or trying to calm her down but fuck it, she was right. Maybe someday she'd have to learn to control her cup-throwing urges but it wasn't my job to change her and apologising for her would be telling her I didn't like who she was.

"Now imagine it's the last Switch. There are no more

Switches. You can never again buy and sell cabbages in Animal Crossland. Wouldn't you be furious?"

He squinted at her, taking it in. "Yeah, I guess I'd be pretty raging," he admitted.

Meabh smiled her *I just won an argument* smile and the boy made a go-on gesture.

"All right. Tell me about the environment or whatever."

At midnight a dad chased us off his drive and we realised we had to stop. We got in the car one last time and I drove everyone home. Angela told me to drive the car into school tomorrow and she'd get it then. Meabh cried again and thanked everyone. The girl had a lot of emotions. Kavi tackled her for a hug first, squeezing her so tight she coughed. Then everyone piled on at once. I got smushed by all the bodies but that was OK because I was so happy for Meabh to see that she could be herself and still find people who'd show up for her.

When we dropped Laura off she smiled at Kavi as she got off his lap and out of the car. "You have my number," she said, leaning in through the window. He nodded, somewhat dumbfounded.

I wanted to leave Meabh off last and sneak up to her bedroom and have her give me a lecture about how to correctly get her off, but tonight was not the night. I needed to go home. I still had to look after my mother.

31

In registration the next morning I ticked the box next to Meabh's name, walked over to the folding table Ms Devlin had set up, and dropped it in the slot of a shoebox. It wasn't very ceremonious. Meabh was hovering near the tables, trying to crane her neck and see who voted for her. She narrowed her eyes at people giving her dirty looks and I had to pull her away and remind her that they were not giving her those looks because they didn't vote for her but because she was crawling up their arse and making them uncomfortable. I caught Holly's eye a couple of times. Her eyes were puffy and red and seeing that made me want to cry again, so I stopped looking. I was relieved when the bell rang.

I squeezed Meabh's hand as she went off to Physics and tried to calm the butterflies. In my head I counted all the people last night who'd said they'd vote for Meabh. Then I tried to count all the ones who I thought had meant it. I texted the others and asked them how many they thought were going to vote for Meabh. They sent me back variations on the theme of *I don't know* or in Angela's case, *Stop asking me this, I'm not bloody psychic.*

Meabh was too nervous to eat lunch so Kavi and I sat on the steps in front of the entrance and ate his father's homemade bacon and egg muffins while Meabh paced up and down. I'd suggested behind the prefab for lunch but Meabh argued she wouldn't hear the announcement from there.

"They're not going to broadcast it over the speakers," I said.

Meabh shrugged, a tense jerky shrug. She was too wound up even to speak.

Ten minutes before the end of break, Ms Devlin walked out of the doors.

"There you are. I've been looking for you," she said to Meabh. "Come with me."

Meabh looked stricken. It didn't stop her from shooting me an I-told-you-so stare, which I took to mean if we'd been behind the prefab, Ms Devlin wouldn't have found us there. Kavi and I scrambled up and Ms Devlin shot us a look.

"I don't need you two."

"That's OK, we don't mind," I said.

"You have class in a few minutes," she said firmly.

I held my hands up and fell back. When Meabh looked for me over her shoulder, I mouthed, *We're right behind you.*

We followed ten steps behind the whole way and when we arrived at Ms Devlin's office, I could see that Holly was already inside. Ms Devlin started when she saw us.

"I thought I said you had class," she snapped.

"Yeaaah," I said, like it was obvious. "We're on our way there now."

"There are no classrooms over here except mine."

Kavi and I exchanged a glance.

"Huh . . . weird."

Then she sighed and, deciding to ignore us, guided Meabh into her office. Kavi and I pressed our ears against the door.

"Like old times," he whispered.

"It was two weeks ago."

"Old times." He smiled wistfully.

Ms Devlin's clipped PE voice carried through the door. I could tell she was trying to temper any heightened emotions with her no-nonsense attitude.

"I wanted to let you both know the result before we announce it. You've both done exceptionally well and it was very close. I don't know if that makes it better or worse, but only eighteen votes separated you."

I closed my eyes.

"Holly, you will be the next student council president."

I didn't want to open my eyes but I could hear shuffling and footsteps that told me if I didn't move I was going to get a door to the face.

Kavi, Meabh, and I sat up on the balcony. Meabh pulled her knees up to her chest and wrapped her arms around them. She'd discarded the boot across the room and she didn't even limp when she wasn't wearing it. I waited until she was ready to speak.

"I'm so embarrassed," she said. "I worked so hard and I did everything I could and it came down to people not liking me."

"It came down to eighteen votes. Out of four hundred," Kavi pointed out.

"It should have been a landslide. I was the better candidate. I could have done so much good."

"I know you. You still will. You won't let a silly thing like losing get in the way," I said.

She burst into tears.

"What is it?" I asked, alarmed. "Should I not have mentioned the L-word?"

"It's not that." She shook her head. "It's that you're right. I will still try and do it all even though I'm not the president."

"What's wrong with that?"

"I'm so fucking tired," she sobbed. She cried for a few more moments. Kavi rubbed her back, and I held her hand. Then she sucked in a huge breath and wiped her eyes with her free hand. She looked at me with a guilty expression. "When Ms Devlin said that I didn't win, a tiny part of me was glad. I thought, *Thank God, I already have too much to do.* And then I felt the whole weight of it all crashing back down on top of me. My foot is healed. Dad's going to expect me to go back to camogie. Mam's going to want me to go back to yoga. To 'relax'. I have a cello exam in six weeks. And . . . and I was hoping I'd get to spend some time with you."

I gave myself a second to let that all wash over me.

"Maybe you should focus on your own problems for a while instead of fixing the whole world," I said. "You should talk to your dad."

"He won't understand."

I thought about how he looked at her like she was sent straight from heaven to make his life worth living.

"I don't think that's true. I think you're afraid of disappointing him. But the worst thing that can happen is he's disappointed. He'll get over it. You broke your own ankle. Doesn't that tell you something?"

"Hah." Meabh laughed bitterly. "I guess. What if he looks at me differently, though? What if he doesn't understand?"

"Then we'll figure something out from there. Between the three of us we'll work something out."

"But then I'm letting everyone down who would benefit from my ideas." She seemed genuinely distraught at the thought.

"That's one way to look at it." I smothered a smile. "Or perhaps we're not the only people in the world who can do things. We've done stuff. We've already helped people. But before we tackle the rest of the world, I think we need to sort out our own shit."

"We?" she asked.

"Yeah. Me too. My life's a disaster. I'm running around fixing other people's problems, and that's not a bad thing, but my own life is on fire. I'm failing every class. And . . ." I hesitated. If I said this part out loud, there would be no taking it back. "And my mam is drinking again. If I tell anyone, there'll be a social worker at my door before I know it and I don't know what will happen then."

I watched Meabh and Kavi take in what I'd said. I saw the pieces click into place for Kavi. Meabh nodded slowly. I held my breath and for a second all I could hear was my heart beating. All I could feel was fear that I'd said too much.

"Then we'll figure something out from there," Meabh said firmly.

Kavi nodded, and he reached over Meabh and squeezed my shoulder. "We'll be here, whatever happens."

We sat together for a few minutes. And then Holly appeared on the balcony. She looked young and vulnerable and I felt like I had too much power in this space, with my friends. But it wasn't me she wanted to talk to.

"Meabh?" Holly's voice was so small.

Ever the professional, Meabh stood up, in one shoe and one socked foot.

"Congratulations, Holly. I should have said so before."

"I don't deserve it," Holly replied, and she didn't wait for a response. "I was wondering if you maybe wanted to work together. Share the seat?"

I don't know who was more stunned. Me or Meabh.

"Holy shit," Kavi said.

Meabh looked back at us. I shrugged.

"Thanks for the offer, Holly," Meabh said, "but I think I'm going to have to say no."

I asked Meabh and Kavi to meet me at the end of the day. I didn't want to go home and talk myself out of it.

Meabh squeezed my hand. "I can come in if you want."

I shook my head. "If you come in, then I'll just let you do the talking."

"We'll be right here," she said, and they both slid down the wall outside Ms Devlin's office and sat.

"You can listen at the door if you want," I offered.

Meabh wrinkled her forehead. "Why would we do that? That's weird."

"Hah, yeah. Just kidding."

Kavi and I exchanged a look. I knocked on the door and I swallowed hard to stop from throwing up.

"Come in," Ms Devlin said. She was marking papers and she seemed surprised to see that it was me. "What now? Have you come down with a case of . . . of . . ." She waved her hands, reaching for an obscure illness.

"Flubberygiblets?" I supplied.

"That's not a real one," she said, pointing her pen threateningly at me. "It better not say that on your next note. There's only so much I can take, Aideen."

"It's not that, miss," I said.

"Well, what is it, then?" She looked at me, her face expectant, open.

Did I trust her?

I sat down in the chair opposite her and said what I had to say.

"I need help."

Acknowledgements

I love reading the acknowledgements but when I write them I feel like a tearful starlet at the Oscars and I'm far too grumpy to be this earnest, so I'll keep it as brief as I can.

With thanks to Steph because she has to listen to me have a crisis twice a week.

To my parents for being embarrassing about my books on Facebook and in public, I know you can't help it.

To the wonderful team at Andersen Press. Chloe, my UK editor and all round star, to Rob Farrimond and Paul Black who get two thank yous because I hadn't met them this time last book. Thanks as well to Sarah Kimmelman, Jack Noel, Jenny Hastings and Charlie Sheppard.

Thank you so much to Spiros Halaris, Jenna Stempel-Lobell and Catherine Lee for the beautiful cover.

As ever thanks to my magnificent agent Alice Williams, having someone you trust to sort out the things you don't understand or feel too awkward to mention is invaluable.

I also want to thank wonderful friends, kind authors and beloved readers who supported my last book by reading, pre-ordering, blurbing, reviewing, buying and borrowing.

It means the world to me. Thank you in advance to anyone who does the same thing for *Not My Problem*.

Thank you to the debut group on Twitter who I could alway rely on while writing this book to be supportive and hilarious.

I specifically want to thank Shveta for her wise counsel. Serena for her voice notes. Jill for buying more copies of my book than anyone else. And Izzy. Always Izzy.

Not Darren, you already got a dedication. What more do you want?

A huge thank you to the bloggers, booktubers, bookstagrammers and tweeters who have supported me so far and anyone who supports *Not My Problem*. I know how much effort you put in and I couldn't be more grateful. I want to mention a few of you here: Theresa, Sasha, Ams and Amber. I know there are others but after all this writing malarkey my brain is mushy and if I haven't mentioned you it isn't because I don't appreciate your efforts. Your enthusiasm literally sells books and that means I can write more books. Thank you doesn't seem like enough but that's all I can do.

They're playing the music now so I will allow myself to be gently ushered offstage to adjust my ballgown and fix my eye make-up.

THE FALLING IN

Love

MONTAGE

CIARA SMYTH

SHORTLISTED FOR THE AN POST IRISH BOOK AWARDS
YA BOOK OF THE YEAR

Seventeen-year-old Saoirse is facing a long hot summer before uni. Ever since the breakupocalypse with her ex Hannah, she's been alone and angry, dealing with the hole left in her family by her sick mother's absence. Worse, Dad drops a bombshell: he's remarrying. Enter the scene: Ruby, who might just be the prettiest girl Saoirse's ever seen. A romcom fan and a believer in true love, Ruby challenges cynical Saoirse to try a summer romance with the serious parts left out, just like in the movies. But what happens when the falling in love montage ends?

'An outrageously comic, moving debut'
Guardian

9781783449668

RAYNE & DELILAH'S MIDNITE MATINEE

Jeff Zentner

Josie and Delia are best friends and co-hosts on their own public access TV show, *Midnite Matinee*. They dress as vampires Rayne and Delilah, perform daft skits, and show the weekly so-bad-it's-good low-budget horror movie. But the end of senior year is coming, and with it big life decisions. A road-trip to ShiverCon, a convention for horror fans, may just have the answers the two need – but will Josie and Delia be prepared for life taking some seriously unexpected plot-twists?

'Anyone can break your heart
– Jeff Zentner can also make
you laugh out loud!'
Rainbow Rowell

9781783447992